THE LUFTMENSCHEN OF PLANET BIROBIDZHAN

The Luftmenschen of Planet Birobidzhan

Zvi Baranoff

1

A PREFACE

Tayere khaveyrim, dear friends,

The Luftmenschen of Planet Birobidzhan is a work of fiction. The setting for most of this book is very far away and in the distant future. Although this book is largely about Jews on other planets, one need not be a *Yid* (a Jew) or a *luftmentsh* (a spaceman) to read this story any more than one, for instance, would need to be a Hobbit or an Elf to read a book such as **Lord of the Rings.**

This book is a future history. To gaze into the future, we will also need to gaze into the past.

Planet Birobidzhan was settled by exiles separated from the Home Planet for a long time. The exiles developed their own unique culture and speak primarily Yiddish. Some awareness of *Yiddishkeit* is certainly helpful to understand this tale. To make this story more accessible, I have included a glossary.

This is a story of displacement, exile, and entrapment by fate. This is also the saga of the few that strive to break free from those entanglements. This story is told from various vantage points, with different voices. The tale spans hundreds of years.

Where to begin? Long before the *Yidden* came to the *gallus* in the stars, we lived on Planet Earth where we were also often displaced. But, that is not really the beginning, either.

The *very* beginning is described in *Bereshis*, what others call Genesis. "When God began to create heaven and earth - the earth being unformed and void, with darkness over the surface of the deep and a wind from God sweeping over the water - God said 'Let there be light' and there was light."

All humanity, we are told, derived from one mother and a single spark. We even all had a single *shprakh*. What that language was, we do not know.

Humanity dispersed globally. Each region developed a unique *Mamaloshen*, I suppose. *Farsheteyt*? I can't say that I really understand, but the *shprakh* of each of us became babbling in each other's ears.

Our Father Abraham originated in Ur Kasdim. Abraham developed a personal relationship with God. Because of this, our *bashert* became distinct from the rest of the *mentshen* of Planet Earth. The relationship with the Creator is our inheritance, but that inheritance is not evenly distributed amongst the Children of Abraham.

What we know of Abraham's immediate family, and those that follow, we learn from the *Tanakh*, the assemblage of texts that others call the Old Testament.

Father Abraham's wife was barren. Mother Sarah, in her old age, offered her servant as a surrogate to bear children. The servant and Abraham's first son are left to fend for themselves in the wilderness because Sarah's reasoning was displaced with jealousy.

I am quite uncertain about how it all ends. Our prophets offer veiled suggestions, but no conclusions. We have no scriptures describing an Apocalyptic End Times as those of other peoples.

The middle is quite garbled. Most of our tale here is likely closer to the end than the beginning. *Es tut mir layd* for a lack of greater clarity.

Our story seems to backtrack and twist in on itself, full of doubt and uncertainty. That rambling is, perhaps, a continuation on the trajectory that reaches back to the very earliest days of the Jewish People. *Ikh vis nisht.*

I suffer from a condition of nostalgia, a dissatisfaction with the present. I long for something better. This life of mine is an anachronism. Maybe that explains it. *Ikh vis nisht.*

A disjointed sense of time and place is not an exclusively Jewish condition. It may be a widespread human phenomenon. A condition of nostalgia and displacement does seem particularly pervasive amongst the *Yidden*.

Questions of lineage fill our *Tanakh* with instances of displaced lines of inheritance, periods of exile, and separation trauma.

Brothers fought within wombs for dominance. Birthrights were traded for bowls of soup. Children were conceived through subterfuge and seduction. Moshe was raised by Pharaoh's daughter. Hadassah married the King of Persia.

These sorts of plot twists repeat throughout our *Tanakh*, reappearing amongst the Nations in barely camouflaged folk tales such as Hansel and Gretel, Snow White, and Cinderella. The Roma fortune tellers use Tarot Cards to retool the *Tanakh* for those lacking a tradition of literacy.

Family roots are taken very seriously by *Yidden*. Perhaps our historical obsession with assurances of ethnicity derives from the obvious lack of lineage purity. We are, after all, of many hues and physical types, mixed and blended.

We mirror this concern with our dietary laws, obsessing on separations. We refrain, for instance, from mixing milk and meat. Nonetheless, the meals that we perceive as Jewish borrow heavily from our Russian, Polish, and Ukrainian neighbors, representing a confluence of cultures.

We tend to blend our foods. Our *kugel*, *gefilte fish*, *kneidelach*, chopped liver, *tzimmes*, and *cholent* all reflect our tendency to bring some order out of chaos, imitating the act of Creation. Our foods are as mixed up as our bloodlines.

Wherever we migrated, we carried our burdens and contradictions with us. We carried *Eretz Yisrael* with us into exile. We carry the habits, values, and customs absorbed in exile from one Diaspora to another.

This was our fate on Planet Earth and continues to be so as we transit across galaxies.

I hope that readers find this introduction and explanation of sorts to be of some use.

A hartsikn dank, a heartfelt thanks, for your indulgence.

2

ON A PLANET SAFE FOR YIDDEN

She stood at the sink, ostensibly washing dishes but mostly staring out the window at the bleak landscape.

How bad had life on the Home Planet been that so many *Yidden* boarded ships and traveled across the void to come here and settle on the Planet Birobidzhan?

She had no way of actually knowing. The last of the ships laden with immigrants and supplies had landed long before her own mother was born and not even a word had arrived from the Home Planet since.

She could, in her dreams, catch a glimpse of a better place somewhere else but this was the only world she knew. She could also imagine a world with pogroms, wars, pollution, grinding machinery, floods, famines, and plagues, dominated by Outsiders of ill intent. But, about that she could not really know either.

What did this world have to offer? The air was breathable. The gravity was tolerable. The ground could be farmed. Most importantly, this was a land without persecution. This was a land without *goyim*. A *Yid* could live here without fear, the founders determined. Of course, she didn't know from *goyim* any more than she knew from *dybbuks* or sea monsters. She truly never knew fear. On the other hand, she really never had much hope.

Out the kitchen window one could see a few bushes, an occasional chicken running about, and then the endless savanna - a whole lot of nothingness as far as the eye could see.

Along one side of the house ran an alleyway. The other side was a shared wall with neighbors that she disliked. In front of the house there was a stoop and a sidewalk and the street.

The children ran in and out of the kitchen, the youngest wearing a droopy and somewhat poignant diaper that was overdue for changing.

She would acknowledge her *kinder*, sometimes with a pat on the head or a scratching behind the ears and sometimes with a swat or a *potch* on the *toches*.

It was all one and the same. She called them *Tantele* and *Mommala* and *Ketschele* and *Yingele* and other such terms of endearment, although she certainly could remember their names when she really needed to, which wasn't very often.

She sighed and sighed again. "*Oy*. Life is hard," she thought.

She mostly had the house to herself. The children ran in and out, this is true. But, mostly they were out and she didn't worry much about them. The neighborhood was safe. The town was safe. A *bissel* larger than a *shtetl* but smaller than a *shtot*.

She knew how *Yidden* lived in the sparse settlements scattered in the hinterlands. There was little appeal to her for that hard life in a small village where everyone knew your every thought, action, and fart.

She had also been to Niu Niu Yark (New New York) and Niu Yerushalaim (New Jerusalem), the two largest cities on Planet Birobidzhan. They were noisy, crowded, dirty, sketchy, and sometimes dangerous places. The theater districts, the restaurants, and the shopping made the occasional visits worthwhile. However, she could not possibly live in either of those places.

No. This town that was bigger than a *shtetl* but smaller than a *shtot* fit her just fine. The view from her kitchen window, however, was beginning to seriously wear thin. She left the wash rag in the sink with the remaining dishes and went looking for her youngest, to change his diaper and take him for a walk.

"*Ketschele!*" she called. "Come see Mama. Let's go for a walk." The *yingele* crawled out from under the table. His name was Dovid but he answered to any term of endearment that his mother chose.

Indeed, he was his mother's favorite and she spoiled him, in her own way. He loved his mother and he loved going for walks with her.

She gave him a perfunctory cleaning, wrapped him in a clean cloth diaper, and dressed him for an outing. She looked in the mirror as she fastened the top buttons on her blouse, adjusted her skirt and tied a kerchief over her hair, assuring that she was properly dressed before leaving her home.

When they reached the first intersection, they could see the corner *minyan* of ne'er-do-wells in the alley huddling in a circle. Her husband, not surprisingly, was in the center, *dreyen* - spinning a *dreidl*. The men were waving banknotes in the air and shouting at each other and at the spinning top.

Her *mann* was shouting "*Gimel! Gimel!*" as the top spun. She stopped and gawked in his direction. The *dreidl* came to a stop and when she saw his shoulders slump, she knew it landed on a *shin*. Now, he would be in a foul mood and broke, to boot.

She took the *yingele's* hand and headed in the opposite direction. "Let's go to the park," she said to her little one.

She didn't consider her *mann* a bad person. She thought of him as mostly unlucky. He worked, on and off. When he did, he would bring his paycheck home. When he worked, he would often come home tired and cranky, but he was always good to the children.

When he gambled, he often lost. When he won, he would bring most of his winnings home and spend that money lavishly on his family.

He never beat her. He never even yelled at her. He drank schnapps a bit, like most everyone, but rarely to excess. He never came home roaring drunk.

Maybe once in a while he would go and lie down with some *kurvah*. Usually, after a bit of a bender and a losing streak at the *dreidl* with the boys in the alley. Afterwards, he would be full of remorse combined with self-pity. He would attempt to make amends, when things bottomed out for him.

No *mann* is perfect. He certainly wasn't. On the other hand, he wasn't the worst. He was her *mann* and she was his *vayb* and they had each other, for better or for worse.

And, he had given her some wonderful children. She loved them all. Even though motherhood was a lot of work, they each brought her *nachas*. She also took some pleasure in her presumption that her two favorite children were probably fathered by men other than her husband.

Her second child, sweet Sadie, the lovely little girl, was most likely the result of a liaison with that gorgeous rabbinical student whose name she couldn't remember.

She met him during the *Sukkos* harvest festival celebration. He was only in town for the Holy Days. It was a semi-rural break from his studies in Niu Yerushalaim.

They made love in a haystack and in a barn and in an open field. She smiled whenever she thought of her seduction of that *yeshiva bocher.* And she thought of him whenever she saw her daughter, the resemblance in her beautiful eyes.

Her youngest, the one whose hand she held, was also probably not fathered by her husband.

His father was most likely the good-natured shopkeeper that smelled like aftershave, with the clean hands and a nice smile. The clothing store was on the other side of town.

He made love to her in the dressing room in the back of the store. They made love standing up, with her skirt hoisted above her waist. He entered her from behind in that little mirrored room.

He made her feel alive. She went to his shop every day for a week, except *Shabbos*, of course. Then she was satiated and she hadn't been back even to that side of town since.

She and Dovid went to the nearby park. The light filtered through the trees. What a lovely day.

The boy climbed on the jungle gym for a while and then the slide. She pushed him on a swing for a bit.

When a small herd of goats arrived, the child ran excitedly to greet them and she followed along as well. The goats brought back happy thoughts of her own childhood and of her own mother, of blessed memory, may she rest in peace.

They meandered towards the far end of the park. There was usually a vendor or two selling food, and so there was that day, as she had expected. They stopped by a cart where an old man was selling *knishes*.

She fished about in the folds of her clothing, retrieving some money - her *knipple* - from it's hiding place.

When she was young, her mother told her that every woman needs her own *gelt*. "Don't rely on a man," her Mama told her. "Not any man, not even a husband. Especially not a husband," her mother insisted. "Men will disappoint you. Men will let you down. Take care for yourself. Every woman needs her own *knipple*."

She took those words to heart. Because of that, she never did without and neither did her children. Not when her *mann* was "between" jobs. Not when her *mann* was on a long losing streak with the *dreidl*. Not even when he was passed out drunk in the arms of some *kurvah*.

She bought a warm *knish*, wrapped in a napkin and returned her *knipple* to it's hiding place in the folds of her clothes.

They sat together on a park bench. She nibbled, pecking at her food like a *foigel*, a bird. Dovid devoured the food, ravenous like a wolf. This child of hers was always hungry, with a seemingly unending lust for life.

They wandered over by the pavilion where the *klezmorim* gathered and listened to the music for a while. She smiled while Dovid danced about. Then, they did some window shopping on their circuitous way home.

Dovid cried a bit outside of the toy store, begging for the airplane he saw displayed in the window. She pulled him down the street with a combination of promises and admonishments.

She had already spoiled the child enough for one day. A mother cannot give her children everything. His tears, they both knew, were just for show and of no real consequence. The tears quickly evaporated.

It was nearly sundown by the time they approached their house. It had been a lovely excursion for the two of them.

When she opened the door, she smelled food cooking. The house had been straightened and swept. There was a vase filled with flowers on the dining room table. Her *mann* was in the kitchen, finishing up the dishes. He smiled when he saw his wife and the child.

He was always glad to see little Dovid. Of all the children, of the entire brood, Dovid was his favorite. Dovid, as well, was happy to find Papa in the kitchen.

"The stars align and it is *mazel* all around!" said her husband. Then, he turned to the *yingele* and said "Dovid, I have a present for you. Come give Papa a hug." The child was in his arms before he barely finished these words and he carried the toddler into the living room where there were actually two presents for him; a toy truck and a picture book.

The *mann* and the *kind* played on the floor while she made herself comfortable by loosening some of her clothing and putting away her kerchief. Her husband could barely contain himself. Words sprung from him like a babbling stream.

"*Oy*," he began. "You wouldn't believe! My luck had been going from bad to worse! Nothing was going my way. Every spin was bad. It was all *nisht, nisht* when it wasn't *shtel arayn*. I was beginning to wonder if one of those *mamzers* hadn't slipped me a loaded *dreidl*."

"I was down to just a few sheckles when I saw you and the little *Ketschele* heading out for a walk. Just then, a beam of sunlight shone on me like a message from the Divine. You always bring me luck, my dear."

"On my next *dreyen* I hit a *gimel*. From then on, it was all *gants, gants, gants*. I was just raking in the cash. Some of those *shtarkers* were probably beginning to suspect me of using a loaded *dreidl, keinehora*." he said and he spit three times to ward off the evil eye.

"So, I gathered up my winnings and left those ne'er-do-wells to their drinking and *kvetching* and licking their wounds. I had *gelt* in my pocket for once and I had better things to do."

"I went and did a little shopping. I bought gifts for all the children and a little something for you, as well," he said. He pulled a new silk kerchief from one of his pockets and handed it to her. Indeed, it was very pretty.

"The other children have all been fed and washed. Let's feed Dovid and put him to bed. We can eat by candlelight, just the two of us."

"Anyways," he continued. "The big news! As I was leaving the store where I bought that pretty scarf, as I was walking out that door, I literally bumped right into an acquaintance of mine and I startled him. He tells me that he was just thinking about me and he has work for me if I wanted and I can begin on *Sontag*. So, right after this *Shabbos*, I am, once again, a working man!"

He smiled at his wife and with that he picked up Dovid, carried him into the kitchen, and got the *yingele* into his highchair.

While her *mann* fed the boy, she headed to the *vashzimmer* to freshen up. There, in the bathtub, she saw a carp swimming. Well, to be more accurate, a fish that they call a carp on Planet Birobidzhan and that the rabbis have declared to be *kosher*. The family would have fresh fish for *Shabbos*.

By the time she had finished freshening herself, her *mann* had the *yingele* fed and his hands and *punim* clean. Her husband carried his favorite child to the boy's bedroom and was reading him a bedtime story.

"My *mann* has a job. There is food in the house. The kids are all well. *Ales iz gut*!" she thought. Immediately, she said "*Keinehora*!" out loud. She didn't want to bring herself or her family any bad luck.

She could hear her husband's lyrical voice as he read nonsense rhymes to Dovid from the boy's favorite bedtime book. She smiled as she remembered how sweet her *mann* was when they were courting and how handsome he was when he stood under the *chuppah*.

"*Abi guzunt*. That's the main thing," she said, to no one in particular.

3

SEARCHING FOR A YENNE VELT

Long distance space travel was no simple feat for our ancestors. The distance from Earth to other potentially habitable and available planets was - and continues to be - vast.

That said, calling the Home Planet "habitable" was becoming more and more of a stretch. Life on Earth had become miserable. Floods, famines, epidemics, toxic waste, riots, genocidal wars, dwindling resources, etc. seemed to unfold daily with no end in sight.

By the early 21st Century, the idea of seeking out a sanctuary from Earth was beginning to get some real traction. The realistic options at that time however were dreadfully limited.

The Earth's moon or Earth's closest neighbor planet Mars and a few asteroids were within reach of the technological capacity. None of those places had an atmosphere that could sustain human life.

The scientists of that time, using the limited technology of the period - that is, telescopes and unmanned probes - searched endlessly for potentially habitable planets.

Well into that century, the best looking potentially habitable planet pinpointed by these scientists was estimated to be about 40 light years from the Home Planet.

The fastest moving vehicle of that time - an unmanned space probe - was crossing the void to humanity's outer capacity at the speed of 36,000 miles per hour (50,000 km/h). At that rate, it would have taken well over 26 million years to reach that distant potential destination. That is a timeframe that is way too long to even ponder.

By the middle of that century, the options began to look slightly more hopeful. This was fortunate because the outlook for life on Planet Earth was looking truly dreadful.

As telescopes and space probes improved, several closer potential planets were pinpointed. Additionally, the speed of intergalactic travel had been significantly improved upon. These two factors combined to shorten the very abstract travel time from millions of years to possibly a few hundred years, give or take. Still out of reach, perhaps, but more tantalizing than imagined beforehand.

Also, the technological capacity to place humans into a state of semi-incapacitation through advanced cryogenics had been developed to the point where it was theoretically possible to *store* passengers for decades without significant damage to the individuals. So, if the travel time could be shortened to a few decades, mass migration would then actually become a possibility.

Perhaps what we think of as mystical is the outer edge of what science has yet to understand. Or, perhaps science is our way of trying to understand the esoteric.

One scientific theory proposed that there are wormholes in the void that essentially fold space/time and that traveling through a wormhole would allow one to go very far in hardly any time.

Kabbalists have spoken of traveling great distances in a troika or on foot or in a meditative state through divine intervention. The Baal Shem Tov, for instance, was famous for such feats. So, the rabbis found the idea of folding space/time to be quite plausible. After all, isn't that exactly what the great sages of blessed memory had done?

Wormholes were theorized for a very long time. The first time one was discovered was in the middle of the 21st Century. The scientists were blown away. The rabbis shrugged.

That first wormhole was within a couple of years traveling time from Earth. An unmanned vehicle was programmed to enter the wormhole, or the Tunnel as it was later named, pass through the length of it and to exit what was theorized to be the other side.

Assuming that the ship survived, it was programmed to do some relatively minor localized exploration and then attempt to reenter the wormhole from the other side. The ship would then return to Earth, if such a miraculous and mystical voyage was possible, with a trove of intellectual wealth. The roundtrip would take around five years.

The whole project was viewed with much global skepticism until the unmanned craft actually re-emerged from the Tunnel and began to broadcast data towards the Home Planet as it sped that way for the next two and a half years.

With the reappearance of that craft, a major shift in perspective occurred. Before that, the idea of dropping down a wormhole seemed rather similar to the plethora of other hair-brained ideas.

During those aimless preceding decades, a vast array of Messianic Cults proliferated on Earth. Religious Revivalism was one response to the dismal conditions everyone was facing.

The *mishegoss* about a Messiah was not confined to the *goyim*. *Yidden* also hoped for the *Moshiach*, and we were certainly in need of Divine Intervention.

Several Messianic Cultish movements arose among the *Yidden*. They were collectively referred to as Neo Sabbatai Zevi Cults. That is probably an oversimplification but not by much. The results were about the same as those of the historical cult. A million or so *Yidden* followed the Cult Leaders to apostasy and conversions.

The discovery of the wormhole came no time too soon. It may indeed have been Divine Intervention as some believe. Of course, the sheer bull headed determination of humanity, scientific curiosity, and the financial interests of the corporations invested in the space industry are all factors as well.

A fold in space/time is a useful metaphor for understanding a wormhole. It falls short, however, in explaining the problem of communication through a wormhole.

In most of space, as vast as it is, communication is straightforward. A message can be sent and it will be received in relatively real time...that is, the time it takes for radio waves or light to transpire the distance. The fold blocks normal, straight line communication.

Now, imagine yourself as a child living in a multi-story building with a friend living down the hallway. If each of you step outside of your apartments, you can easily wave, shout or roll a ball to each other.

However, if your friend's family were to move to an apartment on another floor of the same building, rolling a ball up and down the hall would no longer be possible even though the linear distance between you and your friend would not have been greatly altered. To see each other, one of you would need to ride the elevator. In this sense, the wormhole is akin to an elevator.

To mix metaphors one more time, actually traveling through a wormhole is far more uncomfortable and disconcerting than riding an elevator. The few that have made the voyage wide awake compared it to being flushed down a toilet or sucked up by a tornado.

It is fortunate for all concerned that most people that transpired that passage did so in a state of cryogenic disconnection rather than full consciousness. It is certainly not something that any rational human would choose to do a second time!

To resolve the communication glitch, a workaround was required. The solution, although fairly simplistic, was expensive. Two communication satellites were positioned at opposite ends of that cosmic Tunnel.

On either side of the Tunnel, data could be sent by radio signals to the waiting satellite. The data then was transferred by relay drones through the Tunnel to the parallel operating satellite. From there, the message could be resent as easily as rolling a ball down the hall.

This facilitated the unmanned searches on the opposite side of the wormhole. Those exploratory ships could travel without limitation and send back the discoveries without wasting travel time on a return trip. At this point, the search for livable planets within the technological reach of humanity began in earnest.

The ownership of the exploratory ships, of course, was in the hands of profit oriented corporations. The searches were yielding important hints as to possibly habitable planets.

No corporation actually owned any of those planets but the information about the conditions and the coordinates that provide the location were proprietary. These corporations were like real estate agents. The information gathered was being sold to the highest bidder, piecemeal. The more information about a planet provided, the higher the cost until a final purchase of map coordinates were settled.

The *Yidden* were not the only ones looking for a way out. Anyone that could afford to possibly relocate certainly would be willing to pay the piper.

Earth's very wealthy wished to acquire the closest and most desirable planets. They intended to hire the staff required to maintain the affluence they were used to.

Some corporations were in search of ways to expand their enterprises. Other religious, social, and fraternal organizations also were hoping to find a *Yenne Velt* - Another World - to live on.

Before the coordinates were purchased, the Agency representing our ancestors knew enough about the planet to know that it was habitable, but not a whole lot more. This limited information had been expensive, dripped and dribbled as an enticement. Eventually, the Agency chose to place their bet and spin the *dreidl*, so to speak.

They knew that this world circled a star similar to the sun they were familiar with. They knew that the pull of gravity was slightly less than Earth's pull, but not significantly. They knew that the air was breathable, the soil was tillable, that there were oceans, lakes, rivers, and some forests.

They were aware that there were creatures that resemble Earth's birds, fish, and mammals. Some beasts looked much like the buffalo that once roamed widely in North America. They had no way of knowing if any of those life forms were edible, if they could be domesticated, or if they would be deemed to be *kosher*.

They also knew that the travel time to the possible New World was just under eighteen years. This seemed to be a good omen. The number eighteen had always been considered good luck for Jews, corresponding to the numerical value of the letters of the word "*chai*" which is Hebrew for Life.

Later on, many wondered if more attention should have been placed on the fact that "just under eighteen" might have meant just shy of what was needed for a satisfying life. However, that was later and a matter of hindsight mixed with regrets.

Now that a mass evacuation was beginning to be seen as plausible, practical steps were needed to make the action possible.

Ships needed to be purchased and outfitted. These ships could not be purchased off a lot, like a car, boat, or trailer. They needed to be made to order and paid for before the manufacturing even began. To maximize the carrying capacity of each ship while reducing the production cost, the ships were built for one way traveling.

The amount of fundraising involved was massive although much of the funds were actually raised by schoolchildren.

To organize the safe evacuation of all the Children of Israel became the rallying cry, with the implied promise that no one would be left behind.

An historically unprecedented level of cooperation developed amongst the *Yidden*, a people far more accustomed to disagreement, argument, and interfamilial struggle than working in unison for common goals. Of course, the unified public facade was dependent upon a whole lot of backroom deals, intricate negotiations, and complicated compromises.

How realistic was the plan? The number of *Yidden* on the Home Planet was estimated to be around twenty-five million. That is certainly a lot of people but all told it was less than half of one percent of the global population.

A little more than half of the Jews lived in the North American Federation, which was the political alliance of the countries formerly known as Mexico, the United States, and Canada. Most of these Yidden lived in New York City or within one hundred miles or so.

Around a third of the *Yidden* lived in the Jordan River Federation which was a delicate political tinkering consisting of what had been known as Israel, Palestine, and the Kingdom of Jordan. Previously, the area had a variety of names and governance of different sorts. So, the gathering of the Tribes was helped along by the fact that so many were already concentrated.

Abstractly, *Yidden* from any part of the world were equally eligible for transit. In practice, the first flights originated in the North American Federation and subsequent flights continued from there and also from the Eilat region of the Jordan River Federation. Those that lived within an easy traveling distance from the launch sites certainly had some advantages over those in more far flung regions.

Of course, the Exodus was on a purely voluntary basis. Clearly, not every Jew was keen to sign up. Some had other loyalties and plans. There was also a small, but vocal, religious minority of contrarians that opposed the project on a theological basis. So, in reality, not everyone would be evacuated. Nonetheless, the practical difference between transplantation of ten, fifteen, twenty-five or thirty million people is academic.

In theory, every *Yid* had an equal right to transport. However, the early ships could only carry tens of thousands of passengers in suspended animation and packed like sardines or herring. How long would it take to transport millions? What priorities were set when determining who received passage?

The first ship out had its own unique set of criterion based on the principle that the entire survivability of the settlement on the planet would depend on their achievements.

While the subsequent ships would be laden with travelers in cryogenic suspension, it was determined that it would be best for trained cryogenic technicians to be on hand for "defrosting" the passengers. So, primarily for this reason, on the first transport ship the trip took place in normal experienced time.

On the first ship, besides cryogenic experts, traveled those that were determined to be indispensable for establishing a new space colony. This included a full medical staff, construction experts, those familiar with a wide range of hydroponics and greenhouse operations, animal husbandry, and the establishment and daily operations of farms.

The above were the sorts of folks necessary for any new long-term expedition. The foundation of this new colony also took into consideration what would be needed to protect and cultivate *Yiddishkeit*.

Included on the first transit were *rabbis*, *shochets* and those that oversee *kashrus* for *hechsher* certification, scribes, teachers, book publishers, librarians, vintners, those familiar with the construction and maintenance of *mikvahs*, poets, musicians, and experts in Jewish burial practices. Also, their spouses and children were included.

The Rabbinical authorities insisted that all food transported would be *Glatt Kosher*. Some in the scientific community had suggested rabbits and guinea pigs would make for a good protein source, at least as a transition food. This option was dismissed offhand by the rabbis.

Fertile chicken eggs and a few cryogenic goats were stored on board as future sources for meat, upon arrival on the destination planet. Cows were deemed to be too large for transport. Great hope had been placed in the belief that the buffalo-like creatures would serve as a food source. To rabbinical and general disappointment, they were declared to be not *kosher* at all.

There was, however, another creature that resembles the wild hogs of Earth. This beast was dismissed at first because of the way it looked. However, some adventurous settlers hunted these "hogs" and found them to be quite edible. Once the carcasses were examined closely, it was determined that the "hogs" have split hooves and chew their cuds. The hogs also were found to be fairly docile and easily domesticated.

The rabbis were concerned about the optics of the matter but, after considering that there were no *goyim* to cast aspersions, they eventually declared the animals *kosher*. For the *Yidden* of Planet Birobidzhan, ham, pork, and bacon derived from the native *kosher* hogs became a dietary staple.

Until that point, the *Yidden* were hungry a lot and had become increasingly frustrated by a daily diet of potatoes. The words and melody of the *Bulbes* song - "Monday, Potatoes! Tuesday, Potatoes!" etc. ad nauseum - seemed to float everywhere. Some suggested, with only a touch of irony, that the song should be the official Planetary Anthem.

Passage on subsequent ships was decided by a point system based on a questionnaire as well as one's skill set and the results of a series of detailed health examinations, combined with a lottery. In theory, the system was free of bias. In practice, the subsequent population of our Planet Birobidzhan was determined by the process and that is worthy of some analysis.

Membership in a Jewish organization, a Jewish education, knowledge of one or more of the Hebraic languages (particularly Hebrew, Yiddish and Ladino), certain skill sets, and close family that have already migrated were all factors that improved one's odds of being selected.

Space and weight are the determinants in loading a vehicle for intergalactic travel. Every cubic centimeter matters. Every kilogram is of significance. There is only so much interior capacity.

The average weight for an adult living in the North American Federation was around 80 kg. Weight was a key consideration. No one over 93 kg was accepted under any circumstances.

Fertility was considered of importance. Priority was given to women of child bearing age that tested high on a fertility scale and showed an emotional and psychological likelihood of birthing and raising lots of *kinder*.

It was determined that it was unsafe to place anyone under the age of twelve in cryogenic suspension, so no one under that age was transported. Pregnant women were also not transported.

Particularly amongst the religious, it became a common practice to join a transport shortly after weaning a child, but before becoming pregnant again. Their children would be raised by relatives until they reached the age of twelve when they would be bumped to the front of the list for transportation.

Additionally, many of the twelve year old girls would be married to a cousin or another member of their close knit community, which assured the transport of the *Bar Mitzvah Bochur* along with his young wife.

There was additionally a general cutoff age of forty. Because of these parameters, the average age of new setters fell into that youthful range.

As far as cargo was concerned, everyone could bring some personal possessions, but precious few. There were predetermined necessities that took precedence over any personal choices. Some were to guarantee the physical survival of the pioneers. Other cargo were there to assure our spiritual needs.

It was determined, for instance, that a prayer book should be provided for every emigrant. A copy of the *Tanakh* was provided for every family unit. Every male was provided with a set of *tefillin*, a *tallis* and a *tallis katan*, whether or not he was in the practice of using these. Multiple sets of dishes for maintaining a *kosher* kitchen were required for each family. Sufficient quantities of *kosher* wine needed to be loaded on each ship until the Planet's wine production was up to the task.

The settlement was nominally free of an official theology. The scientific community was central to the foundation. Secularists were amongst each of the new waves of settlers. Nonetheless, the number of religious, Yiddish speaking newcomers continued to be the dominant trend as long as settlers continued to arrive from the Home Planet.

On Earth our planet was known by its coordinates which were designated by a combination of numbers and Greek letters. In the early days of the settlement, no one thought much about what to call this world. The early settlers were just busy trying to stay alive.

Some neo-Zionists called it *Eretz Yisrael* although most of the religious settlers considered that to be sacrilegious. Others referred to *Yenne Velt*, which simply means Another World. However,*Yenne Velt* has the historical connotation of being a euphemism for the afterlife and seeing this place as a type of death was already too easy without bringing that to mind on a daily basis.

The ships arrived from Earth on somewhat of a regular basis for a while. The new arrivals were welcomed with celebration and the early pioneers were optimistic people. However, by the anniversary of the First Landing, far less than a million immigrants had arrived.

The following year, the ships began to arrive less frequently. Additionally, the new arrivals seemed less impressed by the opportunities and culture of their new home.

Then, after a few years, no new ships arrived. Even more disconcerting, no new messages had been relayed from the communication satellite by the Tunnel. There was no way to know what had become of the Earth, the other *Yidden*, or the rest of humanity. We had been left to our own devices, perhaps for eternity.

Long ago, back on Earth, Yiddishists and Stalinists came up with a common dream of establishing a Jewish Republic as part of the Soviet Union. Poets and ideologues led the way. The Soviet Government presented the *Yidden* with a land grant, and free one way transportation. The land that the Soviet Politburo chose for the *Yidden* was far to the east along the border with China.

This Jewish Republic was as far as conceivably possible from any Jewish intellectual or cultural centers or any place where *Yidden* had historically lived. There, Yiddish was made the official language. Publishing houses were established for Yiddish poetry and Communist propaganda. Yiddish theater was encouraged. There were Yiddish road signs. Yiddish was taught in the schools. The lettering on the headstones in the cemetery was in the *Mamaloshen*.

The land was harsh, with little to offer. The Bira and the Bidzhan rivers flowed through the region from which the name Birobidzhan was derived. This was the first post-Biblical establishment of Jewish autonomy.

Our home was at first called Planet Birobidzhan sarcastically. Before long, however, the name stuck. This planet was a Jewish Land in a desolate place. There was little sense of hope. Yiddish had become the semi-official language. What else could we call this place? *Yidden* pondered that question and no other answers came to mind.

4

ANOTHER GLOBE, PERHAPS?

Long ago, on the Home Planet, Earth, there was an ancient Russian Empire controlled by an aristocracy and ruled by a Czar. Under the Czar, *Yidden* suffered from limitations, oppression, deprivation, and the occasional pogroms.

In the Russian Empire, Jews could only live in a region known as the Pale which was at the western end of the Empire in the border regions where competing imperialist powers contended for control.

Armies marched through with flags displayed and much exuberance. Governments came and went. No matter what nation laid claim, life in the Jewish villages remained about the same for centuries.

When everything went as well as could be expected, there would be potatoes *(bulbes)* and onions *(tsibeles)*, a bit of black bread and maybe some *borscht*. On Friday night, perhaps a *schtickle* of fish or chicken, a glass of wine and some white bread.

This was the world that Mendel was born to and this was what he expected from life.

Towards the end of the 1800s, life had become noticeably more difficult for the *Yidden* and many began to consider a life beyond the Pale. Millions emigrated during those years, including some from the *shtetl* where Mendel lived.

Some of Mendel's childhood friends became Zionists. They sang songs in Hebrew. They dreamed of a Land for Jews where they could walk tall and live on communal farms. They went off to a place they called Palestine.

Other childhood friends went to the Americas. Some went to New York, where the streets, they said, are paved in gold. Others went to Buenos Aires, where great opportunities existed for enterprising *Yidden.*

A few of his acquaintances had gone to South Africa. It was there that diamonds could be found just lying on the ground. In almost no time one could be wealthy, with a little effort. So, he had been told.

Mendel stayed in the *shtetl* of his birth, satisfied with his lot. *Bulbes* and *tsibeles* with a bit of black bread were not so bad. Why should he go looking for trouble?

In the beginning of the twentieth century, the Russian Empire was in turmoil. Great changes were afoot. Some of Mendel's childhood friends joined the Bolsheviks in the struggle to overthrow the Czar.

When the Bolsheviks came to power, the Russian Empire was no more. In its place a new government arose and was called the Union of Soviet Socialist Republics.

Everything was new and nothing was the same, he was told. The old power structure was gone. All men were equal. The workers now ruled and the capitalist class was destroyed.

Mendel still ate black bread and maybe a *bulbe* or a *tsibele*. A *schtickle* of fish or chicken was just a dream, but all told, his life had not changed much.

Shortly after the overthrow of the Czar and the installation of the Bolshevik-led Workers Paradise Government, a madman and paranoid narcissist with an evil temperament floated to the top of the pond as is the tendency of scum. Joseph Stalin, may his name be cursed for eternity, led Russia into an extensive period of non-stop terror with an irrational bureaucratic tinge to it.

It was towards the end of the 1920s, with a madman as the Party Leader and Head of State, the Politburo had determined that the *Yidden*, now free, needed a Jewish Republic - a piece of land with a Jewish character and culture - that reflected the values of the new Communist State.

With much fanfare, red flags blowing in the breeze, commissars and Yiddish poets urged the *Yidden* of the Pale to head east, to a new Jewish Land.

Far from the Pale, along another frontier adjacent to the Chinese border, a desolate and uninhabitable place where the Bira and the Bidzhan Rivers flowed, they determined in their wisdom that the Jews of Russia could remake themselves.

Upstanding writers, poets, and Yiddishists urged the *Yidden* to move to the Birobidzhan Republic. Some went, but Mendel stayed put. A bit of black bread and maybe a *bulbe* or a *tsibele* and life goes on.

In the Jewish Republic of Birobidzhan, there was terrible housing, little work, failed gardens, and not enough of anything. That was how things were going there at the best of it. Then, the purges began. Those that were summarily executed were the lucky ones. Many others were sent to Gulags where they worked themselves to death.

Meanwhile, to the west, dark clouds were rising. A stubby colonel, failed artist, and sociopath named Adolf Hitler, a curse on his name as well, seized control of Germany, another country with imperialist fetishes.

These two crackpots found common cause for a short while. While they played lovey-dovey, they divided up all the land that spread out between Russia and Germany. Then, a lovers quarrel broke out which led to a messy divorce. When it reached full scale warfare, the battles raged across the Pale.

Mendel was drafted into the Soviet Army. He fought when he had to. He learned to keep his head down and he lived as a grunt private. The army sometimes fed him *borscht*, but not often. He could sometimes find a piece of black bread or a *tsibele*. Somehow he survived the war.

The madman Stalin held the reins of Russia until his death in 1953. During those years, life was hard for everyone. Of course, life was especially hard for the *Yidden*.

After Stalin's death, everyone breathed a little easier. Life improved somewhat. The gulags had largely been dismantled and the purges had mostly ended. The starving was alleviated. Slowly some reforms took place.

By the 1970s, the Soviet Government began to issue a limited number of exit visas. Mendel decided one day to go down to the office and apply for a visa. Maybe he could go and live somewhere else in this world where *bulbes* and *tsibeles* were plentiful, fish and chicken were available, and one could have a bit of white bread and a glass of wine on a Friday night. Why not?

Mendel waited in line for the proper forms. He sat on the hard bench and filled in the paperwork with the stubby pencil that he was given. He stood in line to turn in the forms. He waited all day in the crowded outer office for his name to be called. It was nearly closing time when he heard a badly mispronounced version of his name being called. Mendel shuffled into the inner sanctum where his fate would be decided.

The bureaucrat that would determine Mendel's future looked up from behind his desk. Mendel fidgeted a bit, his cap in his hand. "Yes," said the bureaucrat. "Where is it you want to go to?"

The question caught Mendel unaware. He hadn't thought about where he wanted to be. He simply could no longer remember what held him there in Russia and imagined abstractly that there must be a better place. He stammered and stuttered.

The bureaucrat looked up from the papers he was shuffling. He saw before him an old veteran from the Great Patriotic War as that period of senseless bloodletting was known in Russia.

The government bureaucrat took a breath and his heart softened a bit. "I cannot issue an exit visa without a destination. You must tell me where you want to go and then I can put my stamp on this piece of paper and you pay the fee and you get a visa. It is as simple as that. Where do you want to go?"

Mendel also took a breath and felt a little more at ease. "Well," he said. "I suppose I should go to the Land of Israel. That is the country for the Jews, is it not?" Israel was the newfangled name for the place that was called Palestine when he was a youth. Some of his childhood friends had gone there back before the Revolution and the War.

The clerk felt a bit more at ease, now that he had something to write down on the blank line of the form. Just as his pen was about to touch the paper, Mendel spoke up. "Wait!" he said. "I am thinking, there they have war and the economy isn't so good. Maybe I don't want to go there." The clerk looked up, and sighed.

"Maybe I go to America. In New York, the streets are paved in gold. But, in America there is racial strife and crime and poverty. No. I don't think I want to go to America." The clerk shook his head.

Mendel considered other choices and just as quickly wrote those choices off. South Africa had apartheid and might be heading into a civil war. Australia had poisonous snakes and large crocodiles. The pictures of Canada that he had seen reminded him of Siberia. In Chile they speak Spanish. Germany is full of Germans.

Finally, the clerk, who just wanted to finish up his paperwork so he could go home, took a globe off of a shelf and placed it in the middle of his desk. He gave the globe a light spin. "Surely there is some place on this globe that you want to go to."

Mendel watched the globe spin. He looked deep into his heart. Then he spoke up. "Please, kindly bureaucrat, commissar apparatchik, comrade clerk sir...perhaps, just maybe, you have another globe?"

At that time, there was no other globe to even consider. We were all in exile then as we are now but our *galus* was limited to the Home Planet. We have since extended our exile out into the great void. Some of us landed on Planet Birobidzhan. Here on Planet Birobidzhan, there are no government officials to grant us exit visas. We have nowhere else to go.

At least on Planet Birobidzhan, *bulbes* and *tsibeles* are plentiful, fish and chicken are available, all sorts of breads and cakes can be purchased at the bakery, *borscht* is as cheap as *borscht* and there is always wine for Friday night.

5

BERESHIS: TRANSPORT AND TRANSFORMATION

It was the first of the starships with many more scheduled to follow. The ship was loaded with Jews headed to begin the settlement of a distant planet. The ship had been carefully built and the selection of passengers went through a vigorous vetting process.

Only around twelve hundred *Yidden* would travel on the first ship and a lot of responsibility was laid on their shoulders. The future of the Jewish People was contingent on the groundwork that would be done by the volunteers on the initial transport.

A second ship, with tens of thousands of passengers in a deep sleep would follow within a couple of months. Over the next few years, if all went well, most of Earth's twenty-five million *Yidden* would be transported in this manner.

The cryogenic technicians, other technical support teams and the spiritual leadership on the first ship needed to be in place when the subsequent transport vehicles began to arrive.

Great hope and expectations were held by all involved in this complicated enterprise. The ship had been named

Hatikvah - The Hope. Bands played and banners waved. Crowds of family, friends, and well-wishers cheered. The volunteers walked to the ship that would be their home for the nearly eighteen years of the voyage.

Eighteen years is a very long time to be cooped up in even the most comfortable and spacious of ships. Eighteen years is long enough for cultural differences to bubble up into conflicts as well as for social interactions to result in significant shifting of attitudes.

The blending and altering of beliefs and practices that occurred amongst the passengers of the *Hatikvah* would have been astronomical to an outside observer, if such an observation had been possible. Surely, some of the passengers found the cultural shifting disorienting.

The changes, however, took place over nearly two decades in an organic manner, lives developing over time. These changes altered the perspectives of the passengers and the future course of life on Planet Birobidzhan.

The settlers that followed, arrived by the tens of thousands, cryogenically frozen, in ships packed like canned herring. The developing culture of the world where they were defrosted, made their heads spin. The way they got there was enough to make them feel disoriented without the additional digestion of the cultural oddities of those of the First Landing.

The traveling time for all the ships was the same. For those of the First Landing, eighteen years of traveling was experienced. For those arriving afterwards, no real time had passed. When defrosted, they felt something similar to a hangover or perhaps a touch of the flu. Within a day or two, those symptoms passed. In their minds, they had been on Earth just yesterday.

The subsequent settlers arrived the same age as they were when they had left and with their attitudes and perspectives intact. Those that had preceded them on the *Hatikvah* had all been significantly altered by the trip.

The volunteers on the *Hatikvah* were chosen primarily for the specific skills that they had to offer that would be useful for the settlement of the target planet. The demographics of the *Hatikvah* were somewhat older, better educated, and among the more secular volunteers, a higher percentage male than all of the following flights.

The more religious adult volunteers were slightly older than future flights and made up of highly specialized experts and their wives. However, they also brought along their children. This was the only passage that included children because on all the rest of the ships the passengers were cryogenically preserved and it was determined that it wasn't safe to freeze those under the age of twelve.

One might reasonably have suspected that the primary cultural fault line aboard the *Hatikvah* was that which separates the most religious from the most secular. That presumption would be, quite frankly, wrong because of multiple reasons.

To begin with, the divisions that separate the various ultra religious factions are deep with a lot of historical animosity. The ideological conflicts and personal grudges that can be traced back to centuries of Earth history were carried aboard the *Hatikvah*. The representatives of the various factions were on their best behavior and committed themselves to papering over their conflicts but that did not go so far as to result in a common agenda to establish a theocracy. The ultra religious were also, all told, a minority of these migratory pioneers.

The more secular of the volunteers lacked the philosophical and ideological passions binding themselves to fixed positions. There were no particular secular axes to grind.

The result of this mix was a strong influence of religious sentiment without coercion. Proselytizing for or against any of the sects was considered gauche and unacceptable.

One of the very few conflicts during that long trip from the Home Planet to the Planet Birobidzhan that actually came to blows - and injuries - did involve a Rabbi, but had nothing to do with religion or philosophical matters. The rabbi was caught cheating at chess.

6

A LANGUAGE, A JARGON OR BABEL?

Finding a common language for the pioneers wasn't a simple matter. The overwhelming majority of those aboard this first flight were from the North American Federation.

English was the most widely spoken language from that region of Earth, but Spanish and French were also regional languages with representation aboard. There was a sizable contingent Hassidim from Québec, predominantly Montréal, that spoke French and Yiddish with strong French accents.

There were also some Europeans including a fair number of doctors from Germany. German was their primary language which made Yiddish fairly comprehensible for them.

There was a sizable number of Yiddishists that had studied and taught Yiddish in universities. They were committed to the ideal of making Yiddish a modern language of the new settlement. There were also those that were aboard, particularly the ultra religious, that grew up in homes that spoke Yiddish.

The university educated Yiddishists were highly critical of the colloquial Yiddish that was widely spoken. The academics derisively referred to the Yiddish in use as Yinglish. For instance, it was far more common to call a window a "*vindow*" than the more correct "*fentster*". As inclined as the Yiddishists were to try and educate on the matter, people spoke the language as they were used to.

Any hope for linguistic purity was delusional. What became the common language of the voyage, and eventually the common language of the settlement, was a hodgepodge. The language spoken was a reflection of the people. They found ways to communicate across the divisions that separated themselves from each other. That which grew organically developed into the forms of speech that we are now familiar with.

7

THE WORK AT HAND

For the eighteen years of traveling time, there was little real work and nearly no responsibilities for these pioneers. The ship's course was set by computer. No piloting, or human intervention whatsoever, would be called for until the time came for landing on the new world. The larder was filled with a more than sufficient, although less than exciting, supply of *Kosher* MRE - Meals Ready to Eat. Those aboard the *Hatikvah* could just sit on their hands for eighteen years and fulfill their mission.

It would be incorrect to say that there was no work to be done and surely ongoing idleness is contrary to human nature. However, many were aboard with focussed skills that had no purpose whatsoever on the *Hatikvah*. The number of people with skills that were useful in transit constituted a workforce of many times more than required for the work at hand.

Perhaps the most redundant of those on the first flight was the financial committee. Their mission, upon arrival on the new planet, involved the printing of currency and the establishment of a market economy. Printing money would be the easy part for them. It took years, however, before those pieces of paper had any exchange value whatsoever. For eighteen years in flight, the committee met once a week...to play poker.

There were enough medical professionals for a small hospital. They were tasked with setting up such a facility on their arrival. On board, there was little to do. The passengers had been pre-screened for physical, mental, and emotional health. The medics provided annual health checkups, bandaged an occasional bruising and staffed a twenty-four hour clinic without anyone working more than a couple of hours a week.

The ship was designed with hydroponic growing in mind. The idea was that some food could be grown enroute and the shipboard system would be up and running planetside while greenhouses were being set up.

The farmers, greenhouse technicians, and hydroponics experts were all antsy to do something - and everyone was quickly bored with the pre-packaged space food - so lots of fruits and vegetables were soon growing and meals were greatly improved.

The Agency had provided carefully preserved fertilized chicken eggs with the presumption that they would be activated on arrival. However, some of the eggs were hatched and the *Hatikvah* may have been the only intergalactic flight ever to include free range chickens.

Even with all of these gardening activities, however, there were ten times the number of experts on board than were needed on the ship for that purpose.

There were six pilots aboard. One would be required to land the vessel which would mean a couple of hours work at the end of the trip. Once planetside, however, those six went on to establish the homing beams and landing fields for all of the rest of the landings.

They later formed the Birobidzhan Pilots Association. They entertained children with model airplanes, built some planes big enough to fly a few passengers, and eventually established somewhat regularly scheduled flights between Niu Yerushalaim and Niu Niu Yark. Most everyone referred to this as the Birobidzhan Air Farce, somewhat cynically.

There were design and construction experts on board that clearly had nothing to do before arrival. In truth, they wouldn't have a whole lot to do once there either. The ship was packed with prefabricated parts for all the primary construction. The pieces snapped together like children's building blocks.

Concerning the religious experts, the *shochets* had nothing to do until there were enough chickens to allow for an occasional culling. The birthrate was high enough to call for a couple of *mohels*, perhaps. Both of these professions were overrepresented. There was virtually no need for *kashrus* inspection but there was a full crew of *hechsher* authorities.

Of course, for the Rabbis, life on the ship was probably very similar to what their lives were like back on Earth. They studied Holy Books and prayed. They bickered with each other over minor theological differences. They paid attention to the holidays and gave advice to those who would seek it out. The *Rebbetzins* also lived much as they had before. They had babies, raised children, and maintained households.

The *Rebbetzins*, perhaps unexpectedly, stepped up to fill a void when the hydroponic gardens began producing. The wives of the various Rabbis established and oversaw the kitchens and feeding stations that freed everyone from the tedium of MRE.

- The *Rebbetzins* worked together in a way that transcended the ideological and cultural differences of the various sects that their husbands represented. The selfless service of these women was recognized by all aboard the *Hatikvah*.

8

TRADITIONS, FAITH & FAMILIES

As far as the Rabbis keeping track of the various holidays and other aspects of Jewish rituals that are time sensitive, space travel raised some serious concerns resulting in some interesting solutions.

On Earth there are observable determinants that ceased to be accessible on an intergalactic flight. According to Biblical law and millennia of tradition, *Shabbos* begins Friday evening at sunset. *Shabbos* candles need to be lit before the sun actually sets.

For the purpose of determining when *Shabbos* begins, time is a very localized matter which differs according to longitude and latitude, as well as seasonal shifting. For instance, Boston, New York, Philadelphia, Pittsburgh and Miami are all in the same time zone but for *Yidden* in each of those cities candles were lit at different times from one another.

Likewise, *Shabbos* ends after sunset on Saturday evening. The viewing of three stars in the sky is how Earthbound *Yidden* determined that the holy day has passed.

The Earth-bound Jewish calendar is lunar, with an elaborate periodic adjustment to bring the lunar calendar in line with the solar for seasonal consistency. A new moon determines the beginning of a new month.

Beyond the Earth, the Earth's moon serves no value for measuring passing time. On an intergalactic flight, there is no sunset. Beyond the solar system, the sun of the Home Planet cannot be seen whatsoever. Likewise, stars are always visible from the observation deck. On the *Hatikvah*, another system was needed for maintaining traditions.

The solution agreed to before the *Hatikvah* launched was that the ship would maintain New York City time for the entirety of the voyage.

The entire ship was designated as *Shomer Shabbos*. Of course, much of the daily operations of the ship were fully automated. Those aspects were uninterrupted, reminiscent of the old *Kosher* hotels on Earth that had elevators that stopped on each floor so no one would need to push any buttons on *Shabbos*.

Nonetheless, everyone was aware of when *Shabbos* began each week and there were real changes in patterns of activities for all aboard. Movies were shown six afternoons and evenings a week. There were no films Friday evening or Saturday afternoon. The public areas were generally used for playing cards, Scrabble, backgammon, chess, and similar activities. Those did not take place in public on *Shabbos*. All the public Beep-Beep Cookers were disabled from just before "sunset" Friday and would not operate until after "sunset" the next day.

Of course, the activities in private were not subject to public mores. What one did in one's private space - or a private meeting space with the blinds pulled down and the door closed - was a private matter.

The *Hatikvah* did not have a dress code, per se. A consensus for such would have been impossible to reach. Some of the biggest divides between the various religious factions had to do with types of clothing, hats, scarves, and other variants.

The one common agreement that could be reached was a general commitment to public modesty. Of course, the more devout dressed far more conservatively, with each of the sects having their own standards.

Many of the secular women adopted aspects of the religious dress standards, in public settings. Some discovered and appreciated that a skirt was easier to lift or slip out of than removing trousers. A skirt simplified casual liaisons. That was certainly an unintended consequence of the rabbinical meddling.

As already stated, the most religious pioneers were married couples raising hoards of children. There were also some married medical professionals and farming couples.

The unattached were disproportionately male, at a ratio of nearly three to one. Some singles formed committed relationships and sealed that under the *chuppah*.

Women that were so inclined wielded quite a bit of freedom to exercise choice. They were highly educated, independent women with healthy libidos and lots of free time on their hands. Over the years, some settled into relationships that were certainly marriage-like, with two or three men if that fit their temperament.

The various holidays that dot the calendar helped to provide relief from the ongoing sameness of daily life of long distance interstellar travel. The Rabbis coordinated the ritualistic aspects. Even the least observant aboard grew to appreciate an excuse for a celebration.

On Earth, the High Holidays were generally acknowledged by most *Yidden*. Passover and Hanukkah were also widely adopted by even those with only a tenuous attachment to ritual and religious structures.

Everyone *kvelled* with pleasure when the first potato *latkes* were served on the first shipboard Hanukkah. Of course, this was long before the food shortages on Planet Birobidzhan.

In the early days after landing - for the first couple of years - as one ship after another arrived, it seemed that all there was to eat was potatoes. At the time, some wisenheimers suggested that the *Bulbes* Song should be made the official Anthem of the Planet...as if!

Anyway, on this flight, as the years dragged on, even the holidays that were considered inconsequential on Earth gained importance.

For instance, the holiday of Purim became very popular. The cross dressing and the drunkenness of Purim that was exhibited by the otherwise staid rabbis reminded some of Mardi Gras in New Orleans. Soon, Purim became a social highlight for everyone on the flight.

After a couple of years, the influence of Mardi Gras seeped into the shipboard Purim celebrations. Nudity, with the cover of masks and body paint, was accepted with little notice and no conflict once the third Purim celebration on the *Hatikvah* rolled around.

By the time of the landing on Planet Birobidzhan, a certain level of exhibitionism and debauchery had become a standard part of the Purim festivities. No matter how the Rabbis that arrived on the subsequent flights felt about it, on Planet Birobidzhan, unfettered celebration of Purim had become traditional.

The birth rate of the religious women of this transport contributed directly to unforeseen cultural shifts aboard the *Hatikvah*.

Back on the Home Planet, the overall birth rate had dropped significantly over the century before the first flight. The average birth rate on Earth was just a bit over one child per mother. For the *Haredi* and *Hasidic* women, six, eight or ten per mother was the norm.

On Earth, the births were fairly evenly divided between male and female. Because of a space anomaly, the number of female births aboard the *Hatikvah* outnumbered the male children.

For the children aboard, marriages were often arranged at a fairly young age, with the traditional *Shidduch*. The increased number of female births, however, complicated the matchmaking process.

Over the years of drifting through the void, however, there were also drifting social changes.

Some of the doctors and farmers that had little inclination towards religious observations at the beginning of the voyage had drifted into the rabbinic circles as the years dragged on. Formerly secular men began attending regular *minyans*, *donning tefillin*, and wearing fringes. These men in their forties grew long beards and wore black hats and then stood under the *chuppah* with very young brides.

On the shoulders of these early pioneers, the culture of our new homeland, Planet Birobidzhan, was built.

9

THE TOWN OF FIRST LANDING

First Landing sits at the approximate center of Planet Birobidzhan's most populous continent. It is a dusty and wind-blown industrial town, at the eternal crossroads. The horizon is flat and unimpressive in every direction. First Landing is the third largest city on Planet Birobidzhan. It is a dreadful place.

Nearly every building in First Landing was constructed from prefabricated materials that had arrived on board the various transit ships or made from the hulls and cannibalized innards of those ships. Best described as a shanty town, it exudes a sense of decay and projects an aura of disintegration.

Few people would consciously choose to live in such a place. There is very little reason to stay put in a place such as First Landing, other than inertia. Of course, for some inertia is the primary force of their existence. That is really the best explanation for the continued habitation of First Landing after so many generations.

The intention of the Founders was for this place to be primarily a transit station. The spot was chosen because it was flat and central. These two factors made it the ideal landing spot for the ships coming from Earth. After landing and orientation, it was assumed that the *Yidden* would flow outward in all directions, filling the land.

Generations after the last transport from the Home Planet landed here, First Landing remains a transient location. First Landing is situated about halfway between Niu Yerushalaim and Niu Niu Yark. The continent's two main highways cross here. The airport and a train station serve as a regional hub.

First Landing has the largest slaughterhouse and meat packing facility on the planet. The Currency Printing Press and what can roughly be called the Central Bank is located there. There is a scattering of small *shuls*. A distillery produces a balm for the tedium of existence. Birobidzhan's only zoo is in New Landing, a monument of sorts to the disjointed thinking of the Agency planners.

The original greenhouses are still functioning in and around First Landing. These facilities grow winter fruits and vegetables. The planet's first vineyard and winery is situated nearby, on the outskirts of town.

For nearly eighteen years, the intergalactic starship the *Hatikvah* traveled through the void from the Home Planet. The trajectory was preprogrammed and automated. For all those years the half dozen pilots on board had no responsibilities other than to wait for the starship to arrive at the coordinates of our new homeland.

When the place that would eventually be known as Planet Birobidzhan was reached and orbiting was set, only one pilot was required for the landing. Nonetheless, they all met on the flight deck. The pilots worked closely together, scrutinizing charts and computer projections, in order to determine the best place on this planet to land. Wherever they put down would serve as the entrance point for all new arrivals for the foreseeable future.

When the *Hatikvah* was safely landed, the passengers were tasked with establishment of the infrastructure for the survivability of the new settlement. The pilots focused on building and maintenance of the landing site and providing electronic guidance for the subsequent unpiloted transit ships.

It can be said that in this aspect, the planning by the Agency and the presumptions and projections of the Earth-bound were right on target. This aspect of the settlement worked out just fine. However, not much else worked according to plan.

On Earth, the publicly stated official position expressed by the Agency was that the entire planetary Jewish population of twenty-five million would be transported in short order. Realistically, no one expected that to actually unfold. It was widely assumed that most of that population - perhaps as many as fifteen to twenty million would leave the Home Planet.

The optimists suggested that could be accomplished in ten years or less, not counting the actual transportation time, of course. The pessimistic position was that it would take twice as long. No one projected that before the third year of active transports, the flights would grind to a halt with significantly less than a million *Yidden* actually transported.

The skyport that the pilots had built and maintained is now the airport. Flights of a ten passenger plane between Niu Yerushalaim and Niu Niu Yark operate six days a week with a short stop at First Landing. The old observation tower and telescopes are used by amateur astronomers. Of course, a sighting of a ship from The Home Planet - or anywhere else - would be a huge event. No one realistically expects any outside contact these days.

The end of the immigration flights played havoc with the various presumptions held. Much of what passed as planning was based on the idea that supplies and personnel for settlement were to arrive in conjunction with timely needs. For instance, it was presumed that schools would not be a big priority for the first five years so teachers and school supplies would arrive later. They, of course, never did arrive.

For the eighteen years of the *Hatikvah's* flight and for the first couple of months on the new planet, there were sufficient varied food supplies for everyone. The Founders had grown accustomed to a consistent supply of fresh produce. The relative comfort of the living quarters on board the *Hatikvah* continued to provide shelter for them on this new planet.

The first of the void-transcending herring tins arrived just a couple of months after the *Hatikva*. There were 10,000 cryogenically preserved *Yidden* on board. As the cryogenically stored loads of new immigrants began arriving by the tens of thousands, the capacity to feed everyone satisfactorily was thoroughly strained and housing for the new immigrants was sketchy.

Upon defrosting on a strange planet, the new immigrants were housed in substandard dormitories and fed a diet consisting mainly of potatoes. Starvation was not an actual danger but there were shortages of everything with the exception of potatoes for the next three years.

According to the orientation before flight - and the master plan - a year's supply of *kosher* MRE would be sent with each cryogenic flight to assure that food supplies would last until the cultivation levels could sustain the population. However, the first of those flights included perhaps an eight month bare minimum food supply. Each subsequent ship held less supplies than the one before it. The Agency, it seems, presumed that the pioneering spirit would suffice if supplies dwindled.

The financial committee was certainly capable of getting the printing press up and running quickly. They printed plenty of cash. However, there was no real way to determine the value of the money and virtually nothing to spend the money on. There was a need for devising a distribution system for necessities in short supply. Ration coupons were far more important to those immigrants than paper shekels.

On Earth, it had been determined that the currency of the new settlement would be called the Shekel and that its value was equivalent to the Dollar. All potential immigrants were given the opportunity to transfer dollars to the Agency on Planet Earth in exchange for credit in shekels upon arrival on Planet Birobidzhan. That was the case for the passengers of the *Hatikvah* and the first of the subsequent flights.

As time elapsed, the Agency found that there was a growing reluctance to exchange hard cash for abstract promises. As an incentive, the rate of exchange increased. New immigrants thus arrived shekel-rich with their wealth duly noted in the ship computers. On arrival, they would receive stacks of nearly worthless cash.

The dollars the Agency acquired, they spent on Earth to purchase the ships and supplies for the next waves of immigration. The financial model was essentially similar to a pyramid or that of a ponzi scheme. The payoff for the immigrants was eighteen years away on a distant planet.

There was no direct accountability for the plans made by pencil pushers and accountants on Earth.

It was presumed that a market economy would be developed. No one really had a clue how that would happen or how long that would take.

It was also presumed that at some point intergalactic trade would develop and that ships would be outfitted for return flights and flights to other settled planets. Generations later, those hopes have yet to be realized.

It was presumed, on Earth, that the large bison-like creatures that roam our planet were similar enough to cattle to be a source of *kosher* meat. This was a false hope. For the first few critical years, meat was in very short supply. After a few years, it was determined that the wild hog-like creatures that the rabbis first disdained are actually *kosher*. At that point meat became plentiful as the *Yidden* learned to appreciate the *kosher* ham, pork, and bacon.

When the first few flights arrived, they were greeted with excitement and hope by the earlier immigrants. New people and fresh supplies held promise. The feelings of hope and promise soon began to fade as an account of the situation became clearer.

Supplies were inadequate. No one could make sense of the decisions made on Earth as to what was needed here on Planet Birobidzhan. Perhaps the Agency was just clueless. Perhaps they were making purchases based on calculations that were beyond comprehension. Perhaps there was a payola factor.

The initial charter for the settlement provided no formula for governance. Very little that resembles a government has ever developed here. There is no military, secular courts, police, public schools, jails, taxes or welfare. Also, virtually no public planning. In the early days, a lot of decisions were temporarily put off until those with more expertise arrived. Of course, those experts never arrived.

We do have rabbis - lots of rabbis - and rabbinic courts. However, because of the plethora, none of them carry a whole lot of weight. They can each, for instance, rule concerning marriage and divorce, dogma and theology, even declare excommunication. They can also contradict each other. If one is unhappy with a ruling from a *Beit Din*, a different answer to the question at hand might be found at a *shul* literally within a stone's throw.

There are historical reasons for the relative weakness of rabbinic authority on Planet Birobidzhan. The rabbis that arrived on the *Hatikvah* had been transformed by their time in transit. By the time they had reached the new planet, they had all developed a fairly laissez-faire attitude about most matters.

When the subsequent flights arrived, the rabbis that came along were much younger than those from the *Hatikvah*, so were inclined to give their elders leeway, treat their decisions as precedence, and follow the example of those that arrived earlier.

This is not to say that the rabbis did not have some real world matters to grapple with upon arrival. For those that traveled on the *Hatikvah*, ship time had been pinned to the Earth time of their departure point. Upon arrival, the clocks and calendar needed resetting.

The days of the week were certainly consistent. The daylight determined the time of the day. The moon was a whole other factor. On Earth, the new month of the Jewish calendar begins with a new moon. On Planet Birobidzhan, there are two moons. The cycle of neither moon is the same as the Earthly moon. Additionally, the seasons in this new land were significantly different from those of the Home Planet.

The rabbis had plenty to argue over concerning how to define time and the order for traditional celebrations under these totally new conditions. Of course, rabbinical arguments have a long tradition.

Not long after the two major cities of Niu Niu Yark and Niu Yerushalaim were settled, a major *Yeshiva* was established in each of these cities, as well as multiple minor ones just to add to the confusion. Each of the major institutions reflected an opposition to the other on almost every issue. It took years to reach a general consensus on the issues surrounding the calendar.

The new immigrants that arrived after the *Hatikvah* were predominantly very young. The Agency, it seems, believed that what was needed were young men with strong backs and women of a breeding age. So, what the immigrants lacked in education, they compensated with inexperience.

Those that had arrived on the *Hatikvah* were more skilled, far better educated and much older than the fresh arrivals. It was their mission to try to motivate the growing number of youthful immigrants to take on the task of exploring and settling the vast and empty planet.

An initial analysis of the planet projected that it could optimally sustain a population of five to seven billion people. Even if all of Earth's *Yidden* had been delivered at once, the Planet Birobidzhan would be sparsely populated for a very long time. This may have been why the Agency chose to ship absolutely no type of birth control - no condoms, no diaphragms, and no birth control pills - of any amounts on any of those ships.

Five major projects were seen as essential to those with any interest in planning.

The founding and development of the two major cities, Niu Niu Yark on the west coast of the continent and Niu Yerushalaim on the east coast was deemed paramount. The locations for these cities were chosen because of the deep natural harbors. A good harbor would provide a logical jumping off point for outward expansion to the rest of the planet.

The harvest of hardwood trees for lumber was considered essential for any advanced construction. In the southern part of the continent, the forest to sustain such an industry offered itself to developing.

Also to the south of First Landing were mineral deposits for potential mining.

The production of a wide variety of food to sustain the growing population required settlements in rural areas and the creation from scratch of an agricultural economy.

The piles of near worthless cash did not excite the new settlers. Ship load after ship load of immigrants arrived. The young people filled up First Landing waiting for inspiration and motivation. Other incentives besides illusory wealth were needed to encourage the youthful arrivals to take on such tasks.

Potatoes at every meal and nightmares of potatoes was the most compelling argument for carrying on the pioneering experiment. The potato has a rightful place in the history of Planet Birobidzhan.

Probably, the tedium of potatoes was more significant motivation than all of the planning and tinkering of ideologues, the theorizing of theoreticians, the philosophies or theological positioning of rabbis and sages on the Home Planet or PlanetBirobidzhan.

Der mentsh planirt aun got lakht. (Man plans and God laughs.)

10

A PERSONAL HISTORY OF AN EARLY SETTLER

My Grandfather was one of the earliest settlers on Planet Birobidzhan. He had, in his long lifetime, become one of the wealthiest men on the Planet. At the time of my Zaydeh's passing, he had left a significant fortune to be divided amongst his heirs.

The responsibility of sorting through his personal effects fell on my shoulders. In a desk drawer, I found a journal filled with various notations, accounts, and observations, including the essay that I reproduce here with no comments or editing.

It was certainly never my ambition to try to scratch out a living as a subsistence farmer. On the Home Planet, I had never even been to a farm. I was raised in a city with no agricultural training. I never even had a garden. I had started at the University and imagined that I was destined for commerce or perhaps law.

However, some issues arose. One thing led to another. My academic career was on the skids. It looked like I was going to lose my relatively comfortable position as a university student...and, even more importantly, the military deferment that resulted from my status as a student.

Emigration to another planet had suddenly become the least disagreeable option, if it could be arranged. Being accepted for passage, however, was more complicated than simply getting one's name on a list. Bookings were limited and a broad set of factors were considered to determine who received passage.

However, I did end up on Planet Birobidzhan and many years were spent growing potatoes and shoveling chicken shit.

My little corner of Planet Birobidzhan did not have much to offer. From what little I had seen - and from all that I had heard - it wasn't any better anywhere else. I frankly never had a whole lot of that pioneering spirit and what little I did have rapidly faded.

I wasn't much thinking about anything and I was paying attention to even less when the rooster's crowing pierced the clouds of self absorption that surrounded me.

"*Kukuriku, kukuriku!* Is that all you have to say?" I asked the rooster. He looked at me, tilted his head, scratched behind his ear and then crowed once more.

I can't say that I am surprised. Quite frankly, if he had something else to say besides *kukuriku* and managed to articulate it, that would certainly be something. He wasn't much for company or conversation but neither was I. I suppose we each settle into patterns and make the best of it.

Anyway, he was being awfully persistent with all that calling and strutting and flapping and such. I looked at the rooster.

The rooster cocked his head to stare off at the skyline to his left. I turned my head towards whatever it was the bird was gawking at. I stared at the empty horizon...and then I saw the streaking across the skyline.

I had arrived on one of the earliest transports. For a while, shiploads of settlers and supplies arrived with regularity every few weeks. Before long, however, the time between new arrivals began to stretch. Now, more than seventy years have passed since the last transport. So very few Earth-born can be counted on Planet Birobidzhan.

Life on Birobidzhan has normalized, so to speak. At the time, our lives were all in upheaval. We were almost all very young and inexperienced. We were on a vast planet full of unknowns. We had limited tools to work with and shortages of basic necessities. And somehow, we still each had to find a way to *macht a leben*.

My financial situation - if we can even use the term "financial" to discuss those early years of life on Planet Birobidzhan - was truly insecure. In the early days of planetary settlement, a lot of outcomes were determined in very informal ways. Family, friends, *mazel*, random rabbinic proclamations, *chutzpah*, and the prevailing winds were the things that mattered most and nearly all "business" involved these factors.

There were a lot of paper shekels in circulation but they held virtually no exchange value. Necessities were rationed, if available. For instance, each person could receive approximately two and a half cups of "*Shabbos* wine" per week. No amount of money could get you any more than that. In the early days, the paper shekels were used by gamblers and accepted by prostitutes. One could also buy rotgut schnapps with currency.

Family connections were way more valuable than cash. Relationship to those on earlier flights was one of the key factors in selection of a position by the Agency. My very passage on board one of the earliest transports was largely contingent on a hastily arranged marriage.

The young woman's familial connection to a prominent rabbi on the initial transport assured her place on board, if she were married. We met one day and became engaged the next. We married the morning of the launch and were placed in cryogenic sleep before consummation of our marriage.

My wife's family connections were enough to get us passage but not enough to gain either of us much pull once we arrived. The family "business" was a *yeshiva* in Niu Yerushalaim. We had absolutely no positions there. She was considered a "troubled child" by her family. Securing her safe passage off of Earth was all that they had to offer.

My family had arranged what I thought to be a significant level of monetary security. They had sold some property and cashed in some bonds. They added some modest savings to that. It all went into my personal account along with the little bit of *gelt* I still had from my *Bar Mitzvah*. The money in my account was all transferred to the Agency before we left the Home Planet. It was exchanged at what we thought to be a very favorable rate of three shekels to each dollar.

My family's assumption was that the money would have some value on the newly settled world. It would be many, many years before the paper shekels were worth anything except for the ephemeral vices, possibly decorating, or perhaps insulation if one had enough.

So, once we were defrosted and semi acclimated, we were faced with some very tough choices. I was not inclined to lumberjack or mining work. There were no shops or commerce to speak of at the time. The *kibbutzim* were full of socialists, secularists, and Hebraists. Niu Yerushalaim and Niu Niu Yark were dominated by the *yeshivas*. The Town of First Landing was rapidly filling with disenchanted and disillusioned new settlers.

We determined that one of the new *shtetls* and a small homestead was our best option and maybe doable. We put on our best front and made an effort to make things work. Well...at least for a while.

It had been nearly a year since the last ship had arrived from the Home Planet. The sighting of a ship was a big deal. It was heading to the port in the Town of First Landing. My little farm was not far from there. I decided to head there myself.

I told the rooster that I was going to town and that he was in charge while I was gone. He walked along with me for a while and then headed back to the chicken pen and his personal frustrations there. The two hens continued to fend him off. They wanted nothing to do with his self-important "*Kukuriku*!" or any other aspects of his rooster ways.

We were two of a kind, myself and that rooster. My wife had given up on the homesteading *shtick* in a little more than a New York minute. She was dazzled by the bright lights and easy ways of a nearby *kibbutz*. She went for a movie. She stayed for the communal meals and lesbian orgies. For the time being, the rooster was the closest I had to a friend and confidant.

My little farm was part of a *shtetl* that was so new that it didn't even have a name yet. The walk from there to the Town of First Landing is over two hours.

Fortunately for me, my neighbor *Reb* Goldman was driving his "Jeep" - Just Essential Parts - into town to pick up supplies. He picked me up along the way, shortening the trip to something like a half hour.

The time shaved off of that little trip by bumping along in that minimalist vehicle was not all that significant. More importantly, the fortuitous ride led to a serendipitous partnership that transformed both of our lives and guaranteed the security and wealth of our families.

When we arrived at the Space Port, the cryogenic technicians, of course, were on hand. The standard transports had each carried around 10,000 tightly packed passengers in a state of suspended animation and it was the task of the technicians to safely "defrost" the new arrivals.

The technicians were surprised by the ship's manifest and what they found on board. There were only a few hundred human passengers on this transport. The balance of this shipment carried an odd assortment of supplies and a very large number of Earth's endangered mammals.

The technicians followed the directions to defrost the people first. The passengers were biologists and zoologists. They had been sent to Birobidzhan to establish a zoo.

Groggy zoologists oversaw the unloading and unfolding of pre-built cages and wildlife habitats. Everything was included. Even a gate with a sign reading *Zoologisher Gortn* in both Yiddish and English, just in case there was any doubt as to what the Agency had sent our way. The future Birobidzhan Zoo began to take form adjacent to the Space Port.

When we arrived at the Space Port in *Reb* Goldman's pitiful excuse for a car, the place was busy with essential workers as well as crowded with curious and excited onlookers. Some of us were busy trying to figure an angle on whatever action there might be from the limited cargo of this rare transport that the crowd was already calling Noah's Ark.

The Agency had previously determined that it was uneconomical and nonviable to ship cattle. On Earth it was presumed that we would derive *kosher* meat mostly from the buffalo-like creatures that are roaming our savannas. This proved to be baseless optimism. At that time, we still presumed that the native wild hogs were *traif*, which was unfortunate ignorance on our part. Up until the arrival of Noah's Ark, the only Earth creatures on Planet Birobidzhan besides us *Yidden* were chickens and goats.

Meat, and even eggs, were still seriously limited. The arrival of breeding pairs of Earth mammals had everyone salivating even before the beasts were defrosted.

A gaggle of rabbis and *shochets* descended on the scene and inserted themselves into the middle of the fray. Someone needed to differentiate between the *kosher* and the *traif* and discourage hungry *Yidden* from trying to barbeque monkeys and hedgehogs.

Through and in spite of all this *balagan*, we pushed, haggled, elbowed, cajoled, *schmoozed*, and negotiated. Rabbis were gesticulating. Laborers were *schlepping*. Technicians and zoologists were trying to maintain order.

We managed to get our hands on a breeding pair of Argali sheep which originated from the Himalayas. We got them packed into a crate and dragged, pushed, and wiggled them towards *Reb* Goldman's Jeep. This is how *Reb* Goldman and I began our sheep herding partnership. We envisioned piles of *gelt* by cornering the planetary mutton trade.

We did not realize how long it would take to build a herd. We also never imagined that the rabbis would declare the native wild hogs to be *kosher* and that the *Yidden* of Planet Birobidzhan would so readily take to ham, pork, and bacon.

We earned a few shekels from the sheep over the years. We earned more from their horns, making *shofars* from them, than we did from the meat but nothing spectacular.

That is not to say, however, that this odd pair of Asian mountain sheep didn't play a role in initiating a very profitable convergence. We must certainly give credit where credit is due.

As we loaded the crate into the Jeep, I noticed a small packet of seeds on the ground by the back wheel. Perhaps it had been lodged in a crevice of one of the crate or maybe someone had dropped it or it had blown there. I slipped it into my pocket and gave it no further thought until I got home and we had our new livestock settled in.

To be perfectly honest about it, I didn't give that packet a whole lot of thought at that time either. A tiny amount of seeds was in the package labeled European Pennyroyal. The picture provided was none too impressive. The information provided suggested that they would grow in marginal soil and that the leaves were used in Italy to season lamb.

I scratched up some dirt behind my house and tossed the seeds in without any real expectations. The herb grew voraciously in that plot and expanded with vigor, displacing native grasses and weeds. I soon had a field filled with the stuff.

Evidently, that tiny packet was the only one of its kind to make it to Planet Birobidzhan. I had a monopoly, so to speak, for an obscure herb for seasoning lamb. Of course, lamb was still a luxury item but we had plenty of seasoning.

The word got around that I had lots of the stuff. I soon had growing consumer demand for this obscure seasoning.

When consumed as a tea, European Pennyroyal has the capacity to terminate pregnancy. We live in a world where birth control is non-existent and doctors are very reluctant to perform an abortion.

European Pennyroyal filled an important niche market. So, while the sheep raising enterprise was no big success, I split the profits from the herbal sales with *Reb* Goldman because a partnership is a partnership and none of it would have been possible if he hadn't picked me up in his Jeep that fateful day.

11

ACKNOWLEDGING THE BICENTENNIAL

(Excerpts from *Der Zhurnal)*

Der Zhurnal (the Journal) is the oldest and probably the most respected publication on Planet Birobidzhan.

Before the 200th year of planetary settlement, *Der Zhurnal* asked a wide range of writers to address our history and culture. Planet-wide, the call was answered. From the *shraybmashin* (typewriters) the essays below - covering a broad range of topics arrived.

The original essays were all published anonymously in the newspaper, to give each contributor the widest possible range of free expression. The editors also published a large table top book which turned out to be a financial disaster. Quite frankly, no one wanted to face a commemorative book on the subject of monumental failures while relaxing at home. Many of these essays are certainly well worth reading in their entirety, nonetheless.

The bicentennial of the First Landing on Planet Birobidzhan is worth noting, even if we have serious reservations concerning the original logic of this planetary settlement and the obvious failures to achieve any of the original goals.

How should we mark the Bicentennial? There are no celebrations planned. No one is thrilled to be living here. There are not even any commemorations scheduled. Well, maybe some of the rabbis will be fasting and tearing their clothes and throwing ashes and dust about.

Nonetheless, there is reason for introspection and examination of our founding and development. Two hundred years gives us a significant amount of history separate from the Home Planet. This is as good of a reason, and as good of a time as any, to examine the trajectory of our history.

Presented here are condensed highlights, with some minor editing for clarity and to reduce redundancy, with much thanks to the editorial board of *Der Zhurnal*.

THE TATTERED CONNECTION

(From Der Zhurnal)

The First Landing was full of hope and possibilities. Two hundred years is certainly enough time for retrospective considerations.

Perhaps the foreshadowing of the soon broken contact should have been evident, but it wasn't. Even when the span between the arrivals of new ships full of immigrants began to widen, no one predicted that the flow of new arrivals would simply stop without a warning or another word from the Home Planet.

When our ancestors concluded that our new home had lost all contact with the Home Planet, the only possible assumption was that something had gone terribly wrong.

What that *something* was led to all sorts of groundless speculation. War and social upheaval? An unspeakable environmental disaster? No one could know but everyone had an opinion.

Some even suggested that the *Moshiach* had come to gather up the remnants of our people and fly them on the backs of eagles to the Promised Land. We were left out of the incoming, they suggested, because we had abandoned our trust in the Holy One, Blessed Be His Name, by leaving the Home Planet.

ECONOMICS: CRONYISM & NEPOTISM

(From Der Zhurnal)

The two most commonly heard utterances in Yiddish are *Vas?* (what?) and *Farvas?* (why?). This perhaps reflects the Jewish traditional attitudes of questioning everything.

On Planet Birobidzhan, the phrase *Aun Vas?* (and what?) became the most widely heard of all spoken words, reflecting the Planetary distrust of all aspects of what could roughly be labeled as economics on Planet Birobidzhan.

In the early days, everyone seemed to have lots of money. The money, however, was of limited value. There was so little that one could actually purchase. Manufacturing had just barely begun. Agricultural products were hardly available. Wood and minerals were nearly non-existent. Earth originated supplies were scarce. If one had something of value, exchanging it for currency of uncertain value seemed foolhardy.

A prevalent business practice arose that was commonly called "*Aun Vas*". When coming to an agreement on the price of merchandise, it would be the number of shekels... "*aun vas*" to close the deal. Cash alone was seen as highly speculative and tenuous. Sellers preferred something more tangible.

There was no planned economy or single model for economic development. The economic structures of enterprise fell into roughly four somewhat distinct categories.

The rabbinic structures - this would include the *yeshivas*, the *shuls*, the *moyels*, the *sochets* - all operated based on family connections. These were controlled by the various sectarian dynasties. Decisions and advancement were also determined to some degree by meritocracy.

The mining and lumber industries were essentially corporations or syndicates.

The *kibbutzim* were, at least in theory, collective enterprises, as were some worker-owned and operated businesses. The brothels, for instance, were, and still are, all worker-owned and self-managed cooperatives.

In the *shtetls*, individualism and family enterprise were the norm.

THE JEWS HARP

(From Der Zhurnal)

Rather than the Yiddish *der bromayzer* or the German *Maultrommel*, we generally use the English name Jews Harp for that quaint instrument. This is exemplary of the way our language developed here on Planet Birobidzhan.

Whatever we choose to call those twangy music making objects, nearly every one of us owns at least one. *Farvas* (why) so many Jews Harps, you ask?

Agency policies that drastically limited space allotted for supplies, the lack of resources available on Planet Birobidzhan, the tedium of daily life, and the vast amounts of paper money were all factors. That, and the nature of two brothers, Moshe and Mendel, from Tennessee.

The brothers were amateur musicians. Because of the incredibly limited space allotted to each passenger for personal supplies, the brothers decided to each carry a Jews Harp, an instrument which fits comfortably in any pocket.

Upon arrival on Planet Birobidzhan, the boys had a lot of time on their hands. They spent a lot of that time "fiddling" on their Jews Harps. Bored settlers were attracted to the sound and pleased by any distraction. The boys, having the only ones on the planet, cultivated a following, of sorts.

One thing led to another and soon they were making, and selling the noisy *tsatskes*. They would sell them for a shekel or two. No one considered the money of any value and most people had plenty of cash with nothing to spend it on.

The teenagers sold Jews Harps like hotcakes. *A bisl aun a bisl vert a ful shtisl.* Those shekels began to add up. One day they were selling the *tsatskes* from a pushcart and then they opened a store with an impressive sign: **Moshe & Mendel's Jew Harp, Tsatske aun Muzik Krom**, complete with a picture of a harp - a real, historic, full size harp that had once been the logo of an Irish beer back on the Home Planet.

A LANGUAGE OF OUR OWN

(From Der Zhurnal)

Long ago, on Planet Earth, Yiddish was often referred to as a jargon, or *zhargon*, rather than a *real* language. Some considered Yiddish to be a patois or a creole, a bastardized conglomerate and a crude construction.

Yiddishists, particularly writers and academics, worked diligently to dispel this belief that Yiddish was substandard. Dedicated Yiddish linguists attempted at every turn to prove the legitimacy of the *Mamaloshen*.

In the early days of planetary settlement, Yiddishists and the Hebraists argued passionately for language purity. Occasionally advocates for Ladino as well as other Judaeo-linguistic streams also pushed for representation in the establishment of an *official* and *authentic* planetary *shprakh*.

The *Yidden* of Planet Birobidzhan generally ignored the debates and considerations of the intellectuals. Yidden continue to communicate as our predecessors had back on Earth, making it all up as they went along. With no embarrassment whatsoever, Yiddish speakers mangle grammar and pronunciation as well as carelessly introduce new words from other languages.

The language we speak here, after two centuries without any contact with the Home Planet, is assuredly a form of Yiddish unique to Planet Birobidzhan. If contact with Earth is ever reestablished, and if *Yidden* can be found there, finding a common language might be seriously difficult.

FREE RANGING CHICKENS

(From Der Zhurnal)

The prevalence of chickens on Planet Birobidzhan can be seen as a combination of successful planning and the sheer tenacity of chickens.

The *Hatikvah*, the first ship to land here and the only ship that passengers traveled in "real time" rather than cryogenic preservation, had free-range chickens aboard. Those passengers on board had a steady supply of nearly daily eggs and chicken for every *Shabbos* and Holy Days.

Upon landing, with the knowledge that new settlers would be arriving by the tens of thousands, a crash course in chicken breeding began.

One of the few opportunities offered to new arrivals was the chance to try one's hand at raising chickens. Settlers were offered a breeding pair and some received a rooster and two hens. The pairs were commonly called Adam and Eve and those sets with the extra hen were called Adam, Eve, and Lilith.

Settlers were urged to refrain from culling eggs to begin with, to allow for a population growth. Hens, given the opportunity, can really be "fruitful and multiply" and bring forth a lot of descendants. At six months of age the next generation are mature and can start breeding.

On the Home Planet, chickens faced all sorts of threats. Their lives were tenuous. Those in captivity lived short, relatively protected lives that generally ended in slaughter. They were, nonetheless, subjected to a wide range of predators such as foxes, cougars, and hawks as well as domestic dangers such as dogs. Those that lived "in the wild" also risked death by cars, trains, and other industrial threats.

Chickens on Planet Birobidzhan live in a *Gan Eden* of sorts, a virtual Paradise. On Planet Birobidzhan, chickens have no natural predators other than man.

The chickens of Planet Birobidzhan have moderate weather, lots to eat and plenty of bramble to hide in when on the run and avoiding humans. There are a lot of chickens on the run. The *Yidden* that received birds for breeding had little experience with raising animals or, for that matter, construction of shelters. Chickens are fairly ingenious at escaping.

The result is that far more chickens are running wild than domesticated. At first, the *Yidden* spent an exuberant amount of effort trying to contain their birds. Then, they tried to mark or brand the chickens. Rabbis were constantly being called in to settle arguments over the rightful ownership of wayward chickens. Eventually, everyone threw their hands up in the air and accepted fate.

Chickens on the loose are no longer considered as property, but more like wild fish. The Chicken Protocol is rooted in those early days. Anyone with a net is free to gather chickens. Anyone willing to crawl through the bramble where the chickens brood can freely gather eggs.

HOSPITALS & MEDITSINISH GORTNS

(From Der Zhurnal)

Back on the Home Planet, there was a widely held belief among the Nations that *Yidden* dominated the medical profession. This was never actually the case. Jews did, however, have a significantly disproportionate representation as doctors.

When the relocation project began, many highly trained medical professionals signed up for transport and received preferential placement on the earliest ships.

The initial voyage of the *Hatikvah* included a top notch crew of doctors and nurses, entrusted to establish a state of the art, high end hospital upon arrival. That hospital, equal to the finest facilities of Earth, was built and staffed in the boomtown of First Landing. The First Landing Hospital also served as a training center and essentially a Medical University.

Quality medical facilities were also soon built in both of the major *groys stadts*, Niu Yerushalaim and Niu Niu Yark.

The *kibbutzim*, on the whole, developed state of the art clinics that served their membership as well as the outlying unaffiliated settlers. The lumber and mining corporations maintained emergency clinics to deal with industrial accidents. Some of the larger *shtetls* soon had clinics as well.

The *Magen David Adom* is what the loose volunteer networks that tie together all of the medical facilities and emergency transportation is called. The name Red Shield of David derives from the Hebrew and an association of similar purpose that operated on Earth long ago.

Large swaths of our Planet Birobidzhan, however, have little or no clinics, emergency or other. Visiting doctors do make some rounds and offer somewhat impromptu services, particularly vaccinations and such. In the smallest *shtetls*, an actual doctor or nurse is as rare as hen teeth, even after two centuries of planetary settlement.

In even the tiniest of *shtetls* we have *Yidden* that have self-trained in emergency care and have an extensive familiarity with herbal remedies with an extensive *Meditsinish Gortn* (medical garden) to serve as a pharmacy of sorts.

LITERACY AND EDUCATION

(From Der Zhurnal)

Planet Birobidzhan has a literacy rate of nearly 100%. Certainly higher than any region of the Home Planet at the time that we lost contact. We have a Medical University that is spectacular and we have *Yeshivas* that are stellar.

Back on the Home Planet, some form of public education funded through taxation operated planet wide. Schooling was available to nearly every Earth-born child, and was largely compulsory.

On Planet Birobidzhan, of course, we have no such thing. We have no government to determine what is compulsory or to collect taxes and disperse funds therefore we have no public education or school system. Perhaps that makes our literacy level all the more impressive.

Perhaps, if we hadn't been cut adrift from the umbilical connection to our Planet of Origin so soon after the First Landing and early settlement of Planet Birobidzhan had begun, our processes of education may have developed differently. Probably so.

The Agency back on the Home Planet determined the supplies and personnel for each shipment. It was assumed on Earth that early child education would not be a pressing matter for the first few years. Teachers and school supplies were not prioritized and then the flights stopped.

The birthrate on Planet Birobidzhan is still high compared to the historical rate on Planet Earth. In the first few years, before the use of herbal concoctions to alter fertility cycles had become widespread, the birthrate was extraordinarily high. There were a lot of babies born in the first precarious decades of settlement.

Some of the earliest settlers were highly educated and inclined toward homeschooling their offspring. A more significant factor was the preponderance of rabbis with little to do. The rabbis envisioned it as their duty to educate the young. They reached back to a traditional form of schooling called the *cheder*. The *cheders* were one room schools.

Unemployed rabbis became *melameds*, that is, teachers. Children as young as three were given a rudimentary education, mostly consisting of learning the *Aleph Beis*, how to read, and some simplified religious studies. So, the children all learned to read. For a few shekels the young ones were out of their parents' hair for a few hours a day.

After around a half dozen years with a *melamed*, the parents and the students had decisions to make. Some children headed to *yeshivas* for more advanced religious studies. Most entered into some form of apprenticeship, to learn a useful trade.

12

DOVID'S NESHUMEH

Dovid's mother certainly tried to tie him to her apron strings. When he was a little *pisher*, she seemingly was held by an emotional bond to him unlike that of any of his eight older siblings.

She fondled him and used terms of endearment. She breastfed him more often. She weaned him more reluctantly and much later than any of the rest of her brood. Dovid's mama also postponed enrolling him into a *cheder* until he was very nearly five.

Maybe it had something to do with his *neshumeh*, his inner spark, that was her reason to treat this child differently than the others.

Perhaps it had more to do with his mother's firm decision that this child would be the end of her cycles of birthing. After his birth, the midwife's assistant visited often and began supplying her with the herbal tea blend that kept her menstruation regular, freeing her from the blessing or curse of pregnancy.

So, night after night, Dovid slept with one hand on his mother's breast and the heels of his feet digging into her husband's ribs. This went on, almost as if it was a plan.

Any effort on his mother's part to keep him at home, however, had no long term effects. When Dovid turned three, he still had eight siblings below the age of *Bar Mitzvah*. Dovid had plenty of role models for mischief seeking and for avoiding parental authority. Beyond that, a passion for adventure burned so brightly inside of him that it was nearly impossible to conceal or suppress.

Beginning before he was even out of diapers, Dovid had an uncanny ability to disconnect, dismantle, and reverse engineer everything within reach. He would bend, break, remold, mangle, and chew on everything. He wanted to know how everything worked and what everything tasted like.

It is not uncommon for children to ask "Why?" repetitively. Dovid, however, rarely did so. What Dovid would ask is "How?" He wanted to know, for instance, what made clocks tick and would find out - often to the frustration of the clock's owner.

And, in spite of a late beginning at *cheder* Dovid mastered the *Aleph Beis* and was an exemplary reader quite early. He quickly worked his way through the *melamed's* books and the knowledge that the *melamed* had to offer. The teacher was quite aware that his young pupil was destined for advanced studies beyond the limited walls of that *cheder.*

One day, when Dovid was ten, he was found lying on the ground. His eyes were wide open but he exhibited no obvious awareness of his surroundings nor of the worried family and neighbors that encircled him. He was carried, in this condition, back home. A doctor, a rabbi, and an herbalist were summoned.

Hours passed with the doctor checking Dovid's pulse, temperature, reflexes, etc. The rabbi prayed. The herbalist made a relaxing tea to calm the anxious family.

The doctor suspected that Dovid was suffering from a fit connected to some form of latent epilepsy. The rabbi hypothesized that Dovid was possibly possessed by a *dybbuk*. The herbalist expressed no opinion and continued to care for the frazzled nerves of the worried family.

After several hours Dovid sat up. He looked around and smiled contentedly. Then, he closed his eyes and slept peacefully. A broad series of medical tests were performed on the child over the following weeks. No cause for the incident could be determined.

Dovid told none of them about the mushrooms he had eaten or the visions that he had experienced. It was many years before he let anyone know about those experiences. He was, after his initial encounter with the fungi, very careful to conceal his experimentations and assure that he was in a secure place before again ingesting the mushrooms and entering into trance-like conditions.

On the Home Planet, over the tens or hundreds of thousands of years that humanity dwelled there, the flora and fungi were pretty well understood. Through generation after generation of experimentation, we knew which are edible and which are poisonous as well as the ones that had medical value or psychoactive potential.

Planet Birobidzhan doesn't have thousands of years of human experience. Our presence here is a mere blink of an eye. Our ancestors brought the seeds and cuttings from Earth to assure our needs. They held a significant degree of mistrust for what grew wild on the planet where they had settled.

The flora of Planet Birobidzhan are still mostly a mystery to us and the fungi even more so. Only a relatively handful of native plants are considered to be safe for human consumption. Many are known to be poisonous. Children are sternly warned against eating random plants and to refrain from even touching the fungi.

What compelled Dovid to eat the Mushrooms of Planet Birobidzhan? It seems that they called out to him and he answered their call.

13

THE OCTOGENARIAN AND THE YOUNGSTER

It is generally acknowledged that those younger than thirteen cannot enter into contractual relationships on their own. While it is not unheard of for those as young as ten to become apprenticed, that sort of contract is usually initiated by the youth's parents.

When the man from First Landing known as *Der Profesor* knocked on the door with a briefcase containing an apprenticeship contract, everyone was caught unaware except for Dovid, of course...because the contract was his idea.

Unbeknownst to his mother, Dovid had, since he was seven, been regularly walking the three miles - and occasionally catching a ride on a goat cart - commuting from his small *shtetl* to the airport in First Landing almost daily. There, he met with the members of the Birobidzhan Pilots Association and learned to build and fly model airplanes.

Der Profesor was the honored patriarch of the Birobidzhan Pilots Association. An old man by any measure, he maintained a library at the airport and served as a mentor to the youngsters that showed particular promise.

Dovid was the youngest of those that gathered at the First Landing Airport. He could disassemble and improve on all the working models. He could troubleshoot and repair the broken ones. He was working his way through the books in the library. In his "spare time" Dovid was teaching himself English and German.

It was no wonder that *Der Profesor* took a liking to Dovid. *Der Profesor* was a wellspring of knowledge and it was little wonder that the boy was drawn to such an inspiration.

It should be noted that it was after the mushroom induced trance-like experience that Dovid's interest in flight turned to rockets. The simple camaraderie of the Pilots Association was no longer enough for the boy. He needed to know the *how* of rocketry and the intricacies of intergalactic travel. That required study, research and experimentation. And that required the guidance of *Der Profesor*.

Of course, the immigration ships that brought settlers from the Home Planet to Planet Birobidzhan two centuries earlier were designed for one way travel. On arrival, they were stripped for useful parts and repurposed to support the settlement. Much of First Landing has a shanty town feel to it precisely because so much of the city is built from repurposed transport ships.

At the time, it was presumed that travel *from* Planet Birobidzhan would commence at some point in the future when the settlement was completed and intergalactic trade was plausible. However, the new arrivals of immigration ships simply ended and contact with the Home Planet was severed without warning.

The First Landing Airport is developed on the original landing field. It now serves as a transportation hub for our limited airplane service. Additionally, there are the observatory facilities that now mostly serve amateur astronomers.

There is also the substantial library that features thousands of books and most of the computer systems from the initial *Hatikvah* ship, which were quite extensive, as well as some of the limited computer equipment from the subsequent automated transports. This is the library that is sustained by the Pilots' Association and is under the guiding hand and tutelage of *Der Profesor*.

So, after meeting with Dovid's parents and discussion that largely went beyond their comprehension, the contract was signed by *Der Profesor* and Dovid's mother.

From then forward, Dovid's time in the *cheder* was reduced to just a few hours a week and the greater part of his education came officially and directly under the supervision of *Der Profesor*.

The octogenarian and the youngster were often seen taking long walks together. They spoke to each other on the widest variety of intellectual topics, casually shifting between Yiddish, English, and German. They mostly ignored those around them when walking through the city streets, absorbed in their exchange.

As Dovid grew taller and *Der Profesor* continued to age, the old man would lean on the boy for stability as they walked. *Der Profesor* was well versed in all sorts of esoteric knowledge and young Dovid's mind was a sponge.

Their discussions invariably focused on space travel, various fuels and energy sources, galactic mapping, and rocketry. How they approached these subjects, however, was rarely direct. For instance, in Greek mythology, Daedalus formed wings from wax to enable flight. His son, Icarus, suffered by flying too close to the sun. *Der Profesor* insisted that Dovid absorbed the lessons that the mythology had to offer possible intergalactic travelers.

14

FLIES AND MUSHROOMS

We are *blessed* with two kinds of flies on Planet Birobidzhan. Both are incredibly annoying and quite plentiful. Neither species is native to Planet Birobidzhan. Neither were imported intentionally. Both types of flies have adapted well to the environment of Planet Birobidzhan.

The one that we call a *ferd flig* or horse-fly tend towards individualized torture and biting. Those that we call *hoyz flig* or housefly swarm and buzz one's eyes and nose.

We do have houses on Planet Birobidzhan but the houseflies do not show any particular preference to our homes. Perhaps they were more inclined to houses back on Earth. As far as horse-flies are concerned, perhaps they had an affinity for the creatures called horses back on Earth.

We have no horses here. I am no more familiar with a horse than I am with a Leviathan or a whale or a bear or a unicorn or a kitten. And yet, after all these years and the unfathomable space distance, each of these still seem to influence our lives.

Besides the *ferd flig*, we say that an industrious man "works like a horse" and we give our children hobby-horses to play with. The rabbis speak of the Leviathan as if they have personal experiences with it. We may say that a fat person is "as large as a whale". Teddy Bears and other sorts of *beralas* are in our toy stores and in every child's nursery. We call our dearest children *ketscheles* as if kittens were something we know and love.

I assume that unicorns, however, are mythological, although perhaps they once lived on Earth as well. Perhaps when the *Moshiach* comes and we are transferred to a *Yenne Velt* - a better world, we hope - we will once again know those creatures and perhaps even unicorns.

It is plausible that the flies arrived with the first settlers on the *Hatikvah*, but that seems highly unlikely. Even if pests of these sorts had found a way onto that flight, we can rightly assume that the volunteers aboard, with plenty of free time on their hands, would have found a way to exterminate such during the nearly eighteen years of traveling.

It is more plausible that flies arrived with the *Zoologisher Gortn* on the transport that is colloquially known as Noah's Ark. The most likely pathway was for larvae to have traveled in the digestive tracts of the cryogenically preserved animals that were sent to us to populate our zoo.

That the Agency determined that our barely settled planet was somehow in need of a zoo is really quite curious. Over the years, there has been an incredible amount of speculation concerning their decision making process. The prevailing consensus is that some degree of payola must have been involved.

The animals chosen for us by those Earth-bound bureaucrats were breeding pairs of a wide variety of Earth mammals. None were domesticated creatures. No pets. No working animals. No livestock. Also, no sea creatures as we were not equipped for an aquarium and no very large animals such as the elephants or even the larger wild cats because of the limited transport space.

As near as we can guess, the animals were chosen to have no practical use. Nonetheless, there were a few attempts to find practical uses for the gift we received from the Home Planet. Various wild sheep and goats have been bred and are being raised on farms with some success.

There is also a farm that has been raising zebras for nearly two centuries with a vague hope to turn them into something pony-like. With an awful lot of encouragement, zebras can be convinced to pull a wagon with a light load. Of course, goats are easier to train and cost less to keep.

Shortly after the zoo was established, a male mountain lion broke free from confinement. The creature roamed the lightly settled outskirts of First Landing for a good part of a year, before returning to free his mate. The resulting pack that soon came to be wreaked havoc on goat herds and chicken flocks. The mountain lions were hunted down and exterminated.

A pair of lemurs slipped out and found sanctuary in a forested area not far from town. The lemurs were fruitful and multiplied. They have adapted so well that many people assume the lemurs to be native to Planet Birobidzhan.

One summertime *Shabbos*, shortly before Dovid's thirteenth birthday, the boy went for a long walk on his own. He walked through the forest where the lemurs lived and past the zebra ranch. From just beyond the zebra ranch, one can see the mountain where a cold stream originates that runs into the valley and towards the ocean. Parts of the stream can be seen but much of it is obscured, blocked by rolling hills and stretches of forests.

The day was hot and Dovid was being pestered by both kinds of flies, seemingly taking turns. He headed into a shady cove of trees, seeking some relief from the flies and the hot sun. There, he found mushrooms growing and the swarm of flies parted, leaving the boy in peace.

It had been nearly a year since he had last found and eaten any. As in the other times, the mushrooms seemed to speak personally to Dovid and direct him. He harvested their flesh and chewed upon it in the cool shade.

There he sat, calmly waiting for the trance-like stage to begin. A light breeze blew through the valley below. A mist cleared and in a bend of the stream a clear pool of water came into view.

This was the swimming hole where the young *kibbutzniks* swam naked. Despite the distance, the young woman came into focus with an unparalleled clarity. Dovid was certain that this was his Bathsheba, the destined love of his life, his *bashert*.

Dovid looked on from the distance, feeling drawn to another as never before. The mist returned, covering the swimming hole and obscuring his view. As this happened, the full effect of the mushrooms took hold. He sat there for hours, disconnected from the physical world around him.

15

AN OTHERWORLDLY HAVDALAH

It is subjective to describe Dovid's mushroom experiences as trance-like. That is certainly what it would appear to be from the outside, looking in. However, that is not how Dovid perceived the time *interacting* with the Mushrooms of Planet Birobidzhan.

From the first encounter when he was ten until Dovid's most recent, each of the half-dozen sessions felt like an immersive seminar of sorts. Knowledge and understanding seemed to be poured into him to the point of overflowing.

It felt something like getting a drink from a waterfall or a powerful hose. He couldn't possibly have absorbed it all. Certainly, not on his own. As of yet, however, he had spoken to no others about these seismic psychic and emotional floodings that had been transforming him.

The encounters each began in the same way. After chewing on the fleshy fungus a calmness came over Dovid. A sense of overall comfort and peacefulness enveloped him. His breathing slowed. The physical world seemed to fade away before the encounter began in earnest.

Dovid perceived a curtain opening or something like a veil lifting. Then, he saw a hand stretching before him holding a scroll. The scroll unfurled before him with lettering that he didn't recognize.

As if hearing the words spoken but yet unspoken, or perhaps spoken directly to his mind, in Biblical Hebrew, quoting directly from Ezekiel, with utmost clarity, Dovid perceived a voice that wasn't quite a voice speaking.

These are the words he heard each time: "Son of Man, open your mouth and eat what is offered. Son of Man, feed your stomach and fill your belly with the scroll that I give you."

The perceptions from that point became panoramic. Sound and sights blended. Time lost all meaning. Space unfolded. Colors blended. Void and form would coincide and Dovid would witness the moment of creation.

Gasses and solids would blend and move outward at unfathomable speed as they formed innumerable stars with planets circling each star. When the expansion rested, a peaceful field would unfold, covered with mushrooms. The expanse above was always a star-filled night sky of unfamiliar constellations.

Following this sequence that he began to think of as a standardized introduction, something that could be understood as more akin to a lecture or instructional film began.

Dovid would see, feel, and hear multi dimensional puzzles being assembled, diagrams, maps, and charts protracting, building blocks stacking, architectural blueprints unfolding, great flowing motions of immense patterns of cosmic winds, dust storms, and hurricanes moving about.

For Dovid, in a very personal way, unasked questions were answered. Mysteries were resolved and then new questions were raised and new mysteries arose. With each session, earlier lessons would repeat with greater rapidity, laying the groundwork for the advancement.

Dovid was unable to determine a direct line between the mushroom guidance and knowledge absorbed. Nonetheless, he found that he was able to approach practical matters in unique problem solving ways with a sense of knowing that could not be easily explained. That capacity certainly would catch *Der Profesor* and his associates by surprise.

How could it be explained that a child from a *shtetl* could intuitively understand metallurgy, complex physics, star mapping of distant galaxies, the process to create new liquid fuels, and more? Surely, no other possibilities than either inherent genius or the guidance of a superior intelligence. Dovid had yet to share the source of his inspiration.

As each of the previous programmings headed towards conclusion, the vista of the field with the mushrooms returned. Then, as if self-constructed, a craft assembled amongst the mushrooms. There would be a blast of light and the craft would lift into the star-filled horizon. Dovid would see from the vantage point of the rising rocket and then that sky would fade and he would once again be aware of the physical world around him. After another half hour or so, he would be able to move about.

On that hot *Shabbos* afternoon, not far from the zebra ranch, in the woods above the swimming hole, the general pattern continued. Fields and hills of flowering plants unfolded. Schools of fish, herds of land beasts, flocks of birds, and swarms of insects whirled about.

Then, in a distinct break from the pattern, a clearing of sorts in the imagery occurred and the bend in the stream where the *kibbutzniks* swim came into focus. The young woman that Dovid was enamored with filled his vision and then the vista of the field with the mushrooms returned.

In the place where he would have expected a craft to form, a human phallus rose to full erection. Above the phallus, filling the sky, a pair of legs spread themselves and the entire skyline was a human vagina. When the phallus reached climax, the horizon exploded with a glorious array of unfamiliar stars.

Dovid's normal consciousness slowly returned and the world around him came into focus.

The sun had set. The *Shabbos* on Planet Birobidzhan had concluded while Dovid was immersed in the otherworldly. Through the trees, the familiar sky was visible. Dovid remained reclining on the ground, gazing at the firmament.

Dovid, a boy on the cusp of turning thirteen, thought about the *Shechinah's* arrival at the moment of the *havdalah*, the conclusion of the Sabbath. He considered the separation between the holy and the common place, between the *Shabbos* and the work week. And he contemplated the possible lessons of the mushroom induced visions.

While walking back to First Landing, Dovid determined that the time had come for him to confide in *Der Profesor* about the mushrooms. As he approached the airport, however, the lights downtown grabbed his attention.

While certainly not as vibrant or exciting as Niu Niu Yark or Niu Yerushalaim, First Landing does have a small entertainment district. The bars, restaurants, bordellos, shops, and cafes in that downtown district reopen after the *Shabbos* concludes and stay open late.

The entertainment district offers a reprieve for those that need more of a separation between the *Shabbos* and the beginning of their work week than that of a burning braided candle and a sip of wine from a shared cup.

Dovid headed towards his favorite cafe for a cup of strong tea. Tomorrow, he assured himself, would be soon enough for that discussion with his mentor.

16

COURTSHIP & MARRIAGE

Previously, he had only been to this cafe occasionally in the afternoon and only with *Der Profesor*. At those times, the cafe was always sparsely occupied, a quiet place for them to drink tea and talk.

Dovid entered the cafe and found it that evening to be quite crowded. *Klezmorim* were playing upbeat music. Waiters were bustling about and shouting orders to the kitchen staff. The tables were full of customers, laughing and talking loudly to each other.

Dovid maneuvered his way through the tightly placed tables filled with customers, towards the back room. While looking for a place to sit, he was simultaneously second guessing his decision to go downtown on his own on a Saturday night.

Though intelligent and wise beyond his years, Dovid was, after all, still a somewhat awkward twelve year old. A *bar mitzvah* and adulthood was still a few months away. He actually almost turned to leave when he saw her sitting along the back wall, surrounded by friends in animated conversation. There, in the cafe, was the young woman that he saw from a distance that afternoon. And then again within the mushroom vision. This was the beauty that he thought of as Bathsheba.

Dovid approached and then stopped. He stood there, staring, with his mouth slightly agape. How could he tell her, without sounding ridiculous or worse yet, creepy, that this meeting was a matter of *bashert*, destiny, fate?

The cultural barriers must have seemed enormous to him. The woman of his vision was surrounded by her peers. They were *kibbutznik* youth, with all the swagger and bravado that entails, from the way they dressed to the way they spoke. Additionally, they were all past the *bar mitzvah* point, the age of emancipation. He was a twelve year old, seen by the world as a child. The thirteen and fourteen year olds that he faced were adults.

Dovid bit his lip and focused his mind on making a good impression. The more he thought about that, the more of an impossibility that seemed. His clothes were ill-fitting hand-me-downs. Their clothing was all well fitting and stylish. His hair was disheveled and his *payos* hung at odd angles, flopping about with every move of his head. They all had sharp haircuts and no side curls. His *tzitzis* fluttered with each step, while their fringes were unseen and possibly not even worn. Needless to say, he looked and felt provincial.

The *kibbutzniks* were all wearing what they call their "town clothes". In order to maintain minimum standards of the social norms, *kibbutzniks* generally adapt their dress when they leave the *kibbutz*. By striving for *minimum* standards, their acquiescence to social norms come off as flagrant disregard. The young men were all clean-shaven. Their heads wore *yarmulkes* of little consequence and with an attitude of flippancy. The women wore skirts that barely came to their knees. The sleeves of their blouses cut off somewhere around their elbows. The conformity felt artificial, which it certainly was. All told, the *kibbutzniks* presented an image of exuberant modernity.

He reminded himself that he had flown in airplanes and that he knew more about liquid fuels and explosives than anyone on Planet Birobidzhan. Somehow, those things didn't make a difference concerning a first impression. He looked and felt like a country bumpkin. To top it off, he was just standing there, staring.

"It looks like you have an admirer," one of the fellows said to her with a bit of a snicker. Dovid felt as if the entire room had turned in his direction but he was only concerned about one person. She looked in his general direction and smiled.

"He's kinda cute, in a way," she responded to her friend's gibe while continuing to smile abstractly although seemingly taking little notice of Dovid.

Dovid threw caution to the wind and took another couple of steps closer to the table. "The cafe is crowded tonight and I am here by myself. Would it be alright if I join you?"

The young woman looked him up and down. *"Bitte. Zitsn do,"* she said, indicating the seat next to her. "My name is Rifka Leeba, but everyone calls me Bat."

Without missing a beat, Dovid said "*Ich bin Dovid und du bist mayn Bat-Sheba.*"

Dovid ordered a glass of tea. He drank it *shtetl* style, with a sugar cube between his teeth. The *kibbutzniks* were all drinking fancy concoctions with whipped cream and chocolate sprinkles and such.

The *kibbutzniks* looked at him sideways and then went on with their frivolities, mostly ignoring the boy. Dovid quietly drank his tea. Rifka Leeba, however, drew the youngster into conversation and somehow the two of them found common ground.

When her *chaverim* decided to head out, Rifka Leeba stayed behind. She and Dovid sat in the cafe, conversing until closing time. Then, they walked together through what remained of the night and together watched the sun rise, before they each returned to their homes.

Over the next few weeks, coincidence, serendipity, and plan brought the two young people together often. They shared secrets. They spoke of their dreams and aspirations. Rifka Leeba took Dovid to the bend in the creek where they swam naked. Dovid took Rifka Leeba to the woods above the creek where he had seen her from afar. This was where they first made love.

The young woman was just a bit more than a year older than Dovid. At some point, that sort of age difference would be irrelevant. In just a few months, the boy would reach the age of emancipation. But, for the time being, he teetered on the edge of adulthood and was in awe of the older woman that had accepted him as an equal.

It may have been presumptuous of him to ask for her hand before he was old enough to stand under the *chuppah* but she readily said yes, even knowing that meant waiting until after his *bar mitzvah.*

Dovid brought his Bat-Sheba to the *shtetl* to meet his family. The *shtetl* where Dovid's family lived was not as primitive as Rifka Leeba imagined from his description of his early childhood. Many of the streets were paved. There were stores and parks.

The family home was small, but well maintained. Rifka Leeba was a bit nervous as they walked towards the house. She fidgeted with her clothing, trying not to look too much like an outsider. She didn't know what sort of a reception she would receive from Dovid's family, particularly his mama.

The house felt a bit empty. Dovid's mama was there alone when they arrived. Her husband was away, perhaps working. All of the older siblings had moved out and were already raising families of their own. Dovid had his apartment at *Der Profesor's* place adjacent to the airport. He was only at the family home on occasion.

Dovid's mother served tea, with sugar cubes and biscuits. Rifka Leeba attempted to drink the strongly brewed tea through a sugar cube held between her teeth before giving up and drinking her tea unsweetened. A tension hung over the room. It came to a head when Dovid's mother turned to him and said, with no preamble or forewarning, "Go outside and *play*. I need to speak with this woman."

Dovid opened his mouth, the beginning of a protest forming on his lips. He looked from his mother to his fiancée and back at his mother. Then, he stood up and walked out the door.

Dovid's mother, for all appearances, was culturally conservative and reserved. The family home was in a staid neighborhood and projected an essence of tradition. Rifka Leeba held many broad presumptions about *shtetl* life and nothing that she had seen or heard so far would have much altered her presumptions. Rifka Leeba's presumptions left her ill prepared for the conversation that was about to unfold.

The older woman grilled Rifka Leeba about sexuality. The questions were explicit and exacting, without mincing words or relying on euphemisms. Nothing conceivable was left out. Dovid's mother relentlessly asked intimate details about desires, fetishes, positioning, past experiences, menstrual cycles, orgasms, masturbation, family history, and more.

Rifka Leeba was shocked and shaken to her core. She broke down crying. Dovid's mother showed no sympathy or compassion for the young woman. With no wavering or uncertainty, the older woman made it clear that she thought Rifka Leeba to be an unfit match for her son and that the marriage was a terrible idea.

Rifka Leeba was shocked by the questioning and disturbed by the unwavering opposition to their youthful aspirations that was expressed. Most certainly, she was mentally unprepared for what occurred next. Dovid's mother elicited two commitments from Rifka Leeba. She insisted that the wedding would not occur until six months after Dovid's *bar mitzvah* and she insisted that Rifka Leeba would refrain from bearing children before Dovid turned sixteen. The older woman gave Dovid's fiancée a packet of herbal tea and explicit directions on how to use the concoction to regulate menstruation and prevent pregnancy.

Rifka Leeba was wiping away her tears when Dovid reentered the house. Neither of the women spoke to the lad about what had been discussed between them. The walk from the *shtetl* back to First Landing was awkwardly quiet.

Turning thirteen brought major changes to Dovid as he transitioned from boy to man. The contract that his mother had signed with *Der Profesor* expired and was up to potential renegotiation. Dovid became fully emancipated. He became fully responsible for his own finances and personal decisions.

Dovid spent the week at the family home in the *shtetl*. Dovid's birthday fell on a Tuesday that year. The day passed with little fanfare. That evening, Dovid's mother insisted that her husband take the young man to the neighborhood brothel. She hoped that the *kurvahs* would help cure him of the nonsense of his ill-conceived love for Rifka Leeba and their engagement.

The following Thursday morning, Dovid attended the *minyan* at the small *shul* near the family home. He *donned tefillin* and received an *aliyah* when the *Toyre* was read. His mother and his fiancée sat side by side, upstairs in the women's section of the *shul*. A party for friends and family was held that evening.

Six months later, the young couple stood under the *chuppah*, surrounded by family and friends.

17

A JOB AND TWO HONEYMOONS

Those last few months before Dovid turned thirteen were tumultuous and disruptive for him. Coming of age necessitated changes in his relationship with *Der Profesor*. His engagement to Rifka Leeba necessitated his taking conscious steps towards economic security.

Dovid's apprenticeship agreement with *Der Profesor* was, to begin with, somewhat out of the norm in several ways.

Generally speaking, these sorts of arrangements are intended for training a young man in a useful trade. An apprentice to a baker, for instance, learned to bake bread and cakes. Almost always, the apprentice is past his *bar mitzvah* and of an age eligible to enter into a binding contract. The normal period of apprenticeship runs two or three years, although some highly specialized training positions can run five years or so.

The apprentice usually receives a small stipend, but no pay. Sometimes other considerations, such as housing and meals are provided. To be perfectly clear, the contract and the relationship between an apprentice and an employer is almost exclusively a financial matter.

Dovid's contract was signed by his mother when he was only ten. The contract expired with the boy's thirteenth birthday.

What Dovid gained from *Der Profesor* was a diverse intellectual education with no obvious commercial value. Dovid had unlimited access to the library, access to tools, regular mentally stimulating conversations, and a serious training in abstract thinking and academic research.

There was also the *Aun Vas?* as we say. Dovid had an apartment (if we use that term loosely) in *Der Profesor's* cottage adjacent to the airport, a modest line of credit covered at the airport restaurant, and some very little pocket *gelt.*

It needs to be understood that the relationship was not a financial one in any sort of typical way. Rather, it was primarily a very personal agreement. Dovid relished the opportunity to simply be at this font of wisdom. In exchange, he would help *Der Profesor* on a daily basis with whatever was needed.

But for Dovid's intentions to marry, renewing the contract might have been fairly straightforward and mutually satisfying continuation of the status quo. A single man can scrape by on very little *gelt.* A married man, however, needs to *macht a leben.*

Often employers discourage an apprentice from marrying. Sometimes, that discouragement is written into the contract. In this case, however, *Der Profesor* was very supportive of Dovid's betrothal with Rifka Leeba. *Der Profesor* was as convinced as the boy that the youthful relationship was determined by a *mazel* and a force beyond our understanding, a *bashert* that should not be resisted or ignored.

Der Profesor was not able to actually pay Dovid to continue in his position. On the other hand, he really liked and appreciated the boy. *Der Profesor* wanted to keep Dovid around. So, *Der Profesor* and Dovid entered into extended discussion on how best to continue their close association and Dovid's somewhat esoteric education.

For starters, *Der Profesor* told Dovid that he and his family could remain in the apartment, at no cost, for as long as they pleased. *Der Profesor* suggested some remodeling to make the place more comfortable for a family. For instance, the kitchenette was expanded to a full kitchen.

Rifka Leeba arranged for a clawfoot bathtub to be installed in the kitchen. She did so with the help of *kibbutznik* connections. When that work was done, Rifka Leeba discreetly moved into the apartment and oversaw the rest of the renovations while awaiting their wedding.

Der Profesor provided Dovid with a letter of introduction and a glowing recommendation. A nod from *Der Profesor* carried a lot of weight on Planet Birobidzhan. Dovid landed a job doing research and development for Moshe & Mendel's Jew Harp, Tsatske aun Muzik Krom.

Moshe and Mendel were young settlers who put together a nest egg out of scraps in the early days of the settlement when Planet Birobidzhan was awash in currency and lacking in entertaining distractions. The brothers began by selling the tiny twangy instrument known as the Jews Harp while sitting in a park or on a sidewalk. After a while, they had a pushcart and eventually a storefront in First Landing.

Over the years, the brothers added an assortment of musical instruments to their inventory as well as a wide variety of simple toys. By the time they were ready to retire and hand the business to their children, they had a large store in First Landing, another large store in Niu Yerushalaim and two substantial places in Niu Niu Yark.

The name of the company is now truly an understatement. Moshe & Mendel's Jew Harp, Tsatske aun Muzik Krom is one of the largest independent employers, worldwide. Besides the large stores in the biggest cities, they have shops in *shtetls* around the globe and a wholesale operation that supplies businesses that operate in venues that the company considers to be too small to bother with.

Dovid's contract gave him a salary as well as a commission on any products that he developed. The position more so suited him for the *Aun Vas?* (and what?) opportunities. Of course, there were the deeply discounted or free toys and musical instruments for his expanding family.

Also, there were the unspoken but understood advantages that included the global network of suppliers and manufacturers that he had access to. While working full time and getting paid for it, Dovid was able to continue to work on what he thought of as his *real* work, rocketry...and, some day, space travel.

So, at the budding age of maturity, Dovid had secured a place to live, a decent income and had a friend and lover that was soon to be his bride and lifelong companion.

Rifka Leeba had made a commitment to her future mother-in-law. She promised to not bear Dovid any children before his sixteenth birthday. Rifka Leeba intended to strictly fulfill the letter of the agreement. Following the wedding, she solemnly swore to herself that she would make her mother-in-law regret the promise elicited.

Rifka Leeba consumed the emmenagogue/abortifacient tea that her mother-in-law had given her exactly as prescribed. There was absolutely no possibility of a fetus forming within her with such a regimen. She kept that secret from her husband. She kept that secret from the world, with the one exception of her friend, confidant, and co-conspirator, Hannah Leah.

What Rifka Leeba told Dovid, even before they stood together under the *chuppah*, was that she was trying to become pregnant and that having his children would be a great honor. More importantly, she suggested, it would bring *nachas* to his mother. The pleasure of grandchildren for her mother-in-law was a dominant theme in how Rifka Leeba framed the idea of possible pregnancy.

As the weeks and months passed with no pregnancy, Rifka Leeba began to drop hints to Dovid that she might suffer from a condition of sterility. Nonetheless, she urged him to keep trying, suggesting that different positions might help or making love at different times of the day might result in the desired pregnancy. The young couple made love every day, sometimes several times a day, particularly on *Shabbos* when there was no work to do and making love is a *mitzvah*.

During the third month of their marriage, Rifka Leeba subtly began suggesting that Dovid needed a second wife to bear children for him and that her lifetime friend Hannah Leah was the ideal choice for a second wife. Rifka Leeba suggested that they could, perhaps, give this arrangement a trial period to see how it works out.

Hannah Leah was a few months older than Rifka Leeba. They grew up together on the *kibbutz*. They were almost like sisters. They shared everything. Rifka Leeba's friend began to spend more time in the apartment. Sometimes Hannah Leah would be there all day, helping Rifka Leeba or just hanging out.

When out in public, both of the women would dress conservatively. Hannah Leah would wear her "Town Clothing". Rifka Leeba began to dress like Dovid's mother. She wore long skirts. Her blouses had sleeves to the wrists and buttons to the neck. Rifka Leeba's hair was always carefully covered with a scarf when she left the apartment.

Both young women were similar enough in form to wear each other's clothes. Hannah Leah had a bit more curves, slightly lighter hair and was a few inches shorter. In the apartment the young women would make themselves comfortable, dressing as they would on the *kibbutz.* They wore skirts above their knees. Their arms were bare. The top buttons of their blouses were often undone.

One Friday, Hannah Leah came for dinner and stayed the night. Rifka Leeba demurely lit the candles and Dovid said the blessings over the wine. The three friends drank the *Shabbos* wine together which was just a bit sweeter and a touch stronger than usual.

The evening passed in friendly conversation and they each drank a little more wine than they were usually inclined to. Hannah Leah stretched out on the sofa and Rifka Leeba took her husband to bed.

After making love, Rifka Leeba whispered in Dovid's ear of her desire for children and her fears that she may be barren. She told Dovid that her dear friend Hannah Leah would willingly bear children for her. Then she emphasized the spiritual necessity of making love on the *Shabbos* and the unfairness to Hannah Leah to be denied such a *mitzvah.*

Dovid was dozing when Rifka Leeba climbed from the bed. He was sleeping in the darkened bedroom when he was awakened and aroused. When he woke in the morning, Hannah Leah was sleeping in his arms. Rifka Leeba was humming to herself and preparing breakfast in the kitchen.

Any thoughts of a trial aspect to this arrangement were quickly put aside. The family bonds between these three were undeniable. By any standard, the three were already married. The marriage was formalized a few weeks later with a rabbi officiating. A few close friends, including *Der Profesor*, attended the small informal wedding.

It seemed that every time Dovid entered his apartment, one of the women was in the large clawfoot bathtub in the kitchen. She would ask him to bring her a sponge or a brush or for help washing the back or rubbing feet. This sort of thing inevitably led to lovemaking. Making love with one of his wives inevitably led to making love to the other because neither wanted to miss out.

Hannah Leah, of course, became pregnant almost immediately. The two wives, however, kept that knowledge to themselves and they continued to pressure Dovid to do his part to provide them with children.

Soon, however, hiding Hannah Leah's pregnancy became impossible. The expanded belly gave away the secret, at least when she was naked. Soon, even through her most conservative clothing, the pregnancy was obvious.

Rifka Leeba was ecstatic with this state of affairs. She insisted that they all go visit Dovid's mother to introduce his new wife and tell her the good news of a child on the way. If her mother-in-law had a heart attack or a stroke when hearing the news, thought Rifka Leeba, that would be icing on the cake.

18

THE PATHWAY INTO THE STARS

Dovid was reluctant to speak with anyone about his experiences resulting from consuming the Mushrooms of Planet Birobidzhan. He eventually confided in *Der Profesor. Der Profesor* listened intently without interruption, interpretation, or comment.

Dovid recounted how he encountered blooms of mushrooms and how they called out to him, urging him to eat their fleshy tops. Dovid enumerated what he had learned from them so far. The pathway into the stars seemed to be unfolding with a map and an instruction booklet from the unpredictable chance encounters with the fungi.

Der Profesor accepted Dovid's analysis of his experiences. He had no reason to doubt Dovid's perception. Dovid was becoming more monofocused, intellectually committed to space travel. Der Profesor was committed to assisting his youthful protégé.

Putting together such a feat as intergalactic travel would be a monumental task. A complicated assortment of pieces would need to be woven together. It was for these reasons that *Der Profesor* pulled strings to get the young man a position at Moshe & Mendel's Jew Harp, Tsatske aun Muzik Krom. *Der Profesor* knew that a job in research for such a large firm would help serve that purpose.

The mushroom-induced visionary lessons that Dovid continued to receive over the next few years led him to hidden mineral deposits. They taught him simplified methods of extraction. He also learned new processes leading to lighter and stronger materials, better conductivity, reduced friction and other sorts of industrial advantages.

The establishment of the *Yidden* on Planet Birobidzhan was probably unlike any other historical settlement project. Certainly, it was unlike any that took place on the Home Planet. It is true that our ancestors came here as volunteers as well as refugees. In this sense, parallels can be found to some historical Earth settlements. However, very much unlike the history of the overall colonization of the Home Planet, our ancestors did not represent an expanding empire, were not of a unified ideology, and did not come into conflict with any indigenous people.

It may seem to be an anomaly but, although derived from an advanced society, the culture that developed on Planet Birobidzhan was relatively low tech. This was not the result of philosophy, ideology or religious beliefs. After all, the early settlers were not Luddites, the Amish, or hippie Back-to-Landers.

The Home Planet, although in a state of crisis, was an advanced technological society when our ancestors emigrated. It was a buzzing place full of gadgetry and easily accessible energy. Our ancestors were well used to the advantages and comforts that a technological society provides. The volunteers held no inherent oppositional perspectives concerning the use of technology and were certainly dependent on it for the transit and settlement.

There was a presumption that the material support from the Home Planet would continue for decades. The abrupt interruption of our connection to the Home Planet combined with physical limitations and the demographics of the settlers. That determined the stunted technological development.

The initial group on the *Hatikvah* were chosen for the particular skills needed to establish the settlement. They were few in numbers and of somewhat advanced age. Subsequent transit loads of mostly much younger people were theoretically chosen for social cohesion and their potential usefulness for the settlement project.

One needn't be totally cynical to believe that the determination of the later passages was largely based on fertility. The settlement of this new planet began with elderly rabbis and farmers. They were followed by unsupervised youths with no particular skills and a propensity for breeding.

In the early days of settlement, the scavenging of the transit ships provided most of the metals and solar panels that were needed. Wood resources were - and continued to be - plentiful and fairly easily accessible. Cotton, jute, and hemp crops were quickly developed and widely available. Wool and leather became widely available as well.

Planet Birobidzhan has an abundance of potentially useful but largely undeveloped mineral deposits. Mining and manufacturing are still incredibly limited. The largest deposits are in remote areas that are difficult to access. The mining and metallurgy is largely controlled by a guild and is viewed by many almost as if it were alchemy.

On the Home Planet those mineral resources would not have been ignored. Either the driving compulsion of economic competition or the competing national interests of antagonistic states would have necessitated the extraction. When mining could not be effectively developed within the normal exchange of commerce, governments on Earth had the capacity to elicit force to assure sufficient labor. Military draft and convict labor are just two of the policy options that are open to the governments of every country of the Home Planet. Planet Birobidzhan, of course, lacks any form of governance similar to that of the Home Planet.

The people of Planet Birobidzhan did not build power plants or string cables and wires across the horizon. They did not have satellites or cell towers. Electricity was generally available in homes and stores, supplied by solar panels cannibalized from the transit ships. Storage capacity was extremely limited and there was certainly no abundance for maintaining gadgets.

The computer databases on Planet Birobidzhan contain virtually the entire intellectual knowledge from the Home Planet up to the time of our predecessors initial landings. Abstractly, we have always been able to accomplish anything that had been done on Planet Earth. However, having the encyclopedic synopsis is not the same as having the practiced skills or the specialized tools and equipment.

In most aspects of life on Planet Birobidzhan, low technology approaches that were not dependent on electricity, fuels, metals, or minerals were adopted. This was the natural course for development on a planet that lacks the compulsion or incentive for dangerous work under difficult conditions in remote places.

The low technology option was all the more true for toys and musical instruments. Toys here have always been simple things. In the very early days they were mostly homemade, consisting of ragdolls and simple wooden wagons.

As a market for toys developed, the playthings did not become incredibly more sophisticated. Toys in the stores had a little more paint on the wood and glass eyes for the dolls. Later, some metal for springs, gears and such were incorporated. All told, the toys available were about on par with those that were available on Earth two centuries before Planet Birobidzhan was discovered.

Six days a week Dovid ostensibly worked at developing toys. That certainly was how he earned a living. In a very real sense, twenty-four hours a day, seven days a week, his primary focus was somewhere else.

With Dovid's hand at the helm for development, the toys sold by Moshe & Mendel's Jew Harp, Tsatske aun Muzik Krom rolled faster, traveled farther, spun longer, jumped or bounced higher, and balanced better than before. The musical instruments that they sold had improved tone, clearer sound, and smoother action.

Dovid certainly brought improvement, innovation, and creativite changes to the toy and musical markets of Planet Birobidzhan. However, while tinkering with this work, his mind was always in the clouds or, more accurately, in the stars above. There was nearly always a synchronicity between the tweaks that Dovid brought about in a simple wind-up toy or a harmonica and a significant advancement on a totally different trajectory.

Dovid was perfecting rocketry as well as various supportive technologies. He was building the networks to facilitate intergalactic travel. Some of what he was learning also made for better toys or musical instruments. The usefulness for toys and instruments created the economic incentive to develop the resources needed for space travel.

Of course, there is an element of *Aun Vas?* in every transaction that takes place on Planet Birobidzhan. So much so that we hardly notice it most of the time. No one would think of drinking a glass of tea in a coffee house without leaving a tip for the waiter any more than having a chicken slaughtered without giving the *sochet* a wing or a leg in addition to his fee.

We take these things for granted. Mostly it is just a social norm, a form of politeness. However, when practiced skillfully, *Aun Vas*? can be a way to build a personal fortune.

Through his job, Dovid negotiated, traded, and facilitated in ways that profited Moshe & Mendel's Jew Harp, Tsatske aun Muzik Krom. He gave his employer no reason to complain.

The settlement of Planet Birobidzhan was financed through a vast effort of millions of people on a planet with an advanced industrial infrastructure. Any space programs that could be developed on Planet Birobidzhan, essentially from scratch, would also be incredibly expensive. However, the social and financial infrastructure that the Home Planet had simply did not exist on Planet Birobidzhan. The method of financing would inherently need to take a different course.

The imperative necessitated a new perspective on money for the two men. Hitherto, their relationship had been built on a common interest in abstract knowledge without an economic incentive. In truth, *Der Profesor* had spent his life avoiding the complications of financial entanglement. Now, the creation of whole new industries required the consolidated resources that would need to be directly controlled by Dovid and *Der Profesor*.

In the few short years of wheeling and dealing, Dovid simultaneously built a privately controlled fortune for himself and *Der Profesor* and rekindled a sense of choice for the *Yidden* of Planet Birobidzhan.

The sky was clear when the first launched satellite joined the two natural moons in circling Planet Birobidzhan. This satellite, the development essentially financed by Moshe & Mendel's Jew Harp, Tsatske aun Muzik Krom, was owned, free and clear by the partnership of Dovid and *Der Profesor.*

The satellite made possible planetary broadcasting of radio and television as well as other aspects of improved communication. It also proved the technical capacity for more extensive travel beyond the planetary surface.

Worlds beyond Planet Birobidzhan exist. Another life, beyond the meager existence offered by Planet Birobidzhan could now be brought about by the hand of man.

19

ABI GUZUNT

Although it may have seemed at times that they were worlds apart, the measurable distance between *Der Profesor's* cottage adjacent to the First Landing airport and Dovid's family home in the outlying *shtetl* was negligible. It is a comfortable walk along a goat path. Dovid began making the *schlep* to the airport nearly daily when he was a small child. He often traipsed in the other direction since he began living at the airport when he was only ten.

The physical distance was not what kept Dovid from bringing his new wife home to meet his family. His job demanded his attention six days a week. It seemed that matrimonial responsibilities absorbed eight days a week. His loyalty and commitment to *Der Profesor* continued, filling the rest of his calendar. As a newly married man, Dovid was very busy.

The printed invitation to the party was delivered by a messenger. It could not be ignored or declined. Dovid's fourteenth birthday was the rationale for the gathering. The whole *gantze mishpacha* would be at his mother's house.

Rifka Leeba looked forward to the party. She was relishing the opportunity to introduce Hannah Leah, Dovid's *second* wife, with the obvious baby bump, to her mother-in-law. The whole week before the party, Rifka Leeba imagined and reimagined ways to maximize the emotional impact on the older woman. Dovid's mother knew nothing of the second marriage or the progeny on the way. In Rifka Leeba's imagination, her mother-in-law collapsed in shock.

Rifka Leeba's expectations were far from fulfilled. Her mother-in-law showed neither surprise nor anger when the three of them walked into the house. Not even a ripple of disturbance could be observed on the face or in the physique of the matriarch.

Dovid's mother calmly served *babka* and tea. She offered an extra piece to Hannah Leah for the "little one" with an affectionate pat and what certainly passed for a smile. No emotional outbursts disturbed the family gathering, much to Rifka Leeba's disappointment.

Rifka Leeba had stayed true to the letter but not the spirit of the agreement she had made with the older woman. She had promised not to bear Dovid any children before his sixteenth birthday. She had made no such promise for her friends. Hannah Leah gave birth to three sets of twins before Dovid's sixteenth birthday. Rifka Leeba gave birth to her first child the week after her husband turned sixteen.

It was true that Rifka Leeba hated her mother-in-law. It was a simmering, passionate hatred. It was the sort of hatred that grew deeper over time.

Rifka Leeba sat in her chair by the window, breastfeeding her youngest. She watched over Dovid and Hannah Leah as they slept. She loved her husband and her dear friend Hannah Leah and all of their children. This was her family.

"*Abi guzunt*. That's the main thing," Rifka Leeba said, to no one in particular.

20

A DOZEN OR SO...

The presence of young children assured spontaneity and a degree of chaos. The two young mothers somehow kept up with their ever increasing brood and brought warmth and comfort to *Der Profesor's* house.

The children called both Rifka Leeba and Hannah Leah "Mama" and would turn to whichever was closest for comforting or nutrition. Truthfully, none of the children knew which Mama had given birth to them. No outsider could unravel that mystery. The Mamas probably could remember, if pressed.

Dovid certainly couldn't have kept that straight, if he would have been inclined to make the effort. Neither did he know, after a few years of marriage, exactly how many children there were. "A dozen or so..." is how he would usually answer, when asked. There always seemed to be one or more on the way, so to speak, some babies in diapers, and lots of little ones running about.

Dovid was committing more and more time to his job. His involvement in the business brought large gains to his already very successful employer. A major innovation that Dovid brought to Moshe & Mendel's Jew Harp, Tsatske aun Muzik Krom, is the use of solar energy in toys and the *sh-*

pilplats (playground). Small toy cars and trains gained increased mobility. Swings, slides and merry-go-rounds now have colorful lights and musical sound...and promote the stores.

Of course, there was an alternative motive. Space travel, Dovid knew, would require a massive amount of solar panels. Toys and the playground equipment could operate on chips and broken pieces of solar panels. If the chips and small pieces were considered the product, the unbroken panels and larger pieces would become essentially a byproduct. The undamaged panels became available to Dovid at a deep discount. Additionally, all of the purchases of solar panels for his employer flowed through subsidiary associations that funneled money and resources into the space project.

The production of solar panels requires minerals mined from nearly inaccessible places on islands and other continents. Deals, side deals, and back deals needed to be negotiated directly with far-flung mining guild members and boat captains. Dovid found himself often traveling globally. He would be away from home, sometimes, for several weeks at a stretch.

Returning from one such trip, Dovid arrived by ship at the Port of Niu Niu Yark shortly before Purim. He was compelled to stay in the City of Niu Niu Yark through the holiday. Niu Niu Yark is nearly tropical, with summer-like weather year round. Beaches with a fine rose-colored sand attract vacationers from across the continent and are enjoyed by the locals. The waters are calm and ideal for snorkeling. It is not so bad to be stuck in Niu Niu Yark, if one needs to be stuck somewhere.

The Jewish calendar is sprinkled with holidays calling for observance. Obligations, commandments, and traditions dictate our practices on Holy Days. Most of these days are treated with a similar sanctity as *Shabbos*. Work, handling money, lighting fires, and other such activities are proscribed or limited. Additionally, we are told that certain foods must be eaten and others are forbidden or how and where we must sit or items of clothing we must wear or that are forbidden.

Purim is probably the most uncharacteristic and even counterintuitive of all the Jewish holidays. On Purim, we are told that we must listen to the reading of the *Megillah Esther*, we should give gifts of treats, and that drinking to excess is considered a *mitzvah. Das iz alts.* What kind of *meshugganah* holiday is this?

Most Jewish holidays have a Biblical origin, including Purim. The *Megillah Esther* is in our Holy Book and therefore considered a divine work. To a casual observer, it may seem to be out of place, as Scripture. The *Megillah Esther* may be imagined more readily as a novella and a work of Oriental fantasy than a religious tractate. A serious Biblical scholar recognizes the book to be full of perplexity and is likely to come to similar conclusions as those of a casual reader.

For one thing, the *Megillah Esther* is the only book within our *Tanakh* that doesn't mention the Ineffable One and there are no evidently miraculous occurrences or Divine Intervention. Not once. If you don't believe me, check for yourself.

The rest of our Scriptures are full of miracles. The miracles vary widely. Some were very personal, such as Sarai's pregnancy at ninety. Some miracles were simply fantastic such as the Prophet Yonah being swallowed by a big fish and Balaam's talking donkey. There were events of regional significance as the Plagues in Egypt must surely have been, and of global proportions such as the Flood.

In contrast, the *Megillah Esther* is a story of backroom deals, subterfuge, palace politics, seduction, and intrigue. In many ways, the Purim story is a very foreign tale, centered on values of an alien kingdom. King Ahasuerus holds an extended celebration with heavy drinking. After a while, he calls for his wife, Queen Vasti, to entertain his drunken entourage. She refuses and is vilified on this account.

If this had been the story of a Jewish monarch, the Queen would have been the hero of the story for declining an unreasonable request. The King would apologize and make amends, hoping to win back the love and respect of his wife.

In the perhaps fictionalized palace of the Persian Kingdom, a very different set of values is obvious. The King does not react with remorse nor out of passion, jealousy, or even anger. The King's concerns seem to be highly legalistic. He turns to the Royal Consultants for advice.

The Royal Advisors fear the independent actions of a Queen could lead to the unraveling of patriarchy. They recommend the banishment of the Queen. They suggest that a more pliable replacement can be found through an audition of every virgin in the domain.

Through this process, and by hiding her Jewish identity, Hadassah aka Esther married the King. A Chief Royal Advisor hatched a plot to destroy the *Yidden*. Esther steps in to influence her husband. So, the *Megillah Esther* essentially celebrates assimilation and encourages marriage to foreigners. This stratagem results in a significant number of slaughtered hooligans at the hands of the *Yidden* and massive conversion to Judaism.

On Planet Earth, the celebration of Purim incorporated costumes and an oddly shaped pastry, the triangular *hamantaschen*. This pastry, it seems, is modeled after the style of hat worn by Napoleon and his troops. The traditional filling for the *hamantaschen* is *munn* which is poppy seeds.

On Planet Birobidzhan, in addition to the traditional gifting of *hamantaschen* and other sweets, *majoun* is also included. *Majoun* is a confection originating from North Africa made from dates, nuts, and hashish or cannabis butter. The prevalence of *majoun* is one of the reasons why the Hebraic name *Tamar,* meaning date, is associated with Purim on Planet Birobidzhan. The other reason, of course, has to do with the Biblical Tamar's costumed seduction of her father-in-law.

The Purim holiday on Earth fell in a rough conjunction with two rowdy holidays of the majority cultures. On the Indian subcontinent, amongst the Hindus there is Holi, celebrated with body painting and the consumption of cannabis infused drinks. In Brazil, Louisiana, and some other Catholic influenced regions of Earth, Mardi Gras is celebrated with widespread drunkenness and a fair amount of public nudity. On Planet Earth, the Jewish People were a tiny minority, living alongside other cultures. The Yidden sometimes adopted the traditions of their neighbors and joined in with the celebrations.

Purim is a raucous celebration on Planet Birobidzhan, and particularly so in Niu Niu Yark. The celebration on Planet Birobidzhan was likely influenced by the way that Holi and Mardi Gras was celebrated on Planet Earth. The festivities start out staid enough in the early evening with a family oriented costumed parade that weaves through the city, leading to the largest *shuls*, where the *Megillah Esther* is read, according to tradition.

Following the *Megillah* reading, the crowds from the *shuls* empty into the streets, led by the rabbis. Bottles of schnapps are passed around while singing and dancing take place. As the night progresses, parents with young children and those with less wild inclination clear the streets.

There is a tradition that on Purim one should drink until one doesn't know the difference between Haman and Mordechai, or, perhaps, you should drink until you can't tell the difference between Queen Vasti and Queen Esther. On Planet Birobidzhan, some wags suggest that at the proper level of intoxication for Purim, one cannot distinguish between one's wife and her sister.

Any other day or night, there is a decorum maintained throughout Planet Birobidzhan, with only a modicum of variations on the *Kibbutzim*. Women's knees are rarely seen on the streets of our cities, and never in our *shtetls*. Sleeves reach past the elbows and usually to the wrists. Blouses, outside of the house, are buttoned close to the neck. Married women cover their heads with scarves.

On Purim, masks are worn by nearly everyone. With the anonymity of masking, inhibitions are often set aside. With faces veiled, the dress norms are also set aside.

On Planet Birobidzhan, it is generally quite warm for Purim. In semi tropical Niu Niu Yark the weather can be downright sultry. Some will, as the night unfolds, be wearing little more than a mask, gauze and perhaps makeup, henna, or body paint. Considering such unrestrained behavior, no one should be particularly surprised that a fair number of pregnancies are consummated on the night of the Purim celebration. This is a factor in the large number of hastily arranged marriages that take place around *Pesach* and the volume of birthing around Hanukkah.

On Planet Birobidzhan, it is not particularly unusual for a first child to be born around seven months after a couple stands under the *chuppah*. The husband will choose to believe that the child born is his offspring. Most of the rest of the year, that is likely true.

For a married woman, a Purim dalliance resulting in a pregnancy has little obvious consequence. However, when an unmarried woman becomes pregnant, a hastily arranged marriage is for the best. If a wedding happens quickly, the social ripples of a Purim dalliance is minimal. If a wedding doesn't take place by sometime around *Pesach*, the young woman begins to swell around the abdomen and neighbors begin to gossip, particularly in the smaller *shtetls*.

The options for an unmarried pregnant woman in a small *shtetl* are extremely narrow. Many *Purim Meydls* leave their homes behind and head to the larger settlements or the cities seeking some degree of anonymity and new horizons. Some will seek out the strangers that fathered their children.

It was early in the winter, not long past Hanukkah. The children had all gone to the *spielplat* with Hannah Leah. Rifka Leeba was drinking a glass of tea, enjoying the rare moments of privacy and solitude when there was a knock on the door.

At the door stood a young woman, evidently from a small *shtetl* by the way she dressed and how she carried herself. In her arms was a newborn baby girl. Rifka Leeba knew at once that this was a *Purim Meydl* on her doorstep. One look at the baby told Rifka Leeba that the child was fathered by Dovid. The infant girl looked very much like Dovid's mother.

In an instant, Rifka Leeba imagined how her mother-in-law would have reacted to such a circumstance. She was determined to resolve this situation in the same calculating way as she believed that Dovid's mother would. Rifka Leeba's face became an emotional vail as she ushered the *Purim Meydl* into her living room and offered her tea.

Rifka Leeba served tea *shtetl* style, in a glass, with sugar cubes. She offered the *Purim Meydl* cookies from the bakery on the dishes reserved for company and holidays. She lulled the young woman into a false sense of security. The swaddled newborn slept peacefully on the sofa, unaware that she was the center of dramatic intrigue. The child's life was on the cusp of a tidal change.

Rifka Leeba did not speak of her husband and paid no attention to the sleeping child. She took even breaths as she spoke in abstractions about vulgarity, sin, and bad choices. She spoke about bordellos and whoring and wantonness. She made disparaging implications of the sort of family background that would result in a woman bearing a child out of wedlock.

Rifka Leeba dug deep and found a reserve of strength and cruelty from a well deep in her soul. She carefully chose each word to inflict pain and suffering, without speaking directly to the situation at hand. The younger woman, hardly more than a girl, lacked the stamina or capacity to withstand the calculated emotional barrage.

The *Purim Meydl* went to the *vashzimmer* to compose herself. Rifka Leeba removed a bur that had attached itself to her shoe. She placed the sharp thing into the fold of the innocently sleeping sweet child's diaper. The baby girl instantly began to cry.

The infant's mother came quickly to the newborn and frantically tried soothing her to no avail. Rifka Leeba looked on with the appearance of sympathy as the young stranger tried rocking the baby, offered her a breast, uttered soothing words, and all the other sorts of things that mothers everywhere do for their offspring. The baby's crying got louder and the young woman grew more frantically agitated.

Rifka Leeba, after a time, stepped in and calmly reached out for the newborn. The *Purim Meydl,* in a state of desperation, placed the screaming baby girl into Rifka Leeba's hands. Rifka Leeba subtly removed the bur as she eased the infant onto her own breast. The baby immediately stopped crying and happily suckled.

Within the hour, the *Purim Meydl* departed with banknotes from Rifka Leeba's *knipple* securely folded into the lining of her coat. The baby remained with Rifka Leeba. When Hannah Leah and the brood of *kinder* returned from the *spielplat,* there was one more addition to the family.

Hannah Leah raised an eyebrow, but asked no questions except for the child's name. Rifka Leeba, sitting with the child cuddling in her arms, shrugged. "Let's call her Tamar," she said and this was how the girl was brought into the family and named.

21

TAMAR'S SKETCHBOOK

By Tamar's third birthday, it was obvious that she was her father's favorite. Dovid strived to treat all of his children the same but his particular affection for this little girl could not be denied. There was a brightness in her eyes that was unique and she seemed to be cut from a different cloth than the rest of the brood.

Try as he would, Dovid could not remember Tamar's birth. Her birthday was celebrated just before the beginning of Hanukkah. Dovid believed her to be Rifka Leeba's daughter because of the child's complexion and hair color, but he couldn't be certain. He had been traveling a lot during those years and some domestic matters were obfuscated as a result. He certainly would not ask.

Once Tamar was fully weaned, she was by her father's side whenever it was possible. Tamar clearly loved her father. It wasn't just that he always had some fruit or nuts or candy in his pocket, although that was certainly a plus. She was particularly fond of delicacies made with dates, her namesake. These were also Dovid's favored snacks.

Tamar was fascinated by everything her father did. She would watch him putter with tools and wiring. When the puttering resulted in lights or sounds, Tamar was thrilled.

It may not have been quite accurate to speak of this young girl as an apprentice. She was, however, at her father's side or in his wake whenever he was not at his job or traveling.

Tamar took an early interest in drawing. Her father had given her color pencils and a sketchbook for her birthday. She carried them everywhere in a small rucksack. Her drawings were pleasant, in a childish way. Dovid encouraged her in a doting manner. Tamar particularly enjoyed doodling when they sat together in wild places where they would hike.

The two were on a long hike near the place where Dovid had first seen Rifka Leeba from afar. The youngster was not much older than five. They were walking side by side when Tamar turned to Dovid. "Do you hear, *Tate*?" she blurted and just as suddenly began running ahead of her father.

When Dovid caught up with Tamar, she was standing in a bloom of mushrooms. They had called out to her as they had done to her father when he was a boy. She was happily chewing on one mushroom and held out another in her hand extending it towards her father. A few minutes later, father and daughter were sitting quietly side by side, each absorbed in their personal mushroom induced trance-like state. Linear time for them faded away.

After an undetermined number of hours, when Dovid again became aware of his surroundings, he saw that Tamar held her sketchbook in her lap. She was fervently drawing highly detailed technical plans surrounded by tightly scripted mathematical calculations and instructional notes.

When Tamar finished, she closed her sketchbook and climbed into her father's lap. The two sat like that without speaking for a while. Tamar was the first to break the silence. "Tate, tell me about my mother," is what the girl said.

"Rifka Leeba and Hannah Leah are your Mamas," Dovid replied. "What do you want to know?"

Tamar looked at her father with the utmost seriousness. "I know that," she said. "I do love them both dearly. But..." and she paused briefly before continuing. "Tell me about the woman that gave birth to me and then brought me to live in your house." Tamar opened her sketchbook as she said that and turned to a finely detailed drawing of a woman on a beach of pink sand, lying on a blanket, wearing nothing but henna and the sheerest of gauze.

Of course, Dovid recognized the woman in the drawing. Before Dovid could formulate a response, Tamar rested her head on her father's shoulder and fell asleep. While Tamar slept, Dovid examined the technical drawings in her sketchbook.

In the sketchbook, Dovid found detailed diagrams of the mushrooms. The next page consisted of instructions for harvesting and transplanting the fungi. The following pages were very exacting directions for building an enclosed mushroom growing environment.

The next morning, construction of a mushroom growing facility began. Tamar took on a supervisory role, assuring that every detail of the plans were meticulously followed. Much to Dovid's relief, Tamar asked no more questions about the woman in her sketchbook.

22

TAMAR'S MUSHROOMS

Carpenters were hired to build the mushroom growing facility, according to the specifications of Tamar's sketchbook. It was built by the airport, adjacent to *Der Profesor's* house, where Dovid and his ever expanding brood continued to live. Tamar supervised the construction. It was assuredly unusual to have a five year old girl overseeing a construction project.

Tamar sat above the workmen, clutching her favorite doll, while watching the work closely. She periodically marched in to assure the correction of the tiniest irregularities in alignment or any misplaced nails.

Tamar would approach with the rag doll in one hand, her sketchbook in the other, and a very seriously pouting countenance. She would insist that the miscreant workman resolve the issue. Then, she would return to her perch with her doll.

After several days, the mushroom cultivation facility was completed, including Tamar's final inspection. The workmen went on to other jobs with less demanding taskmasters. Tamar went out to play.

And while playing, Tamar heard the voices calling to her and she followed the sound. When she came upon the bloom of mushrooms, she carefully harvested as many as would fit into her rucksack in the precise way that she had been shown in her previous trance-like encounter with the fungi of Planet Birobidzhan. She returned to the newly constructed cultivation facility and successfully transplanted her find.

The design of the facility allowed for a perpetual growth cycle. Within a few weeks, the first harvest was made while other chambers were in various stages of growth. Tamar brought the first harvested fungi to her father and Dovid shared them with *Der Profesor*.

Der Profesor had been fascinated by Dovid's encounters with the fungi of Planet Birobidzhan from the time he first learned of them. He scoured the library books and the computer databases to learn all that was available about the entheogenic plants and fungi of the Home Planet, although there was no way of knowing if the experiences of the Earth-bound were relevant.

It certainly seemed likely that the largely religious experiences of those that ate cactus flowers, the roots of shrubs, and various fungi on Planet Earth might be a guidepost for similar experiences on Planet Birobidzhan. *Der Profesor* was certainly willing to find out. However, considering his advanced age, he was not actively hiking through wilderness in a way that would likely lead to a personal encounter with a wild mushroom bloom.

No one had considered the possibility of the cultivation of such until the mushrooms themselves guided Tamar in that way. Cultivation opened up a whole new potential for *Der Profesor* and others to join in the experimental lessons being offered by the Mushrooms of Planet Birobidzhan.

Der Profesor advocated a cautious approach to introducing new people to the experience. The practice of eating these unfamiliar substances and following advice from unknown sources held potentially dangerous and disruptive social consequences.

Tamar did not eat the fleshy mushrooms after the initial consumption for many years. She was transformed by them nonetheless.

Tamar spent hours at a time maintaining the ideal conditions for the mushrooms. Mushrooms grow in dark damp places and thrive on decaying wood and excrement. Cart loads of such matter were delivered to the airport almost daily. Tamar would fill her child-size wheelbarrow using her child-sized shovel and maneuver the poignant growing medium into the beds to feed *her* mushrooms.

Tamar assured that proper temperatures, darkness, and humidity levels were maintained in each chamber. She would check gauges, adding water or adjusting the heat when needed. Sometimes, she would just sit, communing with the fungi. When not directly involved with the mushrooms, Tamar appeared to be a fairly typical little girl, at least to begin with.

Living in a household with more than a dozen older siblings and a gaggle of younger ones, Tamar did not particularly stand out as unusual...at least at first. However, if anyone had taken a closer look, the signposts of disruption would have been evident. Over the following couple of years her odd behavior became obvious to even a casual observer.

Tamar carried an odor of compost and manure with her at all times, even with frequent and assiduous bathing. This may not have been so unusual for a boy living in a small *shtetl*. It was certainly a bit more unusual for a small girl living in Planet Birobidzhan's third largest city.

Indeed, it could be said that Tamar had a relationship with the fungi. Tamar considered the mushrooms to be hers in the sense of her family rather than her property. She perceived the fungi to be like honored ancestors or perhaps even as her *real* mother. The mushrooms spoke to her in a tongue that she alone could hear and understand.

Tamar had always been a quiet child. As the daily meticulous communication with fungi continued, she began to speak less and less to people. Living in a large, noisy family, this change went largely unnoticed for a while. That is, until Tamar stopped speaking almost altogether. On a rare occasion she could be heard, from a distance, holding conversations with herself.

Sometimes, when on a long walk with her father, Tamar would climb into Dovid's lap and listen while he recited simple rhymes and Tamar would hum to herself. It was on such an occasion, a long walk from home on a hot summer day, that they sat in the shade of a large tree. Dovid casually stroked the girl's hair while repeating a nonsense rhyme that he had learned from his mother, the Itsy Bitsy Spider. Tamar turned her head to face her father and spoke.

"*Tate*," she said, "What's a spider?"

Dovid was surprised to hear her words and hesitated briefly before answering. "A spider, I suppose, is some sort of tiny creature that lives on the Home Planet. We don't have spiders on Planet Birobidzhan," Dovid answered.

"Oh," replied Tamar. "Then, this rhyme is a simplified retelling of the Sisyphus myth," the child rejoined before sliding back into silence.

The spinning also was overlooked for a while. Spinning is a common activity for young children. However, the *dreidl*-like gyrations became pervasive for most of Tamar's waking hours outside of her time directly involved with the mushrooms. The only other times that Tamar refrained from the odd cyclical behavior was while drawing and making music. Those activities were encouraged by her family. Everyone felt a sense of relief when the spinning subsided.

It was fortuitous that Dovid had an unlimited account at Moshe and Mendel's Jew Harp, Tsatske aun Muzik Krom. Tamar would enter the store in Downtown First Landing, pick up art supplies or a new instrument and exit without a word. The clerks all knew her and would simply make a notation of the "purchase" to be added to Dovid's tab.

Over the next few years, Tamar mastered one instrument after another on her own. She took no lessons. She studied no theory and didn't read music. She played unaccompanied and oblivious to others. She blended sounds that came from some deep internal reservoir or perhaps from the stars.

Sometime after Tamar's thirteenth birthday she once again ate some of the fleshy mushrooms. It was after sunset and Tamar laid in a field staring wordlessly at the star filled sky. The next day, Tamar entered the family home and began interacting with her siblings and their mothers as if there had been nothing unusual about the last eight years.

It was the summer following Tamar's thirteenth birthday that a traveling troupe of *klezmorim* encamped near the airport and their nightly concerts drew large audiences. Tamar attended every one of the performances. When the troupe moved on, Tamar, with her vast collection of instruments, left with them.

23

INTERGALACTIC TRAVEL CANNOT BE DONE ON THE CHEAP

The years had passed since the launching of the first satellite placed in rotation around Planet Birobidzhan. The satellite brought improvements to communications, worldwide radio reception, and also a steady passive income for Dovid and *Der Profesor*. It was not enough money, however, for all that they hoped to accomplish.

The finances of the satellite was fairly straightforward. There was certainly a fair degree of what could be understood as graft involved, or what is commonly called *Aun Vas?* on Planet Birobidzhan, as is commonly true of most enterprise. The ownership and management of the satellite was a partnership in the control of Dovid and *Der Profesor*. They raised the investment capital, managed the business, and spent the profits as they saw fit without any oversight.

Travel to the stars called for the much larger economic modeling of a corporation or more accurately a syndicate or a cabal, rather than a simple partnership. Massive amounts of capital were needed. There was no straightforward way to raise that kind of capital.

The satellite helped spur a renewed curiosity in the possibility of intergalactic travel. Still, only a fraction of the population expressed any deep interest and fewer still were willing to put their *tuches offen tish* with actual *gelt* for such. We had lived on Planet Birobidzhan for many generations and we had acclimated to that world. Still, some *Yidden* began to step forward, or were drawn in, bringing their shekels to the project.

Investors introduced new complications as each had expectations that needed consideration...or, at least placating. A Corporation requires a Board of Directors that nominally answers to investors that expect a return on their investments.

Much of the technical aspects of the enterprise were essentially being guided by the Mushrooms of Planet Birobidzhan. The mushrooms seemed to understand physics, biology, electronics, fuel systems, and more. Even much of the social aspects were likely manipulated by those forces. The mushrooms played a direct role, for instance, in instigating Dovid's courtship of Rifka Leeba.

What the mushrooms had no concept of is economics or financial matters. The mushrooms left such *petty* considerations to humanity. However, without funding, traveling through the stars could only be hallucinations or science fiction. Interstellar travel is very expensive.

The unvarnished truth of the matter is that the likelihood of any financial return hovered somewhere close to nil. The successful profitability of even that tiniest fraction of a percentage within one's lifetime was even less likely.

Dovid, *Der Profesor*, and the small circle of trusted confidants learned to listen deeply and to tell potential investors exactly what they wanted to hear. All told, the co-conspirators became adept at the art of disinformation and boldface calculated lies to hoodwink investors.

Hands down, investors believed that the greatest financial potential was to reconnect with the Home Planet. Some hoped for repatriation. Others envisioned development of trade between Planet Birobidzhan and Planet Earth.

The consortium assured investors that such a strategic approach would lead to a healthy return on an investment.

To be skeptical of successfully reconnecting with Planet Earth was certainly a reasonable outlook. Over two centuries had passed since communication with the Home Planet had been unceremoniously severed.

All that the settlers at the time of the disconnect could do was to speculate about what went wrong. All of the guessing involved some level of catastrophic occurrence. Something horrible had surely happened but our ancestors could not fathom what occurred any better than Dovid and his associates could two centuries later.

The consortium delved into an extensive profusion of overly optimistic speculation of snafus and foul ups that *could* have led to the severance from the Home Planet that fell short of catastrophic. Maybe, rather than a disaster, communication fell off because someone hadn't paid the phone bill or our brethren on the Home Planet had simply lost interest in extra planetary excursions.

Perhaps, Dovid's band of fundraisers proposed, the Agency had simply gone bankrupt, the pyramid scheme collapsing on itself and there were no funds to even inform the settlers of Planet Birobidzhan. Perhaps Earth had forgotten about us and life on Planet Earth was thriving and we would be welcomed back with open arms. This is the sort of thing that was said to potential investors.

Within the organization, and out of earshot of their marks, those sorts of investors were referred to as Lot's Wife.

Some *Yidden* hoped to make contact with other human settlement planets. The settling of Planet Birobidzhan did not occur in a social void. Other exploration projects were also set in motion at that time.

It seemed plausible that some settlements on other planets were nearby - essentially in the same neighborhood. Investors held hope for trade. However, it certainly seemed unlikely that any other settlement in this particular quadrant would be an attractive trading partner. Likely, any parallel settlement would be in roughly the same condition as Planet Birobidzhan, with precious few opportunities to offer.

Then, there were those that envisioned an expedition of discovery that would return wealth to Planet Birobidzhan. They were promised a wealth of discovery that would be relayed back to Planet Birobidzhan from the very inception of flight.

Of course, none of the stories told to investors reflected the actual intentions of Dovid and his consortium as influenced by the Mushrooms of Planet Birobidzhan. Their intention was resettlement for a small contingent of pioneers. They had no interest in Planet Earth and no concern for the interests of investors.

When sufficient funding was available, the consortium set out to acquire the *Hatikvah*. What could be more fitting than using the vehicle that began, two centuries earlier, the Planet Birobidzhan settlement experiment in the first place? Of course, there were quite a few steps that would need to take place before that would be possible.

After two centuries of sitting on the edge of the airport and serving as an apartment building, entertainment center, and market, there were a lot of diverse interests that would need placating to acquire the *Hatikvah*, before the massive retrofit could even begin.

Many of the apartments were occupied by the families of the original *Hatikvah* passengers. There was a lot of emotional investment in a home where the family can trace ownership back over two hundred years. Apartment buildings needed to be built to resettle these families. Each family wanted a place just a little better than the abode they were giving up. They wanted a better view, higher ceilings, more space, and greater comforts. Each family also expected to be compensated as well for the trouble.

The merchants that operated businesses in the *Hatikvah* each considered their stalls to be prime real estate. A shopping mall was built for those businesses. The original hydroponic growing facilities were still in operation, cared for by some of the descendents of the farmers that had arrived on the *Hatikvah*. They too needed new facilities and compensation.

Around twelve hundred *Yidden* boarded the *Hatikvah* on the Home Planet and traveled on that first ship to initiate the settlement of the world that became known as Planet Birobidzhan. That voyage took nearly eighteen years and transpired in living and breathing very real time. The original *Hatikvah* was designed for one-way travel. The destination was programmed into the automated systems that piloted her through the vastness of galactic mileage.

The rekindled *Hatikvah* faced a different set of challenges and required broader piloting options. When leaving

Planet Birobidzhan, on this flight, those on board were quite uncertain as to where they were headed. They needed to be able to choose to leave any planet they might land on. The propulsion rockets, additional equipment required, and fuel capacity for reentry to the cosmos added weight and took up a considerable amount of space. The repurposed *Hatikvah* would have far less passenger capacity. Far fewer people would be able to travel than on the original voyage.

The corporation continued over these years to consolidate resources and to spend those shekels retrofitting the ship. It was all a monumental task and very costly.

As this work was being done, a tight knit shadowy community of a few hundred pioneers was being formed, drawn together and empowered by semi-regular gatherings where the cultivated Mushrooms of Planet Birobidzhan were consumed.

24

UNAUTHORIZED FIRE

Dovid had an extended and ongoing relationship with the Mushrooms of Planet Birobidzhan. He found them in wild places and consumed them where they grew. Dovid was likely the only person to eat them until his young daughter Tamar heard the Mushrooms calling her. No one had cultivated the fungi before Tamar.

Der Profesor was the first person to be introduced to the cultivated Mushrooms of Planet Birobidzhan. Following his first session consuming the fleshy mushrooms, he was very sure that Tamar and Dovid had discovered a powerful and useful tool. He was also absolutely sure that an uncharted and quite dangerous social terrain was being engaged.

After the hypnotic phase had ended and some semblance of normal consciousness had returned, *Der Profesor* entered his personal quarters and sat in his chair surrounded by books. This is where Dovid found his mentor, with a tome in his lap.

"We risk the wrath of those that won't understand," Der Profesor said to Dovid without looking up from his book. Then, after a long pause, he said "*Aish Zerah*" in Hebrew and then "*Fremd Feyer*" in Yiddish. "We damn well better get some rabbis aligned with us before the mushrooms become common knowledge." With that, he closed his book and went to bed, leaving Dovid alone in his study.

Dovid picked up *Der Profesor's* volume, a copy of the Tanakh. The Book opened to *Vayikra*, what the Greeks called Leviticus. Dovid read about the brothers Nadab and Abihu and their misadventure with a Foreign Fire. Moshe's nephews, Aaron's oldest sons, were consumed by a Heavenly Flame for their audacity in starting a small unauthorized fire. Dovid knew that they ran a greater risk from religious zealots than Heavenly wrath, especially on Planet Birobidzhan which seems to be beyond any Heavenly Concern.

Der Profesor was right that they would need their own rabbis. A minimum of three, to be exact. Any three rabbis were, at least in theory, able to constitute a rabbinic court. If the project had an assuredly sympathetic rabbinic court essentially on call, that would provide a counterbalance to any potential adverse effects of other rabbis and their courts.

Planet Birobidzhan was awash with rabbis. There are always lots of rabbis for hire. With so many rabbis holding so many vastly different opinions on every possible issue, Planet Birobidzhan was assured that there was never an unanimous position on anything.

If there had been significantly less rabbis, the rabbinic courts might have wielded considerably more potentially destructive power. On Planet Birobidzhan, rabbis were plentiful and individually carried very little weight. Most likely, the plethora of rabbinic authorities is what had kept Planet Birobidzhan from becoming a theocracy. When all was said and done, no rabbinic court had the authority to give orders to any of the rest.

Two days later the corporation had six rabbis on the payroll, a few extra just in case. Then, both Dovid and Der Profesor felt secure enough to invite others to learn from the Mushrooms of Planet Birobidzhan.

Invitations for initiates to partake in consuming the Mushrooms of Planet Birobidzhan were only extended to those directly involved with the remodeling of the *Hatikvah* transport ship and those that planned on joining the expedition. With the guidance of the fungi, the project moved steadily forward. Distant constellations began to feel far more accessible and much closer.

25

TAMAR AND THE KLEZMORIM

The troupe of *klezmorim* that Tamar had joined was one of the oldest, largest, and best organized on Planet Birobidzhan. They toured planet-wide, year round. They were well received everywhere they went.

Like most employment opportunities, the entry-level positions open to the very young on Planet Birobidzhan are unpaid apprenticeship roles. However, unlike other trades, there is greater flexibility among the *klezmorim*. A transition of roles within the troupe is far more fluid than among the bakers, shoemakers, bookbinders, or other such trades where an apprentice is bound by a contract and stuck in a subservient position for years.

Tamar, like all the other *chaverim* of this troupe, started out mostly as a general roustabout. She built stages, hung posters, cared for the goats, tuned other people's instruments, cooked meals, washed pots, sang in the chorus, and played her fiddle in the back row.

The *klezmorim* headed east when they left First Landing. They diverted from the highway as they proceeded eastward to set up their big tent in the many *shtetls* that lie scattered between First Landing and Niu Yerushalaim.

Tamar was soon recognized as a virtuoso. Tamar's unmatched skills with an array of instruments inspired awe. The songs that she sang invoked an otherworldliness. In spite of being so very young, her musical talents propelled her into starring roles. She, in return, achieved more comfortable accommodations than most. She rapidly graduated from a pup tent to a private caravan as the troupe moved about.

Tamar earned the respect and affection of the entire crew. In spite of Tamar's status as a headliner and a top earner, she never shied from any of the physical labor, such as erecting or breaking down the big tent. Tamar was always quite willing to assist in the loading and unloading of heavy gear. She fed and watered the goats that pulled the carts of gear. Additionally, Tamar was a wizard at troubleshooting the electronics of the sound system and lighting.

When the troupe arrived in Niu Yerushalaim, a record company brought Tamar into the studio, where she recorded a solo album. The album garnered a significant amount of success. It sold well and the songs were played often on Planet-wide radio stations for many years. The royalties were deposited into a bank account that Tamar set up for that purpose.

The troupe, after an extended stay in Niu Yerushalaim, meandered north and then westward, visiting the remote *shtetls* of those regions until they made it to the west coast. Then, of course, they followed the coastline south, entertaining the fishing villages nestled wherever a suitable cove offered enough comfortable dockage to encourage fishing.

Nearly two years had passed before they arrived in the vicinity of Niu Niu Yark. The troupe encamped on a plateau. In the valley below, the city of Niu Niu Yark was wrapped in a mist. After settling in, and with no performance planned for that evening, Tamar went for a long walk. This was when she heard the Mushrooms of Planet Birobidzhan once again calling her.

Tamar came upon a fresh bloom of mushrooms. She ate some of the fleshy fungus and sat alone as the sky darkened and the stars filled the night sky. Soon, the plateau, the nearby troupe of *klezmorim*, the mist, and the stars all faded for Tamar. Tamar sat transfixed. She was oblivious to her immediate surroundings. What she saw, as if in broad daylight, was the city which was below her in the cloudy mists and blanketed by the darkness of the night sky.

Niu Niu Yark was a place that she had never even seen pictures of. In her vision she was shown that city in great detail. Initially the perspective was an overview of the metropolis from above, transpiring with a rather dizzying effect. Then, the pace slowed as she was moving about through the unfamiliar streets.

In a neighborhood bordering the coastline the pace of the motion became a gentle floating. Here, she saw a large *Yeshiva* and crowds of black-clad students milling about. Two rabbinic students momentarily came into focus. She saw their faces with utmost clarity. They seemed to be in sincere debate as they walked together down the street. Their hands moved about gesticulating for emphasis. Their *payos* swayed as they walked.

Tamar was shown a prominent herbal apothecary with a glass display window and down the street a very inviting bakery. Adjacent to the bakery there was a door with a sign on it, although the writing on this sign was far too small for Tamar to read.

At this point the perspective spun outward until the city was completely obscured by a thick fog. The Mushrooms of Planet Birobidzhan directed Tamar's attention elsewhere. Tamar watched New Landing and then Planet Birobidzhan regress in the distance from a portal as the craft she occupied was propelled upwards. She was shown unfamiliar constellations and planets.

Then, in what appeared to be a shipboard clinic, Tamar saw a rounded abdomen, raised knees, and the encouraging faces of midwives. One baby and then another appeared in the secure hands of the midwives. In the mushroom-induced vision, two baby boys were eased onto her breasts. Then the vision faded.

Tamar was still sitting in the same position, on the ground among the Mushrooms of Planet Birobidzhan, when sunrise brought light to the *klezmorim* encampment. She smelled food cooking from the mobile kitchen and heard the young roustabouts packing and loading equipment. The troupe was preparing to descend into Niu Niu Yark. Tamar went through the breakfast line and then joined in with the work at hand.

26

HERESY, FLIMFLAM AND DEATH

It was valid for *Der Profesor* and Dovid to be cautious about the swirling rumors that they were fostering a Neo Sabbatai Zevi Cult, but probably not for them to be overly concerned.

There were the occasional uttered underbreath accusations of *apikores*. No formalized charges were ever lodged. No grievances concerning the enterprise were ever brought before any rabbinic court. Generally, the discretion of their inner circle, and the rabbis on the payroll, were sufficient to keep chatter about heresy and apostasy to a minimum.

A bigger ongoing danger to Dovid, *Der Profesor*, the corporation, and the project was that the financial house of cards that they were building would collapse before the retrofitted *Hatikvah* was launched. It was essential for the viability of the project that investors were kept utterly in the dark. The financing was a total sham.

The investors wanted to reconnect with the Home Planet. In order to access investor *gelt,* that is what was promised to them. None of the money raised was spent for that purpose. Not a shekel was ever intended for such a foolhardy endeavor.

What the public was told and what actually was being done were very different. The corporation promised a dual-track strategy. One ship, investors were told, was to be sent on an exploratory mission, seeking out potential profits to be derived from nearby planets. A second ship, investors were assured, would be sent on a diplomatic and trade mission to the Home Planet, Planet Earth.

Adjacent to the *Hatikvah* stood another ancient ship. To all outward appearances both ships were actively being retrofitted. Supplies were delivered and craftsmen could be seen coming and going to each of the ships. However, mostly empty crates were delivered to the second ship and no real work was actually done on the interior of that craft.

A dedicated crew of *gonifs* and *schnorrers* worked diligently to make sure that the operation was funded. They were truly committed to the cause. They never let moral considerations get in the way of doing what needed to be done.

Secrets, of course, are difficult to keep. The more people involved in a conspiracy, the more difficult it is to keep it under wraps. There were hundreds of people involved in this operation. The work dragged on for a very long time. Nonetheless, the co-conspirators were a tight knit, intensely loyal group. There were very few leaks.

Der Profesor's stellar reputation, more than anything else, protected the enterprise from excessive scrutiny. The financial reality was kept from the light of day. The true motives of the conspirators and the flimflam did not become common knowledge on Planet Birobidzhan.

Der Profesor was, no doubt, one of the most widely respected people that ever lived on any planet. Planet-wide, people knew and trusted *Der Profesor. "Er zitst bay der mizrekh-vant,"* people would say of him. They trusted him unreservedly and extended that unreserved trust to his associates, as long as *Der Profesor* remained visibly at the helm of the operation.

Der Profesor lived a long and productive life. We bless each other with the hope of one-hundred and twenty years. Few people obtain that age but *Der Profesor* came close. *Der Profesor* was well into eighties when Dovid first crossed his path and decades had passed since that eventful day. There were signs of his aging and slowing down but *Der Profesor* remained healthy, cognizant, and vibrant until the very end.

Der Profesor and Dovid were playing chess in the library. As usual, *Der Profesor* was winning. Most uncharacteristically, *Der Profesor* apologized for feeling tired midgame. He excused himself and went to bed.

The next morning, when *Der Profesor* did not appear for breakfast, Dovid went to check on him. *Der Profesor* was sitting in bed reading when Dovid let himself in. *Der Profesor* smiled wanly. "I have been waiting for you," he told Dovid. "I wanted to talk with you before I go."

"Going, but..." Dovid started but *Der Profesor* weakly lifted a hand to silence him.

"No one lives forever. I have lived a long life in this world and now I am ready for the *Yeder Velt*, the World to Come." This *Der Profesor* said and then he and Dovid were both quiet for a while before *Der Profesor* continued speaking. "Do you remember the day that I first met you, when you were a little *pisher* that could barely dress himself?"

"Of course I do," Dovid responded while blushing slightly. "You straightened out my suspenders and tied my shoes."

"Do you remember what I told you that day?" *Der Profesor* asked.

"You said that I should always remember that I am smarter than my suspenders and that I should be careful not to fall over my own feet," Dovid replied.

"Well," said *Der Profesor*, "that is still true and that is the best advice that I can give you." *Der Profesor* closed his eyes and spoke no more. His breathing slowed and then ceased.

The funeral held for *Der Profesor* was one of the largest ever on Planet Birobidzhan. *Der Profesor* was buried in his family plot alongside his wife and near other family members including some of his children.

As far as the expedition planned for the *Hatikvah* was concerned, it was fortunate that the time of launching was quickly approaching. The protective shield *Der Profesor* provided for the operation was no longer in place. The grumbling of investors became much louder almost immediately after his funeral. Many were beginning to believe that they may have been swindled.

A few weeks later Dovid received a message from his mother. She needed to see him immediately. He put aside what he was doing and went to the family home. For years that house had mostly been occupied by his mother alone. His father came and went.

When Dovid arrived, his mother was in the kitchen. On the sofa, there was a body covered with a sheet. Dovid's mother barely looked away from the dishes that she was washing when she spoke. "I need your help arranging a funeral," she told him. She tilted her chin towards the sofa.

At once Dovid grasped that his father had passed away. He gave his mother a hug. "Of course, Mama, I can help with that," Dovid told her. "Should I stay here while we *Sit Shiva* for *Tate*?"

Dovid's mother stopped what she was doing and looked directly into her son's eyes. Then she spoke without emotion. "I did not love that man. I was married to him so I am responsible for burying him. I certainly will not *Sit Shiva* for him. You do know that he was not really your father, right? There is no reason for you to say *Kadish* for that man, much less tear your clothes and other *mishegoss*. But," she concluded, "we do need to bury him." She went back to washing dishes.

Dovid made all of the arrangements for the funeral. The funeral was attended by his mother, all of her children, and a handful of her husband's ne'er-do-well *dreidl*-spinning gambling buddies. After the funeral, *babka*, tea, and schnapps were served in the family home. The gambling buddies left when the booze ran out. Dovid's mother sent the family off so she could, at last, be alone.

Dovid returned to his own home by the airport. The house felt very empty now, with *Der Profesor* no longer there and most of Dovid's children grown, living elsewhere, raising families of their own. His favorite daughter, Tamar, was traveling with the *klezmorim*. Dovid checked on his wives. They were both sleeping.

Dovid sat in his library. He drank whiskey by himself until he fell asleep.

27

AN APARTMENT IN THE CITY BY THE SEA

Planet Birobidzhan is a sparsely populated world. Most of the *mentshn* live in small settlements and *shtetls.* Generally speaking, life on Planet Birobidzhan is slow paced. The planet's largest city, Niu Niu Yark, on the other hand, is a crowded bustling metropolis.

Niu Niu Yark is truly the business, cultural, educational, and industrial center of Planet Birobidzhan. The geologists and architectural experts amongst the Founders chose the location because of the fine natural harbor. The rabbis designated Niu Niu Yark as the primary city for building the grand *yeshivas.*

Situated in a near-tropical zone, there is a casual ambiance and a laissez-faire attitude there. One might be rightfully surprised by the degree of diversity from a city established to such a large degree by rabbis as a center for religious studies.

Niu Niu Yark is sometimes called the City that Never Sleeps. This is particularly true for the *Tsenter Shtot.* That urban core includes the Theater District. Here one finds the large entertainment venues as well as many smaller clubs, lots of restaurants, hotels, several casinos, the higher class brothels, and a slew of bars.

The *klezmer* troupe had a two week engagement booked in one of the *Tsenter Shtot's* finest theaters. There were two performances scheduled for every day except, of course, *Shabbos*.

The *klezmorim* were settled into their own wing of a large hotel. It was a welcome reprieve for the troupe to stay in one place, sleep in wide beds, bathe whenever they wanted, and to let someone else do the cooking.

Even with the heavy performance schedule, the *chaverim* had time to relax and play tourist in Niu Niu Yark. The city is made up of many neighborhoods and districts with distinct characteristics beyond the *Tsenter Shtot* that are well worth visiting.

Tamar, however, did not play at being a tourist. The morning of her first full day in the city, Tamar went directly where the Mushrooms of Planet Birobidzhan had led her. She headed to Seaside Mea Shearim.

Seaside Mea Shearim is the oldest district of Niu Niu Yark. The *yeshivas* were built here. Much of the district is made up of apartments that serve as bachelor student housing. There is, as well, a neighborhood of mostly married students with young growing families. The district also has a variety of businesses that cater to the students. The families that run these businesses often live in apartments above or adjacent to their shops. Of course, the faculty of each of the *yeshivas*, and their families, also live in Seaside Mea Shearim.

The coastline is made up of dockage primarily used by commercial fishermen. Pleasure boats offering snorkeling trips and the ferry service between Niu Niu Yark and Eilat also utilize these docks. Nearby are dive bars and other sorts of distractions that appeal to fishermen, and an occasional *yeshiva* student. So, in this way, the holy, the profane, and the mundane coincide somewhat comfortably in Seaside Mea Shearim.

Tamar rode the streetcar from *Tsenter Shtot* to its terminus by the docks of Seaside Mea Shearim. From there, she walked past the large *yeshiva* that overlooks the harbor.

As Tamar approached the school, the rabbinic students that she had seen in her mushroom induced vision descended the steps. She walked behind those two, casually observing and nonchalantly eavesdropping. The students were immersed in a debate of *halachic* fine points.Their hands gesticulated and *payos* swayed as they walked and argued from the *yeshiva* to their apartment. The two were *chavrusa* - studying partners - and roommates.

Tamar followed them unnoticed. She learned a lot about these two young men in a very short time. She knew that their names were Baruch and Shmuli. She knew that they were each highly intelligent. She learned their favorite foods, class schedules, and where they lived. Tamar had a pretty good idea where they would be every *Mantik aun Danershtag* and where they ate lunch every *Mitvakh*. Most significantly, she was assured that these two young men were linked to her *bashert*, her destiny.

As Tamar continued strolling along the streets of Seaside Mea Shearim all the sights were familiar. The buildings, the trees, the street vendors, the cobblestones, the storefronts, and more had been imprinted in her memories by her interactions with the Mushrooms of Planet Birobidzhan. Every footstep was preordained.

Tamar came to the bakery with the wide window display. A comforting aroma of fresh baked goods was wafting from the open door. Adjacent to the bakery was the door that

Tamar had seen in her vision, with a handwritten sign tacked to it. "Furnished Apartment for Rent" read the notice in large block letters. The tighter script below, directed anyone interested to speak with Miriam at the bakery. So, Tamar removed the notice from the door and went into the bakery to meet Miriam.

The rental, situated above the bakery, was indeed quite comfortable and appealing. The apartment was being offered on a monthly basis. Tamar rented the place for six months. Tamar negotiated a twenty percent discount on the *dire gelt* for the apartment above the bakery. She paid cash, in full, for the six months. Tamar insisted on daily pastries and *challah* every Friday from the bakery as well as a weekly delivery of wood to fuel the kitchen stove. Tamar's negotiation prowess would have made her father proud.

Tamar returned to *Tsenter Shtot* by streetcar, arriving in the Theater District in time for the *klezmer* troupe's performance. She informed the *chaverim* that she would not be traveling with them when the troupe resumed their touring. This engagement at the theater in Niu Niu Yark would be her last with the *klezmorim*.

The next morning Tamar hired a taxi to transport her possessions to Seaside Mea Shearim. She began to make herself at home, settling happily in her apartment above the bakery. Tamar commuted to the theater by streetcar for the rest of the gig, fulfilling her contractual agreement. Her heart and mind were elsewhere.

28

THE GIRL WITH A FIDDLE

It seemed that everywhere that Baruch and Shmuli went, there was the *meydl mit a fidele*. When the young scholars walked home from the *yeshiva*, Tamar would be on the corner near their apartment, playing her fiddle. An open instrument case with a handful of coins and a few crumpled shekel notes would be at her feet.

Every *Mantik aun Danershtag*, Baruch and Shmuli would *daven shacharis* with a small neighborhood *minyan* and help with the *Toyre* reading. When they left the *minyan* on their way back to the yeshiva, the *meydl mit a fidele* would be on the sidewalk as they walked by. Every *Mitvokh*, Baruch and Shmuli would splurge by eating lunch at a delicatessen near the *yeshiva*. Shortly after leaving the restaurant, they inevitably found Tamar busking.

The weather was nearly always perfect in Niu Niu Yark for playing music outside. The streets of Seaside Mea Shearim provide some of the best acoustic possibilities in the city. Tamar would close her eyes while playing the violin. She played for no one but herself until Baruch and Shmuli arrived.

Tamar always knew when Baruch and Shmuli were nearing. She could hear them arguing from a block away. As they approached her, the bickering would taper off and then cease. At that moment, Tamar would open her eyes, increasing the crescendo of her fiddling.

Baruch and Shmuli, like most *yeshiva bochers,* had little money. They would, however, stop and listen to the otherworldly melodies that Tamar conjured with her violin. The young men would always drop a few *peniz oder a nikal* in her violin case.

Tamar always smiled demurely at the young men, respectfully avoiding direct eye contact. She would watch them out of the corner of her eye as they would try not to stare at her. The *yeshiva bochers* would stand about awkwardly, fidgeting and mostly avoiding the sin of looking directly at the beautiful young woman with the fiddle that played Heavenly music.

Tamar was always dressed in a most appropriate manner. Her long sleeves covered her arms to her wrists. Tamar always wore a skirt that reached down to her shoes. Tamar's attire was exactly what is worn in the most conservative of *shtetls* on Planet Birobidzhan.

Sometimes, when Baruch and Shmuli were nearby, Tamar's skirt would shift enough to expose an ankle. Occasionally, her sleeves would flutter when she vigorously stroked the fiddle with the bow and her bare arms would be momentarily visible. The young men would blush. Tamar would smile, demurely.

For weeks, neither Baruch nor Shmuli uttered more than a few cautious words directly to Tamar. Yet, most assuredly, as time went on, both of these young men fell in love with Tamar. They began to look forward to encounters with the pretty musician. They were no longer surprised at the "chance" meetings with Tamar.

Everyone has to *macht a leben,* but Tamar had no need to play her fiddle on streets corners. The *dire gelt* for her apartment was paid up in advance and there was money left over from her gig with the klezmorim. Tamar had a steady royalties stream from the album she recorded in Niu Yerushalaim, paid directly into a bank account where it sat untouched. Tamar earned a share of the door from a weekly gig at a small club where she performed just for practice. That money was spent on whims and impulses. Tamar drank coffee in cafes, visited museums, attended theater performances, indulged in the occasional snorkeling trip, and bought herself small luxuries, when so inclined.

Tamar was only busking on those Seaside Mea Shearim streets when she could expect Baruch and Shmuli to be walking by. Tamar planned her Mondays, Wednesdays, and Thursdays around staging those seemingly spontaneous short encounters. Tamar sometimes arrived at the precise spot only minutes ahead of the *yeshiva bochers* and packed up her violin as soon as Baruch and Shmuli were beyond hearing range.

Tamar spent Tuesdays at the Herbal Apothecary. She helped the proprietor by filling orders, talking to customers, and straightening up. In exchange, Tamar received a comprehensive education in folk medicine and herbal therapy. Tamar learned how women can govern their cycles, taking control of the terms and timing of pregnancy. She learned that the likelihood of pregnancy occurring during intercourse varies widely. There are days when a resulting pregnancy is quite unlikely and a time when a pregnancy is nearly guaranteed.

Tamar became familiar with the effects of various herbs and the combination of various herbs. She discovered that there are herbs that can shield a woman from an unwanted pregnancy and others that will increase the possibility of impregnation. She also learned that there are a wide variety of herbal mixtures that increase or decrease male potency, and some that promote male vigor.

Tamar absorbed an encyclopedic knowledge of herbal history, lore and science. This was incredibly useful when she counseled customers in the Apothecary. Most of the clients were the young wives of *yeshiva* students and rabbis. They, nearly unanimously, were interested in limiting the number of children that they would bear.

As the weeks passed, so did some of the *yeshiva bochers'* awkward tendencies. Before long, the semblance of actual conversations began to take place such as commenting on the weather or asking about Tamar's health and her family. Then, one Monday, Tamar took the bold step of inviting Baruch and Shmuli to her apartment for a cup of tea and *kikhlekh*.

The yeshiva *bochers* expressed some reluctance, at first. They didn't want to be a burden on a poor street musician. They assumed that she was at least as impoverished as they were. Tamar gave them no reasons to draw other conclusions. Tamar assured them that the baked goods were a side benefit of living above the bakery. She explained that the tea was obtained without cost from the Herbal Apothecary.

In this case, no harm, assuredly, could come from a cup of tea and a cookie or two, determined the *yeshiva bochers*. The young men stayed with Tamar until she finished her impromptu street performance and accompanied her home.

Tamar unlocked the door adjacent to the bakery. Baruch and Shmuli followed her up the stairs and into her apartment. The *yeshiva bochers* stood about, quite unsure of themselves. Tamar settled her guests at a table on the balcony overlooking the street. She went into her kitchen to prepare the tea.

Tamar could hear Baruch and Shmuli begin to argue over that morning's *Toyre* portion. That habitual bickering assured her that the *yeshiva bochers* were beginning to feel at ease. The theological argument had become quite animated by the time that Tamar rolled the samovar onto the balcony. She served the tea *shtetl* style, with sugar cubes, a platter of cookies from the bakery below, and a bowl of dates.

One of the things that Tamar particularly enjoyed about living in Niu Niu Yark is that dates are so readily available. She reminded Baruch and Shmuli that the Hebrew word for dates is *tamar,* her namesake. "The Hebrew *tamar* certainly sounds more *romantic* than the Yiddish *da-tes,* don't you think?" Tamar said with a wink.

29

TAMAR AND THE SCHOLARS

Tea at Tamar's every *Mantik* after *shacharis* became ritualistic for Baruch and Shmuli. The tea time often stretched into lunch. Sometimes the *yeshiva bochers* would *daven mincha aun maariv* at the apartment above the bakery.

Tamar introduced Baruch and Shmuli to a variety of herbal concoctions that she brought home from the Herbal Apothecary as well as serving the more traditional tea that they were used to. The *yeshiva bochers* were always a bit hungry and a few cookies or a *shtikel* of *babka* were well deserved calories and nutrients. In Tamar's apartment, there were always fresh pastries, provided by the landlord from the bakery below. The dates that Tamar served were truly wonderful, a *mechayeh*. Sometimes, instead of dates, Tamar offered *majoun*, made from dates, nuts and hashish. On special occasions there was schnapps.

Once in a while Tamar would tell her friends that she had received movie tickets from the club or dropped into her violin case while she was busking. On those occasions, the three friends would meet in the evening and walk to the nearby Bijou Theater.

At the cinema, Tamar insisted on sitting between the two *yeshiva bochers*. In the darkened theater, Tamar would kick her shoes off and brush a stockinged foot casually against one or the other of her friends. Tamar would lean her shoulders against each of the *bochers* while passing the tub of popcorn.

Sometimes, in that darkened movie theater, Tamar grabbed one of the *bochers* by the knee when something dramatic happened on the screen or slid her palm down an inner thigh if the film was suspenseful. Each assumed themselves to be the only recipient of this sort of special attention. Both were too polite to mention such to the other.

Purim, of course, is on the fourteenth day of the month of Adar. On Planet Birobidzhan it is celebrated with a broad abandonment of social norms. This is all the more so in Niu Niu Yark, partially due to the subtropical latitude and balmy weather. Even before the beginning of Adar, a degree of excitement and anticipation can be felt throughout the city. *Majoun* is sold in every grocery and neighborhood store. Masks and materials for costumes are everywhere. The annual Purim party in the streets of Niu Niu Yark is the biggest party of the year, on the entire planet.

The rabbinic authorities of Niu Niu Yark issue their annual admonishments concerning the holiday, discouraging public nudity and debauchery. The heads of each of the *yeshivas* also offer strict warnings to all of their students. The admonishments and warnings have no effect on how Purim is celebrated.

Tamar's anticipation of the celebration was amplified by her various undisclosed plans. Every aspect involved precise timing.

Tamar intended to leave Niu Niu Yark immediately after the holiday. She had told no one of of this beforehand. Shortly after the First of Adar, Tamar packed up her large collection of instruments, except for her violin, and all of her clothes that didn't fit in her rucksack. She shipped her things to her family home, via Moshe & Mendel's Jew Harp, Tsatske aun Muzik Krom, from their store in Niu Niu Yark to their store in First Landing.

The Wednesday prior to Purim, Tamar woke early. She fidgeted around the apartment for a while, with an air of anticipation. She was looking forward to meeting with Baruch and Shmuli on the street near where they eat lunch. Before leaving the apartment, Tamar wiggled the *mezuzah* that hung by her bedroom door, causing the top nail to fall out so that it was hanging loosely, upside-down by the bottom nail. She smiled to herself. She skipped across her living room and headed down the stairs.

Tamar arrived earlier than usual at the regular *Mitvokh* corner and played her violin more passionately than usual. Tamar's street performance drew a crowd and her violin case filled with banknotes. While playing, Tamar looked off to her left, in anticipation of Baruch and Shmuli. She visualized their presence on the street as if wishing it to be so would bring them sooner.

When the *yeshiva bochers* approached, Tamar stopped playing mid song and spoke to them breathlessly. "I was so hoping that you would come today," she said as if there was anything unusual about them walking down that street after *Mitvokh* lunch at their usual delicatessen. "I have a problem. I need your help," Tamar said emphatically as she packed up her violin.

The *yeshiva bochers* were concerned and assured Tamar that they would help her in any way they could. They asked her what was bothering her.

Tamar took a deep breath and spoke directly to the two young men, looking from one face to another, deeply into their eyes. "A *mezuzah* in my apartment has fallen halfway off. It is hanging upside down by the bottom nail. It needs to be reattached. I want to be sure that it is hung correctly." Tamar sighed. "Can you help me? Please?"

Tamar smiled wanly at her two friends. What else could they do but follow Tamar back to the apartment above the bakery to lend their assistance and expertise?

Along the way, Baruch and Shmuli bickered over the laws and customs concerning the proper care and display of a *mezuzah*. There is the matter of the exact angle and if a *berakhah* needs to be said and what to do if the scroll has been damaged. They presented positions and counterpoints, quoting holy books, arguing the whole way there. Tamar walked ahead of them, smiling in anticipation of her unfolding plan.

Of course, the *yeshiva bochers*, once they were in the apartment, made short work of the repairs. Tamar thanked them profusely and suggested a small glass of whiskey to drink *l'chaim* and in honor of the *mitzvah* performed. The young men were more accustomed to drinking the less potent schnapps than whiskey, but under the circumstances they could not refuse.

The three friends, said a *berakhah,* drank *l'chaim* and *l'chaim once more.* Tamar suggested that they have tea and perhaps a little something to eat. "After all," she said, "it is still early in the day." Of course, Baruch and Shmuli acquiesced.

Tamar served *majoun* and an herbal concoction. She continued to refill their whiskey glasses. Time became irrelevant as the various substances took effect. When the clock showed that it was time to *daven mincha aun maariv,* the young men could barely stand. They mumbled their way through the prayers.

The whiskey had Baruch and Shmuli sloshed. The hashish in the *majoun* distorted their sense of time. The herbal concoctions that Tamar served kept them awake and increased strength and stamina in ways that they could not have anticipated. As the night unfolded, Baruch and Shmuli became detached from the world that they knew. Everything seemed as if to be a dream.

Tamar asked the *yeshiva bochers* if they would like to see her Purim costume. She said that she wanted their opinions as to the propriety of the costume that she had chosen. While Baruch and Shmuli sat on the living room sofa in a quite unfamiliar haze, Tamar turned down the electric lights and lit an aromatic candle, which she placed on the mantle. Tamar went into her bedroom to change.

When Tamar returned, she was wearing little besides gauze. Soon after that, she was wearing even less. Tamar knew that she was ovulating. The moment to fulfill that specific destiny was upon her. The two *yeshiva bochers* sat on the sofa, transfixed. They were both beyond rational thought.

When Baruch and Shmuli descended the apartment stairs and stumbled into the streets of Seaside Mea Shearim, morning was already approaching. The *yeshiva bochers* choose to *daven shacharis* in the privacy of their apartment. They skipped their regular Thursday *minyan* and *Toyre* reading.

Tamar wrapped herself in a comfortable bathrobe. She was absolutely sure that she was pregnant with twins. She was quite confident that both Baruch and Shmuli were very fertile and that their seeds were well placed.

Tamar brewed herself a cup of soothing herbal tea and sipped it contentedly, sitting on the sofa surrounded by fluffy pillows. Tamar stroked her abdomen and smiled.

30

THE TROPICS OF PLANET BIROBIDZHAN

The streets of every neighborhood of Niu Niu Yark were raucous with the celebration of Purim throughout the night. The sounds of the drunken revelers were everywhere. The celebratory noise rippled through Tamar's window above the bakery until nearly dawn.

Tamar was content to be sober, by herself, and in her apartment. Tamar stayed at home, reading, drinking herbal tea, playing her fiddle, and resting. She went to bed early.

The whole next day the city seemed to be suffering from a collective hangover. The remains of the festivities littered the streets. Bits of clothing and gauze were everywhere. Overnight, some alleyways had been turned into temporary improvised urinals. The smell of piss lingered. Some people fell asleep in doorways or on the sidewalk. A few were still sleeping in these odd places long into the day.

Businesses around the city opened late the day after the Purim festivities, or not at all. The bakery below Tamar's apartment opened late and closed early. Tamar was grateful for the pleasant fragrance of breads and cakes baking. She would certainly miss those smells when she moved.

She was very glad for the platter of croissants that the baker's apprentice delivered to her that morning.

The following day, Tamar rose very early. She packed her rucksack and took the time to tidy the apartment before leaving it for the last time. When the bakery opened its door, Tamar returned the apartment key to Miriam. The two women exchanged hugs. Tamar left with a few fresh baked rolls added to her rucksack and walked towards the docks.

Tamar's strolling was casual and pleasant. Tamar felt something akin to nostalgia as she walked past the various corners where she had played her violin, the Herbal Apothecary where she worked, the cafes that she had frequented, and the *yeshiva* where Baruch and Shmuli studied.

Tamar arrived at the ferry station with time to spare. Tamar bought her ticket for the boat trip to Eilat and then ordered tea from a nearby café. She sat at an outdoor table on the sidewalk adjacent to the docks. The tea was served *shtetl* style, in a glass with a sugar cube on the side.

Niu Niu Yark is semi tropical but as one heads south on the ferry into the true tropics, the transition becomes evident. Temperatures rise. The texture of the air changes. Colors become more vibrant. Along the way, traveling on the ferry, the warmth of Niu Niu Yark is replaced by the balminess of the Tropics. The sea is generally calm, making the ferry ride a very pleasant trip.

The Tropics of Birobidzhan are sparsely populated. The Tropics consist of the small *shtot* - actually not much bigger than a *shtetl* - of Eilat and a smattering of very small semi isolated coastal *shtetls* where *Yidden* scratch out a *leben* by fishing. One can travel between the various *shtetls* on a network of goat paths or by boat.

There are no large fishing fleets to be found. There is little industry or commerce to speak of. The region has a small agricultural sector that specializes in growing *esrogim*, the citrus fruit used for *Sukkos*. Other than that, there are very few commercial farming endeavors. Most food is raised in family gardens. There is no mining and no manufacturing to speak of.

Eilat and its vicinity have some tourist draw. There are hotels and restaurants that cater to visitors. Outsiders come to the Tropics mainly in the winter. After Purim, travel to Eilat falls off dramatically. The ferry was not crowded at all. That was certainly how Tamar preferred it.

Tamar stayed on the upper deck of the ferry for most of the trip. She had a fair degree of privacy and an incredible view. The sea was nearly without waves. The water was a beautiful aqua. A breeze blew through Tamar's unraveled hair. The sun was shining on her shoulders when she removed her shaw and on her legs when she adjusted the folds of her skirt, stretching out. Tamar soaked it all in.

The Tropics of Birobidzhan have far more *Sephardic* and *Mizrahi* influence than the rest of Planet Birobidzhan. This first becomes evident to visitors when eating in the restaurants of Eilat. The food served is spicier than what is found elsewhere on Planet Birobidzhan. There are also, one might note, some variants in the *Sephardic* approach to *kashrus* laws and customs, particularly concerning *Pesach*.

Throughout the Tropics the *mezuzah* on the outer doors of most buildings is perpendicular rather than at an angle, which is the planetary norm. Most buildings in the Tropics, in addition to a *mezuzah*, display a *hamsa* to ward off evil. Additionally, the ceilings of porches are usually painted blue as this is believed to help protect a home from evil spirits.

There is a local accent in the Tropics of Birobidzhan with some unique pronunciation. In some cases, the emphasis is placed on a different syllable. In the Tropics, there is a tendency to sometimes use a "t" sound to replace the "s" or "sh" that is more common on the rest of Planet Birobidzhan. On the whole, however, the *shprakh* spoken there is not incredibly different from the *shprakh* of the rest of the planet.

There are quite a few Spanish and Arabic words that spice up the Yiddish spoken in the Tropics of Birobidzhan. At times, the use of one of these words denotes a very different meaning from the more common Yiddish words with the same definition.

If one is speaking about getting something done "tomorrow" one can say either *morgan* or *mañana*. If one is told *morgan* in the Tropics, then the speaker may actually mean tomorrow. If, however, one is told *mañana* it means that maybe tomorrow or the next day or maybe next week or perhaps not at all. The Tropics of Birobidzhan are called the *Land of Mañana* for good reason.

The ferry arrived in Eilat in the early afternoon. The city seemed sleepy, as if just waking from a nap. Most businesses in the Tropics close mid day for an extended lunch and rest in the shade. The local term for this extended afternoon break is *siesta.* This derives from the Spanish word meaning a nap. Indeed, the arrival of the ferry from Niu Niu Yark coincides with the conclusion of the *siesta.*

The first thing Tamar did upon arrival was rent a cozy room at a guest house. She left her rucksack and violin in her room and headed out to see Eilat unencumbered.

Tamar walked about, looking at the colorfully painted homes and the lush gardens accentuated with splendid tropical flowers. She ate a seafood meal in a quiet little restaurant. The dining room had windows that opened to the street and a ceiling fan that circulated the balmy air. Tamar sat on a dock to watch the sun set into the sea.

Tamar was enamored by the Tropics.

31

THE BEACHES AND COASTAL SHTETLS

The guest house that Tamar had chosen was clean and airy. The room was brightly painted and pleasant. The bed was comfortable. The ceiling fan cooled the room. Yet, Tamar could not sleep.

Tamar turned one way and then another. There was no position that allowed for comfortable sleep. She felt like the princess in the ancient tale *mit a bebl* under her mattress. Something infinitesimal and unseen was so disruptive that sleeping in the guest house was impossible.

When exhaustion would start to supersede discomfort and Tamar's eyelids grew heavy, she would then hear the voices, arguing. Tamar would bolt straight up, looking around for Baruch and Shmuli. All around her, there was darkness and the room was empty. The bickering voices would fade and then go silent. Again, Tamar would try to sleep but rest never came.

Tamar had nearly given up all hope for sleep. She went to the *vashzimmer* and splashed her face with water. She looked at herself in the mirror and hardly recognized the reflection. She was very tired and felt very much alone.

Tamar stepped outside and gazed at the view of unfamiliar constellations of the sky south of the equator. The air was balmy and filled with the fragrances of a myriad of exotic tropical flowers. In the courtyard of the guest house, slung between two trees, was a hammock that invited rest and offered an unencumbered view of the sky. There, Tamar managed a few hours of sleep, temporarily freed from the bickering voices for a little while until sunrise.

On checking out, Tamar asked the *balabusta* of the guest house if there was a place in Eilat where a hammock could be purchased. After some hemming and hawing and a bit of negotiation, the innkeeper sold Tamar the hammock that she had slept in. Tamar wrapped the hammock up and tied it to her rucksack. She went from there to a small grocery and then Tamar set out *tsufus* down the goat path leaving town to explore the Tropics of Birobidzhan.

There is very little traffic along the goat paths that connect the coastal *shtetls* of the Tropics of Birobidzhan, especially after Purim. The coastal dwellers prefer to not travel. When they feel compelled to go up or down the coast, they will choose to do so by boat.

The goat paths are used by small children when going to, perhaps, the next closest village to visit friends or family. The older children, like their elders, prefer to go by boat. The paths are used to some extent by the more adventurous of tourists, in season. Most outside visitors, however, rarely explore much past the *shtot* of Eilat, where there is an array of facilities that cater to tourism.

When entering the *shtetls* by goat paths, one is unlikely to see any signage whatsoever. That part of town is thought of as the outer fringe or backside of the *shtetl*, where one might find a dump, slaughterhouse, or some limited and fairly primitive industries. The oceanside and dockage are the outward face of the *shtetls*. On the dock one is likely to see a colorful sign with an exotic town name such as Tangiers, Marrakesh, Caracas, and Habana.

Between the tiny *shtetls* that dot the coastline are some of the most incredibly spectacular beaches to be found on any planet. The sand colors on these beaches vary from pink to peach to lavender. Tropical foliage borders the sands. The warm waters are frequented by large schools of colorful fish. Birds with a cacophony of sounds and colors perch in the trees and fly above in large flocks. The beaches remain beautiful because of their remoteness. The beaches are only accessible *tsufus*. Most people will not walk for miles to visit even the most spectacular beach.

Tamar camped on these beaches that lie between the outlying *shtetls*. She would string her hammock between trees or sleep directly on the soft sand dunes, staying in one place for two or three nights. Camping provided some relief from the arguing voices that haunted Tamar's nights. She suspected that a struggle was taking place within her womb.

Tamar rarely saw another person between the *shtetls*. She mostly had the tropical beaches to herself. She would swim naked and sun herself on the soft sand. Tamar minimized her time in these tiny *shtetls*. She would acquire a few necessities and then head out to another unoccupied beach.

In most of these *shtetls*, there is a small shop that offers a very limited array of consumer goods and a few groceries. On the whole, households in the Tropics of Birobidzhan grow most of their own vegetables, raise a few animals for meat, bake their own bread, and either do their own fishing or buy fish directly from the fishermen.

Market days on *Mantik aun Danershtag* provide more choices than the tiny stores. Tamar preferred to arrive at a *shtetl* on a Monday or a Thursday. On these days fresh vegetables are available and often baked goods.

There are few accommodations to speak of. Some of the town folk have an extra room that they will offer to rent to the rare traveler passing through. Tamar hardly ever stayed overnight in any of these *shtetls*.

When Tamar entered a *shtetl*, she was often accosted by one of the *balabustas*. Tamar would be offered a home-cooked meal and perhaps a place to spend the night. Inevitably, there was a son, brother, or grandson in need of a wife. The *balabusta* would set right into matchmaking. Even after Tamar's swollen abdomen made pregnancy undeniably evident, the matchmaking efforts did not abate much until she became so large that her gait turned into a wobble.

Tamar was not looking for a husband. Some of the young men of the *shtetls* were pleasant enough perhaps for a dalliance. None were the sort that she could imagine forming a long-term association with, much less a marriage.

In the early evening, on the docks of these coastal *shtetls*, the fishermen without homes, wives, and children gather to feed and entertain themselves. They cook fish heads and other less marketable parts from the day's catch along with potatoes and peppers into a thick, seasoned, savory stew that they call jambalaya.

The fishermen serve themselves from their communal pot and drink schnapps profusely late into the night under the equatorial stars. The musicians among the fishermen play their accordions, harmonicas, and Jews Harps. When Tamar felt a desire for social interactions, the docks among the fishermen is where she felt the most comfortable. She would open her violin case and join in with the amateur *klezmorim*. She was always welcomed and also well fed.

Tamar's pregnancy was quite advanced by the time autumn approached. Getting around on her own, *tsufus*, became significantly more difficult. The increased number of tourists entering the region made the Tropics of Birobidzhan less appealing to her than before. Tamar determined that it was time to move on. Tamar found her way back to Eilat and traveled on the ferry to Niu Niu Yark.

Tamar disembarked the ferry in Seaside Mea Shearim. From the distance, she watched Baruch and Shmuli descend the steps of the *yeshiva* where they were still students. She saw them walking towards their apartment, gesticulating and arguing. Tamar smiled as she watched them walking away, unaware of her presence.

Tamar boarded a streetcar by the docks and rode it to *Tsenter Shtot*. She had enough time to go to her bank and close her account before heading to the train station. She booked a sleeper car on the train to First Landing and arrived at her family home relatively rested early the next morning, a very rare congruity of efficiency for Planet Birobidzhan.

32

A PRE-LAUNCH REUNION

Dovid had his crews working in twelve hour shifts, non-stop from early morning on every *Sontag* until late into the afternoons every *Freytag,* with barely a break for *Shabbos*. The sense of urgency was palatable. Dovid and his inner circle knew that they were racing against the clock.

Suspicions about the finances were growing by the day. *Der Profesor* had played a major role in camouflaging the irregularities of the operation. He was trusted globally. *Der Profesor* used that trust diligently and to the utmost in the interests of the project. Dovid was widely liked and even appreciated but he lacked the reputation of his mentor and the innate ability to deceive.

The two track plan was, of course, a sham. There was no actual mission to the Home Planet. As time spiraled forward, the complexity of the lies required more creative subterfuge and illusory constructs.

Initially, the consortium suggested sending a drone on a mission to Earth. This was a low cost approach and was even actually doable. However, there were, indeed, some very practical reasons why sending a drone to the Home

Planet might be a fool's errand. Besides, the idea of a drone had little appeal to anyone. A drone was not proactive enough to capture the interest of deep pocket investors. A lot of *gelt* was needed to finance the *Hatikvah* expedition so a marketable story was needed.

The consortium's public proclamations that a diplomatic and trade mission would be sent to Earth was a lie that needed to be believed by the general public and, most importantly, by the financial victims of the ponzi scheme. The consortium dragged its feet but ultimately had to provide a plausible show. To that effect, they began a mock recruitment process for the supposed mission, resulting in all sorts of public input.

After much back and forth, it was expressed that eighteen men would be picked to represent the religious and business communities of Planet Birobidzhan. An approval process was designed for the fake mission. When the eighteen supposed representatives were chosen, they were housed at a barrack adjacent to the airport. The volunteers were put through a "training mission" for the nonexistent mission. These eighteen volunteers were beginning to get anxious to be on their way. Of course, there was no functioning ship to take them anywhere.

The *Hatikvah* needed to be off the tarmac and heading to the stars, before everything unraveled and Dovid's inner circle faced the repercussions of Planet Birobidzhan's equivalent of a tar and feathering. The guidance that Dovid received from the Mushrooms of Planet Birobidzhan was of no help to sort through such human concerns.

Nearly three years had passed since Tamar had left First Landing with the traveling troupe of *klezmorim*. A few very short letters arrived from her as well as some picture postcards. After an extended gap in communication, and with no explanation, the crates with Tamar's musical instruments were delivered. A few days later, a picture postcard from Eilat arrived. Then, *nisht gornisht*, not a word or a clue as to where she was and what she was doing.

Tamar arrived in First Landing by train early in the morning, shortly after *Sukkos*. The First Landing airport serves as the train station as well so it was easy enough for Tamar to walk to the family home, even with her enlarged torso. Her rucksack was on her back and her violin case was in hand. Tamar's arrival was unexpected. Her family was also unaware of her advanced pregnancy.

The morning light was just creeping over the horizon when Tamar appeared at the family home. At that early hour, Tamar surprised her father. She was nearly as surprised herself to find Dovid already up and working at a feverish pace.

Dovid was thrilled to see Tamar, his favorite child of the "dozen or so" *kinder*. He was also anxious about the work he had been doing. Dovid's first inclination was postponing the reunion until he was done working. Tamar patted her abdomen and said emphatically, "We must eat!"

Tamar presented the same face and gestures that she had used to manipulate Dovid's heart since she was a toddler. Dovid could never resist her demands when she was small and he still couldn't. Dovid put down the box that was in his hands and they headed together to the family kitchen.

33

THE LAUNCH WAS IMMINENT

Tamar left her rucksack and violin in the foyer and started towards the kitchen with her father. Suddenly, Tamar clamped her hands over her ears. "Just stop!" she yelled. "Don't you two ever stop bickering?" she cried out in exasperation. Her face grimaced and she was taking short and grasping breaths.

Dovid gazed alarmingly at his daughter. Tamar was evidently distraught and in pain. He stepped closer and reached out towards her. She flailed her arms about until he stepped back.

After a while, Tamar's quivering stopped and her visible tension receded. Tamar's breathing became more relaxed. Calm returned to her countenance. Tamar pushed back tears and stroked her extended abdomen before she began speaking. "They are always fighting, always arguing. These two, they are just like their fathers."

Dovid looked at his daughter quizzically but refrained from voicing an actual question. They resumed walking towards the kitchen.

The house was a jumbled *balagan.* There were piles of everything, everywhere. There were boxes stacked. There were overflowing trashcans. A sorting process going on.

The retrofit and design work on the *Hatikvah* was finished. Fuel had been loaded. All the mechanisms had been thoroughly tested. The hydroponic gardens were already up and running. The pens for the chickens, goats, and sheep were ready for the livestock. The launch was imminent.

The loading of personal items had already begun. Only some of the family belongings were destined for the stars. The rest would remain on Planet Birobidzhan. Heirlooms were earmarked for delivery to family. Other possessions would be abandoned. Similar calculations and evaluations were taking place in several hundred households in First Landing and the surrounding region.

When the *Hatikvah* lifted towards the stars, around eight hundred Yidden would be leaving parents and children, friends and loved ones, personal possessions, and Planet Birobidzhan behind. Tensions and discordant emotions were at play in each of these households. Everyone felt stressed as the liftoff time approached. Some relationships were strained to the breaking point. It is not easy to leave one's world behind.

For Dovid, Rifka Leeba, and Hannah Leah, no less than anyone else, these were difficult times. Although they were each committed to the plan of leaving Planet Birobidzhan behind for quite some time, they still had much physical and emotional baggage to process.

There were only a handful of younger children still at home, too young to make their own decisions. Most of the family's children were past the Bar Mitzvah age and with children of their own. The *kinder* were busy raising their own *kinder* and chose to remain behind.

In the kitchen, Rifka Leeba cooked. A tea kettle whistled. Hannah Leah nursed the most recent addition to the brood. Tamar and Dovid sat at the table *schmoozing* as they ate. Their conversation spanned the globe, the universe, and galaxies.

Tamar told Dovid about her pleasant apartment above the bakery, in Seaside Mea Shearim, Niu Niu Yark. She spoke of her deep bonds of attachment with her dear friends, Baruch and Shmuli. Tamar most emphatically believed that she was carrying twin boys fathered by each of these nice *yeshiva bochers.*

Tamar spoke in run-on superlatives about the beauty of the Tropics of Birobidzhan. The beaches were spectacular beyond comparison. The people of the region were friendly, open, and welcoming. The food eaten there was flavorful, filled with exotic spices.

To anyone listening, it would have been abundantly clear that Tamar found the people that she loved and a region of Planet Birobidzhan that filled her heart, touching her soul.

Dovid was deeply relieved that Tamar had come home before the departure of the *Hatikvah.* She was, after all, his favorite daughter. He did not want to leave this world without saying goodbye. However, neither father nor daughter were really ready for goodbyes.

They finished breakfast and Dovid was preparing to resume the work at hand. Tamar was incessantly speaking to her unborn children, begging them for a little tranquility, while she helped to clear the table. With no transition whatsoever, Tamar broke off that monologue in order to speak to her father.

"I know that I am not much use these days with physical projects but if you give me a work crew, tomorrow morning I will oversee the transfer of the Mushrooms of Birobidzhan to their new growing facilities aboard the *Hatikvah.*" Tamar patted her abdomen once more.

Dovid was surprised and relieved by Tamar's offer. No one understood the Mushrooms of Planet Birobidzhan better than Tamar. After all, the mushrooms had chosen her.

34

LIFTOFF INTO THE UNKNOWN

The next morning, Tamar was up before dawn. She paced about waiting for her work crew to arrive. Dovid was also up, sorting personal possessions and waiting for enough daylight to resume loading supplies aboard the *Hatikvah.*

Tamar and her crew had the mushroom growing facility successfully moved aboard the *Hatikvah,* although they had to work late into the night. The workmen were none too pleased about the grueling pace and the exacting demands of the supervisor. Some of the men working under Tamar's watchful eyes had built the initial facility. They remembered the little girl with the rag doll that terrorized them over a decade before. They found Tamar, as an adult, to be no less demanding and just as difficult to work for.

The chickens, goats, and sheep were all settled in before sunset. Dovid oversaw the boarding of the poultry and livestock. He appreciated that the complaints from that element were minimal. Dovid was interrupted periodically by other managerial responsibilities. People are a lot more demanding than chickens, goats, and sheep. Passengers had begun boarding. Personal possessions were limited to what each could carry. The emigrants hauled their possessions in suitcases and tied up in bedding. Everyone pushed the limits. No one was pleased when the limits pushed back.

The complaints and arguments from these emigrant *Yidden* mostly were smoothed over with Dovid's intervention, but the effort was exhausting and emotionally draining. Dovid went to bed early and he slept like the dead.

Around midnight, Dovid was awakened by Rifka Leeba. She climbed into bed and pressed herself against him. They made love that night with a passion that rekindled memories of their courtship. The first roosters could be heard crowing before Dovid began to drift off to sleep. Rifka Leeba, however, determined that the time had come for a conversation and that sleeping was not an option. She rested her head in the crook of her husband's arm.

"Dovid," Rifka Leeba began. "I am not going with you. I am staying on Planet Birobidzhan."

"How can that be?" Dovid asked. "You are my wife and my heart of hearts. Of course you are coming with me," Dovid told her. "*Du bist meyn vayb*," Dovid repeated.

Tears ran down Rifka Leeba's face and dripped onto Dovid's arm. She shook her head ever so slightly before continuing to speak.

"All of my *kinder* are here and some grandchildren and there will be more grandchildren soon. I am not leaving them. Also," Rifka Leeba continued, "your mama, *mayn shviger*, is here. She is growing older and shouldn't be alone. She can't live on her own. She needs help. I am going to live with your mama. You will go to the stars without me."

Dovid had not given much thought to his mother's needs since the death of his father. "Mama has other children," Dovid told Rifka Leeba. "They can watch out for her."

"Oh, your mama is a mean spirited and cantankerous old woman. She has driven away all of her other children. Besides that," Rifka Leeba reminded Dovid, "you are the only one she ever showed real affection to. Your mama loved you and now I am responsible for her," she said emphatically.

Dovid looked at his wife. "We could still have more *kinder,* you and I."

Rifka Leeba rolled her eyes and touched her pelvis, just above the patch of hair. "I have not had a baby for more than a dozen years. This well has run dry. There won't be any more *kinder* through me."

Rifka Leeba never told Dovid that she restarted the herbal regimen that she had learned from his mother to avoid pregnancy. As far as Dovid knew, the barrenness that Rifka Leeba suffered from when they were first married had returned. Female reproduction was mostly a mystery to Dovid and Rifka Leeba considered her womb to be none of his business.

Dovid drifted into sleep around first light. When he awoke, Rifka Leeba was no longer in bed. Rifka Leeba was walking in the *shtetl* where her Dovid had been born, along the goat path, towards her mother-in-law's house.

On board the *Hatikvah,* the passengers were nervously awaiting liftoff. Dovid and his technicians were running about the tarmac making the final inspection and last minute tests of equipment. This was when Tamar approached her father.

"*Tate,*" Tamar said, "We have decided to go along." She patted her abdomen. "We discussed it, the boys and I. If there is room for us, we want to go...if we can bring my musical instruments."

The crates of instruments stacked in the house were certainly more than any one person could carry. There was no way they fit the personal property limitations for passengers on the *Hatikvah.* Dovid marked the crates as "Essential Agricultural Equipment" and piled them on a cart to be loaded. Dovid and Tamar were the last to board before the door of the ship was sealed and the final countdown began.

Liftoff was flawless and not a moment to soon. A swarm of angry investors had arrived at the airport. The crowd intended to salvage some of their losses, if possible, and perhaps execute some level of punishment on the perpetrators of the fraud.

Instead of enacting justice, those on the tarmac found themselves standing in clouds of dust, smoke, and fumes. The *Hatikvah* ascended into the sky above First Landing, heading into the void and the unknown.

35

DOWN A WORMHOLE & INTO THE SNOW

A few weeks after the *Hatikvah* left the Planet Birobidzhan behind, Tamar gave birth to twin boys. They emerged, each crying voluminously, healthy and strong. She named her sons Perez and Zerah.

From their first breathing day, Perez and Zerah competed for Tamar's emotional attention, as well as the nutritional sustenance that flowed through her when they suckled. Tamar continued to speak with the twins as she had when they were in her womb.

Tamar told Perez that his father is a *yeshiva bocher* named Baruch. She told Zerah that his father's name is Shmuli. She would tell her newborns that their fathers were busy with their studies but would no doubt seek them out, anywhere in the universe, when they finished their education.

Tamar was the first to use the birthing room of the *Hatikvah* clinic. Over the next few years, there were quite a few births in the ship's clinic, keeping the *Hatikvah's* team of midwives fairly busy.

On Planet Birobidzhan, and probably still on Planet Earth, most children are outdoors for several hours of every day, running and playing in the fields, forests, playgrounds, and streets. On an intergalactic ship traveling through the void, there is no outdoors. The *Hatikvah* had designated play areas for the ever increasing hoards of *kinder* but the children didn't confine themselves to the *spielplat.* The sounds of children crying, laughing, running, and sometimes fighting filled the ship.

Long before Perez and Zerah learned to walk or talk, the brothers were already fighting over everything and nothing. When together, they would pull each other's hair, bite, and scratch. When separated, they would cry and each would seek out the other. They were inseparable and irreconcilable. Tamar would say that they are just like their fathers.

Perez and Zerah, being the first of the *kinder* born on the ship, were the de facto leaders of the pack of *vilde khius* that were the children of the *Hatikvah*. Under the influence of these two, the younger children picked up tendencies that are disturbing to most adults and potentially harmful to other children. This was even before any of these *kinder* born to the *Hatikvah* were old enough for *cheder.*

Of course Perez and Zerah were the first of the transit born to enter *cheder.* It did not take long for the two to test the patience of the *melamed* and push his tolerance beyond capacity. The twins required two classrooms separated by the length of the ship. Individually, each of the *yingeles* wore a teacher out.

Dovid and Hannah Leah doted over their grandsons. They showered them with affection and care. The boys showed love and even *Derekh Eretz* under the watchful eyes of the grandparents. Perez and Zerah would calm for an hour or two at a time when with their *Bubbie* and *Zeida*.

Hannah Leah would bake *kikhlekh* and sometimes sing songs. Dovid would tell the boys long, winding, and totally unbelievable stories about *Moishe Pipik*, a little boy that builds a spaceship from junk he finds. Often, the boys spent the night with Hannah Leah and Dovid. Around the time that the boys began their schooling, they began living with their grandparents full time.

Tamar rarely slept through the night. She would eat *majoun* and play soulful music on her violin late into the night. Then, through the void, she would engage in extensive conversations with Baruch and Shmuli. Of course, she had left the *yeshiva bochers* behind in Seaside Mea Shearim, Niu Niu Yark, on Planet Birobidzhan. The conversations, however, were very real for Tamar.

The *Hatikvah* proceeded, unencumbered on a trajectory through the void. The people on board lived their lives and grew older.

Years transpired before the *Hatikvah* came within range of the wormhole. Traveling through this wormhole was a necessity. A fold in space/time opens up totally new vistas and presents unknown constellations. The actual search for habitable planets could only begin in earnest after transpiring through the wormhole.

Everyone, nonetheless, was aware that going into a wormhole would be an horrendous experience. There was much warranted anxiety before the drop. The emigrants aboard the *Hatikvah* prepared themselves as they each saw fit. Some prayed and fasted. Others took a more proactive approach to warding off the discomfort that they reasonably expected. There was an awful lot of schnapps consumed in the days leading up to the drop into the wormhole.

Nothing anyone did made the transition through the fold of space/time any easier. There was a lot of physical discomfort, much puking, and several spontaneous abortions.

Emerging from the wormhole left the *mentshn* aboard the *Hatikvah* discomforted for days. A melancholy overtook the ship and it was hard to shake. Like a period of bad weather, a cloud hung over the *Hatikvah.* And, like the weather, the cloud that hung over the emigrants eventually lifted and spirits improved.

Several months after emerging from the wormhole, the first planet that showed potential for supporting life was detected by the *Hatikvah's* computer. The technicians named that planet *Rishon*, Hebrew for first. After a closer examination, they had determined that it was not worthy of settlement.

When the ship's sensor alerted the technicians of a second possibly livable world, they all tried to temper their optimism. They named this second planet *Shneya*, meaning second.

As the *Hatikvah* came closer within range of *Shneya*, all of the computer analysis continued to be positive. It certainly seemed that the emigrants from Planet Birobidzhan had found themselves a world to live on.

The planet has breathable air with a slightly richer oxygen mixture than Planet Birobidzhan. It is a bit larger resulting in stronger gravity pull, making everything seem slightly heavier. There is plenty of potable water. It rains heavily in the spring and summer. There are deep and wide rivers that run year round except when they freeze over.

The average temperatures on this planet are significantly lower than on Planet Birobidzhan. Snow falls frequently beginning in early autumn and throughout the winter. The higher mountains have snow all the time. Summers are cooler than the spring or autumn on Planet Birobidzhan. Occasionally snow or hail will occur even in the summer.

The sheep thrive on this planet. Their wool grows thicker and they are meatier than any sheep that are raised on Planet Birobidzhan.

The emigrants found adapting to the cold difficult, although wool clothing certainly helped. The children born in transit, however, made a fairly smooth transition. The parents, born and raised on Planet Birobidzhan, wore multiple layers of clothing and never seemed quite comfortable. The children ran barefoot even in winter and readily shed their clothing in the summertime.

The irony that the Hebrew word for "second" sounds so similar to the Yiddish word for "snow" was lost on no one. It was not long after landing that the new settlers all began calling the place Planet Shney rather than Planet Shneya.

36

FLOURISHING ON PLANET SHNEY

If the *Hatikvah* had orbited that planet in the winter, it is likely that it never would have landed. However, in very early summer, much of that world looked quite appealing.

The air is good. The soil is fertile. There are extensive mineral deposits. There is an abundance of creatures similar to the beavers of Planet Earth with pelts that make excellent fur. There are large docile herds of a bovine sort whose flesh provides a high quality *kosher* meat. Wide swaths of this world are forests that offer up an abundance of lumber. There is much to love about this place. The first few months were enjoyable for everyone.

The emigrants appreciated disembarking, having a change of scenery, and becoming pioneer settlers. The *Hatikvah* had the potential to shelter the emigrants but to become settlers required moving beyond the ship. A small *shtot* was designed and the first houses were built. Extensive gardens were planted. Chicken coops were built. The sheep and goats were allowed to graze and seemed very happy to do so.

Tamar had been self absorbed and socially awkward when she was aboard the *Hatikvah.* After the landing, however, she came out of her shell, for a while. Tamar offered a new design for the mushroom cultivation facility and oversaw the construction. Hinged doors made access easier. The mushrooms from the ship were transplanted to the spacious structure on the outer edge of the planned *shtot.*

Once the facility was completed, Tamar kept a close observation of the growing until the first full cycle was completed. When the first harvest was done, Tamar packed her rucksack and her violin and headed off, *tsufus* and alone, into the uncharted wilderness of Planet Shney.

When winter set in, the fortitude of the settlers was sorely tested. The first year was very difficult. It was very hard for the *Yidden* from the temperate Planet Birobidzhan to adapt to the harsh physical conditions of Planet Shney.

But for the vastness of the void stretching outwards in all directions, these *Yidden* may have been inclined to reboard the *Hatikvah* and seek out a more comfortable place. Facing such a Hobson's choice of perhaps an endless search of space or making do, the emigrants from Planet Birobidzhan built for themselves and their children a flourishing existence from what was available on Planet Shney.

All told, the trip from Planet Birobidzhan to Planet Shney took just under a decade, which is around half the traveling time of the *Hatikvah's* initial voyage two centuries earlier from Planet Earth to Planet Birobidzhan. During the decade of transit, Dovid tinkered with calculations and perfected designs to improve space travel. He came up with several innovations that could significantly reduce transit time and cut production costs, with certain caveats and considerations.

The first winter, when Dovid was essentially snowed in on Planet Shney, he fine tuned his design to a point where he believed it was worthy of sharing. Dovid determined that a much smaller vehicle could be built that would need far less fuel for liftoff. Assuming that the vehicle could be refueled at its destination, far less fuel carrying capacity would be required. Dovid also calculated that food production and preparation space could be significantly reduced if passengers would rely on prepared vacuum sealed and dried meals.

A smaller vehicle would travel quicker and more efficiently than a lumbering ship such as the *Hatikvah*. The vehicle that he envisioned would carry no more than one hundred passengers and ideally less. With a predetermined route, such a vehicle could be fully automated and need no pilot or technicians. According to Dovid's calculations, such a vehicle could be built on Planet Birobidzhan and the travel time to Planet Shney could be reduced to under five years. Of course, this presumed that there was interest on Planet Birobidzhan for travel to Planet Shney.

The passengers would be charged for their transportation with the profits going towards reimbursement of the investors on Planet Birobidzhan. On the return voyage, the ship would carry trade goods, initially furs, to be sold on Planet Birobidzhan with those profits also returned to the earlier investors.

Dovid prepared a drone ship and programmed it to land at the First Landing airport with a signal to alert the Planet Birobidzhan Pilots Association on arrival. Dovid packed into the tiny vehicle an extensive description of Planet Shney, his completed design for the pared down transit vehicle, and his business proposal. He also included samples of the fine furs made from Planet Shney's beaver-like creatures. The drone was launched in early spring.

Neither Perez nor Zerah showed much interest in academic pursuits. Both of the boys did seem to have an affinity and aptitude for the care of sheep. Perez and Zerah liked being outdoors and were quite willing to sleep under the stars for days on end. The boys also had certain volatile and violent tendencies that could be channeled into protecting the sheep from the predators of Planet Shney. Being shepherds fit their temperament.

Sometimes at night, while camping under the stars, the boys would hear soulful violin music wafting from a distance. On occasion, Tamar would approach their encampment and sit with her sons.

When Tamar was inclined to talk, she would tell the boys about Baruch and Shmuli. Tamar would assure Perez and Zerah that their fathers were now learned rabbis on Planet Birobidzhan. Tamar would say that someday soon the rabbis Baruch and Shmuli will come to be with their sons.

The Mushrooms of Planet Birobidzhan thrived on Planet Shney. The hinged doors of Tamar's newly designed growing facility gave the mushrooms a vector to the outside and the Mushrooms of Planet Birobidzhan took full advantage of the opportunity.

The Mushrooms of Planet Birobidzhan were soon growing and rapidly reproducing in the woods on the edge of the *shtot,* near the growing facility. The wind carried the spores and the mushrooms spread for many kilometers that first year on Planet Shney and much further in subsequent years. They grew very well in the dark moisture of the forests that cover much of Planet Shney.

Almost twelve years to the day after the *Hatikvah* had landed on Planet Shney, the first of the ships built to Dovid's specifications arrived on Planet Shney from Planet Birobidzhan. The door of the ship opened automatically and a gangplank lowered to allow the weary travelers to disembark.

The first people off the ship were a pair of rabbis in their forties. They were immersed in a *Halachic* debate and apparently oblivious of their surroundings. They gesticulated wildly as they argued and their *payos* blew about in the wind.

The rabbis paid scarce attention to this new world that they had landed on until the soulful sounds of a violin playing interrupted their *Halachic* argument. Baruch and Shmuli each stopped speaking in mid sentence as they looked about for the girl with the violin.

37

MOSKVE ON PLANET SHNEY

There were well under a thousand inhabitants to begin with on the entire planet, all living in one settlement. It was a bit presumptuous of the passengers of the Hatikvah to call their settlement a *shtot* as it was certainly hardly more than a *shtetl*. However, their intentions were to build a city so that is how they referred to the place even from the beginning.

For the first few months, it was a "city" without a name as the planet was a planet known by a number, Planet Shneya, the Second Planet. When the "winter" snows began in the middle autumn and continued well into spring, their world became known as Planet Shney. Not long after, the settlement that dreamed of becoming a city named itself Moskve in honor of the ancient and perhaps mythical city of Moscow, capital of the Home Planet's icey nation of Rusland.

If Planet Shney was a few degrees closer to its sun or if the sun that it circled was slightly larger and burned a tad hotter, then this world would have been a far more comfortable place for human habitation with a reasonably temperate climate. However, the climate of Planet Shney was far from temperate.

The stars and the planets were placed in the firmament by a hand other than that of man. We are not given any choice in this matter. We do the best we can with what is made available to us.

Planet Shney is habitable for *mentshn*, but only the most hardy of people would choose to live in such a place. Life on Planet Shney is made possible with the help of woolen clothing, fur lined boots as well as fur coats and hats, well insulated housing, efficient wood burning stoves, and solar panels.

The settlement *shtot* of Moskve is situated on the cusp between two distinct environmental regions. The higher altitude terrain of broad plains and mountains is situated to the northeast. This region is more thickly forested and richer in minerals than the rest of Planet Shney. The settlers named the northeast sector Sibir after a cold and desolate region on the Home Planet known as Siberia.

The relatively lower plains to the west and the south are less thickly forested, better suited for agriculture, and somewhat more suitable for human habitation. This is where the pioneers perceived that most further settlement would likely take place. They named this region Eyropa after the Home Planet continent of Europe.

Planet Birobidzhan was settled by refugees. The project was financed largely through the efforts of religious institutions on Planet Earth. It can certainly be construed that the settlement of Planet Birobidzhan had been overly influenced by the religious authority of rabbis, *shochets* and *moyels*.

With the exception of the technicians, agricultural experts, and medical professionals, the initial Founders, those that traveled from Planet Earth to Planet Birobidzhan on the *Hatikvah* two centuries earlier, were nearly all religious leaders. They were entrusted to instill a sense of *Yiddishkeit* and assure a *Halachic* influence for social development. There was a definite disproportionate number of religious authorities.

Planet Shney was settled by adventurous pioneers rather than refugees and exiles. The second voyage of the *Hatikvah* was financed by investors rather than charities.

It can be deduced that the establishment of Planet Shney happened with a dearth of religious influence. *Der Profesor* and Dovid recruited the potential candidates for the *Hatikvah's* second voyage, the one from Planet Birobidzhan into the unknown, based primarily on their practical skills.

"*Nayn rabonim kenen kin minyen nit makhn, ober tsen shusters - yo.*" This , *Der* Profesor said at the very beginning of the process and it served as an underlying principle for the enterprise. Ten shoemakers, or otherwise skilled and committed pioneers, were valued far higher than any nine, or ten or one hundred, rabbis.

On the second voyage of the *Hatikvah* there were certainly less than a *minyan* of rabbis, or even the *nayn rabonim*, or even nine religious authorities of any sort. There were exactly three rabbis, two *sochets* and two *moyels*.

After disembarking on Planet Shney, the rabbis commissioned two *shuls* to be built at opposite ends of the planned *Tsenter Shtot*. The *shuls* are commonly referred to as the Yerushalaim *Shul* and the Niu Yark *Shul*.

The *sochets* formed a partnership to build and operate a slaughterhouse and butcher shop. The bovine creatures that roam in abundantly large herds on this planet are *kosher*. The three rabbis and both *sochets* concur. The creatures are docile and easily corralled. The meat derived from these creatures is believed to be similar to that of cows of the Home Planet.

The business of the slaughter and butchering of the native cattle-like creatures is the sole domain of the *sochets*. As far as the other meat producing animals on Planet Shney, the monopolistic grip is far from secure.

Sheep that are raised in large herds are mostly slaughtered by the *sochets* and the meat is distributed through their butcher shop. However, most shepherds will kill their own sheep and process the meat for their family and friends. The smaller the herd, the more likely the meat will be processed without a *sochet*.

A few goats and chickens are kept by most families on Planet Shney. Probably around half of the goats are brought to the slaughterhouse for *kosher* processing. The rest find the way to the stew pot more informally. All told, very few chickens are brought to the *sochets*. Most chickens come to their end most unceremoniously, with their necks broken before being plucked, cooked and eaten.

The two *moyels* agreed to take turns for any *bris*. They have a true monopoly on that trade, as there are no amateur competitors in this field. However, because of the fairly low birth rate on Planet Shney, both *moyels* also have other jobs.

Tamar was in her mid twenties when she disembarked on Planet Shney. For the first few weeks, Tamar committed herself to setting up the mushroom growing facility and assuring that the first growing cycle was completed.

During those weeks, Tamar lived with her family and immersed herself in reestablishing the relationship with her sons. Perez and Zerah reveled in the attention that they received from their mother. They had sorely missed out on anything resembling mothering from her for most of the long voyage of the *Hatikvah* from Planet Birobidzhan to Planet Shney.

It was not very long, though, before Tamar left the home and the settlement without a word. She headed off with her rucksack and violin, alone and *tsufus*, into the wilderness.

Tamar only saw her family rarely afterwards. Her contact with the other *mentshn* of the settlement from that point on was even more tenuous. When she passed through Moskve she avoided eye contact. Tamar spoke hardly a word to anyone other than Dovid.

It was Tamar's design for the mushroom growing facility, with the hinged doors, that optimized the conditions for the Mushrooms of Planet Birobidzhan to gain their own foothold to grow in the damp forests of Planet Shney.

Once the mushrooms were fully acclimated to the new environment, the relationship between the fungi and the *mentshn* of Planet Shney fundamentally changed.

The Mushrooms of Planet Birobidzhan had played a central, if somewhat obscured, role in the whole extra-planetary enterprise. They inspired Dovid to yearn for the stars and guided his quest over the course of all the years from inspiration to the launch of the *Hatikvah*.

Leading up to the launch, a sizable percentage of the *mentshn* working on the project and those intending to join the expedition had consumed the fleshy mushrooms. They were each guided by the influence of the mushroom induced visions.

On the flight from Planet Birobidzhan to Planet Shney, the mushroom growing facility on board the *Hatikvah* was fully functional and most of the passengers would partake of the guidance offered through consuming the Mushrooms of Planet Birobidzhan on occasion. This was true, as well, for the first few months on Planet Shney.

As the mushrooms spread on their own in the wild, the relationship between the fungi and the *mentshn* changed.

It seems, from a human perspective, that the *mentshn* of Planet Shney simply lost interest in the mushrooms. On the other hand, it is plausible that the mushrooms lost interest in these people because it no longer served the mushrooms any purpose to provide humans with further guidance. The mushrooms stopped calling out to the *mentshn*. When eaten, the mushrooms no longer offered inspiration and instructional insights.

Either way, before the first anniversary of reaching Planet Shney, the residents of Moskve abandoned the upkeep of their mushroom growing facility and no longer consumed the fleshy fungus. That is, everyone except Tamar. She continued to maintain a very personal relationship with the Mushrooms of Planet Birobidzhan and interacted with them quite regularly.

Perez and Zerah continued to live with Dovid and Hannah Leah for the remainder of their childhood, as they had all those years of traveling on the *Hatikvah*. This was the arrangement that they had become used to from when they were quite young.

The boys were raised by their *Bubbie* and *Zeida*. Dovid and Hannah Leah had no more children of their own to raise. Their youngest daughter was a few years older than Perez and Zerah. She was fully weaned shortly after liftoff. She had reached the age of emancipation before the *Hatikvah* had landed on Planet Shney.

Perez and Zerah were not quite ten when the *Hatikvah* landed on Planet Shney. They were rough and tumble youth at the time. They were inseparable and yet they fought almost constantly. The boys gifted each other with bruises, scratches, and black eyes.

If it hadn't been for the sheep, it is quite plausible that their mutual blows would have eventually resulted in very serious consequences. Perez and Zerah began learning how to work with sheep before they turned eleven. By their twelfth birthday, the two brothers developed a fairly smooth working relationship that only occasionally came to blows. They owned and managed their own flock of sheep well before they reached the bar mitzvah age.

Tamar was living in a cave in the mountains. On rare occasions she would venture into town and seek out her father. Dovid gave Tamar a highly efficient wood stove for cooking and heat and a couple of solar panels to provide her with light. Tamar slept in a hammock. She had a few simple pieces of furniture consisting of a table, a couple of chairs and a few shelves that held her collection of musical instruments.

Tamar maintained a small kitchen garden just outside her cave. She grew a few greens but mostly potatoes, carrots and cannabis. She had a small flock of free range chickens. Tamar would collect their eggs when she remembered. In a dark and damp corner of her cave, the Mushrooms of Planet Birobidzhan grew on their own after just a bit of encouragement from Tamar.

When the mood moved Tamar and the weather was conducive, Tamar would find Perez and Zerah while they camped with their herd. Sometimes she would talk with them. Often she would play her violin without speaking. Sometimes they would all just sit by the fire. Tamar's sons supplied her with mutton.

38

BARUCH AND SHMULI

When Baruch and Shmuli were youthful students in Niu Niu Yark, in the neighborhood of Seaside Mea Shearim, they lived in a consistent and predictable manner. The *yeshiva bochers* had come to expect Tamar to be busking on her regular corners at predictable times that corresponded to their consistent routines. Baruch and Shmuli were accustomed to being with Tamar for several hours every week.

After that eventful night just before Purim, Tamar was suddenly out of their lives, gone without a word. Not finding Tamar at any of her normal busking corners, Baruch and Shmuli went to the apartment looking for her. On the apartment door was a For Rent sign.

The *yeshiva bochers* spoke with Miriam at the bakery. They learned that Tamar had returned the apartment key and left with a rucksack, walking down the street. There was no forwarding address.

Baruch and Shmuli had each been enamored with Tamar and both *yeshiva bochers* missed her deeply. They continued their studies that year with a cloud of melancholy hanging over each of them. They knew nothing of Tamar's pregnancy. Then, eight months later, news of the launch of the *Hatikvah* from the airfield in First Landing was heard Planet-wide. The newspapers printed a list of all the emigrants. Tamar's name was on the list.

The years passed. The *yeshiva bochers* finished their studies. Baruch and Shmuli each found positions as teachers and the friends continued as roommates, sharing the same apartment that they had lived in when they were students.

Both Baruch and Shmuli were each regularly approached by relatives, friends, and professional matchmakers with suggestions for a *shidduch*. However, neither of them felt compelled to follow through with any of the potential marriages. They each silently pined for their *Meydl mit a Fidele*.

It was nearly fifteen years after Baruch and Shmuli had last seen Tamar that Dovid's drone arrived at the First Landing airport. The news quickly spread that the *Hatikvah* had landed safely on a habitable world and that planet was rich in natural resources. Furs, minerals, and timber piqued the interests of investors. Those that held bonds, stocks, and promissory notes from a decade and a half earlier had some renewed hope that those pieces of paper might actually be worth something.

The possibility of recouping losses and actually profiting hinged on attracting new investors. The former victims of the pyramid scheme that financed the *Hatikvah* expedition began to recruit others into a financial venture based on a belief that Dovid's propositions and offers were valid. This required either a huge leap of faith or a very deep cynicism.

The construction and launching of ships needed to be financed. Under the most optimistic calculations, any ship sent out from Planet Birobidzhan would return laden with valuable trade goods ten years later. That is a long time to wait and is also dependent on the good will of those *mentshn* on Planet Shney that had so blatantly misrepresented their intentions fifteen years earlier. All financial calculations suggested that the cost of passage would be exorbitant.

The financial interests that could conceivably back such a scheme held no guarantee that the vehicle would actually return at all. Those already deeply invested in the initial scheme were not about to gamble any more of their own *gelt*.

Ultimately, it was decided that the only possible way for such an enterprise to begin would require that passengers heading to Planet Shney fully finance the flight, including the total expense of construction of each vehicle, and a short term profit margin.

To market a high priced ticket on a five year transport through the void of space, the destination would need to be spectacular. The investors that perceived themselves as cheated by Dovid and his associates began to speak in superlatives about the beauty, wealth, and broad potential of life on Planet Shney.

New investment capital began to roll in. Soon the construction of a ship based on Dovid's design began, the first of a planned fleet. The initial transport, and a projected date of departure, was announced. The very limited number of tickets was emphasized. A position on a transport to Planet Shney required a serious personal commitment of a significant amount of *gelt*.

The possibility of wealth derived from furs, minerals, and timber was of little interest to Baruch and Shmuli. Reuniting with Tamar was their only incentive for leaving Planet Birobidzhan. How they convinced their families to finance such a pricey voyage is a wonder. We can suppose that Baruch and Shmuli lied, connived, and finagled. Somehow they raised the money that they needed.

It is hard to imagine what Baruch and Shmuli had expected when they boarded the ship to Planet Shney. There is no doubt, however, that they were following their hearts in pursuit of Tamar, their *Meydl mit a Fidele*. What that actually entailed was a mystery that neither man could logically explain.

No one on Planet Shney had any advanced knowledge that a ship from Planet Birobidzhan would arrive on that, or any, day. I suppose it was simply a coincidence that Tamar was in Moskve and playing her violin when Baruch and Shmuli disembarked.

Baruch and Shmuli found Tamar on a street corner, playing her violin, with an open violin case at her feet. When they approached, Tamar acted as if she had just seen the *yeshiva bochers* a few days before, although nearly two decades had passed and she as well as they were significantly changed.

Tamar played a set on that street corner while her old friends stood watching and listening. When she finished playing, she returned her violin to its case before speaking to Baruch and Shmuli.

Without preamble, Tamar told her old friends that she had a new apartment. She invited them to come home with her for tea. Baruch and Shmuli readily agreed. They followed Tamar, without questioning. They followed her out past the edge of the town, along craggy trails, into the mountains, and to her cave.

As far as caves go, Tamar's abode was fairly comfortable. The wood stove heated water and Tamar served the tea *shtetl* style in glasses with sugar cubes on the side. The three friends sat in the cave and talked as if nothing had changed in their lives and they were still young, in the apartment above the bakery in Seaside Mea Shearim.

Tamar brought out a tray with a sampling of freshly picked mushrooms. She offered the mushrooms to Baruch and Shmuli with no explanations. They assumed that they were being offered appetizers or a local delicacy. Baruch and Shmuli each ate the fleshy fungus without any questions or hesitation whatsoever. They came under the influence of the mushrooms without any preconceived notions.

The visions that Baruch and Shmuli each had under the influence of the mushrooms were remarkably similar in pattern. What they each saw was exactly the same, to begin. Then, the visions diverged and were very specifically personalized.

The cave where they sat faded and disappeared. They were exposed to a disorienting array of shifting constellations, swirling galaxies, and the birth of universes. Time and physical space lost all meaning. When clarity returned, Baruch and Shmuli each saw Tamar reclining in the birthing room, surrounded by the midwives of the *Hatikvah* clinic.

As if they had each been in the birthing room, they witnessed the birth of Perez and Zerah. At that point, their visions diverged. They each saw a newborn brought to their mother's breast and begin suckling. Baruch witnessed Perez as he was fed. Shmuli watched as Zerah received nutrients from Tamar.

The visions proceeded in stopgap motion of each boy growing. Baruch watched Perez progress from a newborn swaddled in a diaper to a toddler beginning to walk to youth at a *spielplat* to young adulthood surrounded by sheep. Perez appeared to be the image of Baruch when he was a *yeshiva bocher*. Shmuli watched Zerah going through the same process. As a young adult, Zerah was the spitting image of a young Shmuli.

The night sky again appeared and they were shown Planet Shney as if from above. They envisioned *shtetls* arising and growing into *shtots* to the west of Moskve throughout Eyropa. Then, they saw mines and mining *shtetls* unfolding in Sabir.

The orientation of the visions shifted once more. Baruch and Shmuli were given a view of Moskve, the city that they had barely seen when they arrived earlier that day. There was the bustling of the market and activity around the two *shuls*.

In the marketplace, they each were given a vision of a woman working at a booth and saw themselves standing beside the vendor. They each saw children that called them *Tate* and the woman beside them *Mama*.

Neither Baruch nor Shmuli were aware of how much time had expired under the influence of the mushrooms. When they regained a sense of normal consciousness and an awareness of their surroundings, they were alone in the cave.

Tamar was nowhere to be seen. After a while, Baruch and Shmuli found their own way to the mouth of the cave. The first light of dawn was in the eastern sky. They *davened shacharis* there at the opening of Tamar's cave and then waited for her return. They didn't have a clue how to get back to Moskve on their own.

When Perez and Zerah were young, aboard the *Hatikvah*, Tamar would tell the boys about the men she said were their fathers. By the time that the *Hatikvah* had landed on Planet Shney, they both already had serious doubts about their origin story.

Perez and Zerah knew enough about biology to understand that they were twins and that they, in all likelihood, probably had the same father. They knew enough about their mother to understand that she had a tenuous attachment to what others deemed reality. They grew to accept their mother as she was and her stories for what they were worth.

Tamar found the brothers on that particular day working with their flock. By this point, her sons were in their early twenties. They both had married and already had children of their own.

Perez and Zerah were quite surprised to see Tamar during the daytime. Their encounters with her were almost exclusively late at night, under the stars. When Tamar told her sons that it was time for them to meet their fathers, the brothers each raised an eyebrow as they glanced at each other before shrugging and following their mother back to her cave in the mountains.

It was mid morning by the time that Tamar returned to the cave with her sons in tow. Baruch and Shmuli heard them approaching. They stepped out of the cave, and found themselves staring at what seemed to be their own youthful mirror image.

The awkwardness was palatable. Perez and Zerah found themselves, equally confounded as the older men, as they stared at their own future countenances. Tamar simply smiled and smiled. No one spoke a word for a very long while.

After a bit, Tamar broke the silence by inviting everyone into the cave for tea. She served the tea *shtetl* style in glasses with sugar cubes on the side. She also produced a plate of cookies from a bakery in Moskve. Somehow Tamar had procured them for this particular occasion.

Perez and Zerah guided Baruch and Shmuli from Tamar's cave back to Moskve. Along the way, all four spoke at once, gesticulating wildly. They argued much of the way. When the dust settled, it was agreed that Baruch was to stay in Perez's house and that Shmuli would stay with Zerah, at least temporarily.

No one on Planet Shney, with the possible exception of Tamar, had anticipated the arrival of the first transport from Planet Birobidzhan with one hundred immigrants aboard.

At the time, there were no hotels, inns, hostels or apartments to accommodate *mentshn* in transit. There was no excess housing whatsoever available. Each of the new arrivals negotiated temporary lodging in the homes of families in Moskve. Nearly one in five homes hosted a boarder.

Everyone, besides Baruch and Shmuli, that had arrived on the first of the shuttle transit ships came to Planet Shney to seek their fortunes. They were gambling their life savings with the hope of finding wealth on this new planet. Most were only in Moskve as a transition point and intended to head off into the wilderness of Sabir to prospect for minerals as soon as they were acclimated.

Acclimatization to Planet Shney was not an easy matter. Although it was summer, the temperatures felt like late autumn or early winter for the new immigrants from Planet Birobidzhan. They all needed woolen clothing, fur hats, and fur-lined boots.

Those immigrants that were heading to Sabir with camping equipment were definitely roughing it. They had less than two months of weather warm enough for such. Very shortly they would either need much more secure housing in Sabir or they would be back in Moskve seeking a warm room and bed for the long winter.

According to the new arrivals as well as the ship's log, the syndicate on Planet Birobidzhan intended to launch a new transit ship approximately every eight or nine weeks. The investors on Planet Birobidzhan were anticipating that Dovid and his associates would quickly load the ship with trade goods for the return flight. The roundtrip for each ship would be nearly ten years.

Of the one hundred passengers, Baruch and Shmuli were the only rabbis. They were also probably the only two people to arrive with no plans whatsoever. They were not seeking fortunes. They were answering a call that was straight to their hearts.

Baruch was warmly welcomed by Perez's wife and their *kinder* readily called him *Zeida*. Shmuli's reception in Zerah's home was quite similar. No one in either household questioned the kinship.

That evening Perez and Zerah brought Baruch and Shmuli to meet Dovid and Hannah Leah. Hannah Leah served tea, *shtetl* style with *kikhlekh*.

Afterwards, the men drank schnapps and spoke late into the night. Dovid offered to help Baruch and Shmuli establish a school. It would be situated approximately halfway between the Yerushalaim *Shul* and the Niu Yark *Shul* in a building that Dovid owned. In exchange for this help, Baruch and Shmuli agreed to waive tuition for all of the family's grandchildren.

Towards midnight Dovid heard a rustling outside and he saw a hooded figure at the window. Dovid opened the window but no one was near the window any longer. They watched as Tamar walked away into the darkness.

No one saw or heard from Tamar again over the following days. After a week passed, Baruch and Shmuli insisted that the younger men guide them back to the cave to check on her. The cave was unoccupied and the wood stove was cold. They walked back to Moskve in silence.

The days turned into weeks that no one in the family had seen Tamar. Her sons assured Baruch and Shmuli that it was not at all unusual for Tamar to be gone for weeks at a time.

A construction boom was just beginning in Moskve. It was projected that housing for five or six hundred new immigrants per year would be required with many of these people living in Moskve. The sawmill stayed busy making lumber to accommodate the demands of the carpenters. In addition to building new houses and apartments, many existing homes added rooms or auxiliary apartments.

Baruch and Shmuli began developing their school without delay. The location suggested by Dovid was centrally located. It was a comfortable walk from both of the homes where they were living. A bakery was directly next door to the school. Several other shops were nearby. The two *shuls* were nearly equidistant.

Every *Mantik aun Danershtag* there was a vibrant market on that street as well where farmers and craftspeople offered their goods directly to the public. It was a Monday morning, after *davening shacharis* that Baruch and Shmuli first attended a market day on Planet Shney. This was the market that they had been shown by the mushroom vision in Tamar's cave.

Cheyna and Freyda were close friends. They were intelligent and industrious. They worked a booth in the market together. They were also both attractive and unmarried.

Cheyna and Freyda sold high quality wool yarn and fine clothing handmade from wool. They sold a lot of socks. Warm socks are very useful on Planet Shney, year round.

Baruch and Shmuli each bought a couple of pairs of socks that first visit to the market.

Baruch and Shmuli had not brought nearly enough warm clothing with them from Planet Birobidzhan. No experience on Planet Birobidzhan could have prepared them for the weather on Planet Shney, even if they had been the rugged outdoor types and that they definitely were not. Baruch and Shmuli had lived the sheltered lives of urban academics in the semi tropical *shtot* of Niu Niu Yark.

Over the next few weeks, Baruch and Shmuli would find reasons to stop by the booth that sold wool clothing that was operated by the attractive vendors, Cheyna and Freyda.

The school prospered, in spite of the relatively low birth rate and few school age children on Planet Shney. The school attracted students and filled an important niche in Moskve. Baruch and Shmuli were a welcome, respected addition to the community.

In addition to the school, Baruch and Shmuli opened an office that served as a one-stop checkpoint for new arrivals on Planet Shney. They offered the immigrants basic supplies as well as extensive maps and topography information. They brokered deals for lumber and solar panels. They also served as something akin to a real estate service.

The business of their school and their secondary enterprise afforded the two men their own modest homes and gave them the freedom to pursue personal interests. Clearly, Baruch and Shmuli were interested in the attractive wool merchants.

The wedding of Baruch and Cheyna was well attended at the Yerushalayim *Shul*. A few weeks later, Shmuli and Freyda stood under the *chuppah* down the street at the Niu Yark *Shul*, a ceremony attended by a similar number of friends and family.

Dovid's entire extended family on Planet Shney attended both weddings with the exception of Tamar. She had not made any appearances in Moskve and had yet to return to her cave in the nearby mountains.

It was nearly midnight and Baruch was sleeping with his wife in the bedroom of the family house. A familiar melody, just barely audible, almost like a dream or a memory, wafting from a great distance, woke Baruch. Cheyna heard nothing and continued to sleep peacefully.

Baruch climbed out of bed. He stepped into slippers, wrapped himself in a robe and walked quietly down the stairs.

Baruch stood with the front door opened briefly, and listened attentively. He was trying to determine if he was really hearing a distant violin playing or if the sound was his overactive imagination. Then, he stepped outside, closed his door behind himself and walked out in search of the *Meydl mit a Fidele.*

Baruch walked a bit and then the melody abruptly stopped. Baruch stood on that quiet street corner, unsure which way to go. Then, the violin music began once again and Baruch followed the sounds.

This went on and on. Baruch would seemingly approach the source of the music floating in the late night air and then the sounds would cease with Baruch standing alone, ear cocked, waiting for the fiddling to begin again.

On the outer edge of Moskve, Baruch saw Tamar playing her violin soulfully, with her eyes closed. The moon was shining brightly above her.

Tamar continued to play her instrument with her eyes shut as Baruch approached. Tamar did not stop playing until Baruch was within arm reach. Then, she opened her eyes, placed her violin in the case and wrapped herself in Baruch's arms.

They spoke not a word between them. They kissed each other passionately. They made love in the soft grass at the outskirts of the *shtot*, under the bright moon. And then, still wordlessly, Tamar was gone in the darkness and Baruch walked alone back to his house. He was home before the sunrise. His wife was still sleeping in their bed.

Baruch spoke to no one about his encounter with Tamar. Who would he have told? How could he have explain it? The night hardly seemed real to him. It was all quite dreamlike.

No one else had seen Tamar either that night or at any other time until a couple of weeks later. Freyda was sleeping in the bedroom upstairs. Shmuli had been a bit restless so he was in his kitchen having a *nosh*. It was an unusually warm night and the kitchen window was open. That is how he heard the violin playing at a distance that dark night.

Shmuli left his house through the kitchen door and followed the sounds of the violin. He found Tamar in a grove of trees, playing the violin under the stars.

When Shmuli approached, Tamar put away her fiddle and enveloped him in her arms. She held him tightly and he returned the embrace. The first roosters were calling when Tamar slipped away and Shmuli returned to his house.

It was only a few days later that a sign advertising a furnished apartment for rent appeared in the window of the bakery adjacent to the school. The sign was only up for a few hours.

Tamar rented the apartment above the bakery. Then, she went to her father's house and elicited Dovid's help moving her modest belongings from the cave in the mountains to the apartment above the bakery.

The next evening, Tamar began performing regularly at a nearby cafe as well as busking on the street. She visited the homes of her sons, staying often for meals and playing with her grandchildren.

The door to the staircase leading to Tamar's apartment was hidden from the street, in the back of the building, near the school's back door which served as an emergency exit.

Every *Mantik* morning, Baruch and Shmuli would walk together to the Yerushalaim *Shul* to pray with a *minyan* and hear the reading of the *Toyre*. Afterwards, they would return to the school together.

When they returned to the school, Shmuli would busy himself with the students. Baruch would step out the back door of the school and climb those stairs to Tamar's apartment.

In the apartment above the bakery, Tamar and Baruch would drink tea, eat *majoun*, and make love in her broad comfortable bed. Baruch and Tamar would eat lunch together before Baruch descended the stairs and resumed working.

Danershtag mornings, the two schoolmasters attended the minyan at the Niu Yark *Shul*. After *davening shacharis* and returning together to the school, Shmuli would leave through the same back door and go up the stairs where Tamar would greet him.

Shmuli and Tamar would drink tea, eat *majoun*, and make love. Shmuli and Tamar would eat lunch together in the apartment above the bakery every *Danershtag*.

Every *Mantik aun Danershtag* afternoon, Tamar played her violin at the outdoor market, with the case at her feet.

39

REMAINING ON PLANET BIROBIDZHAN

Early that fateful morning, a bit before the sunrise, the first light was just edging the horizon. Rifka Leeba left her home on the edge of First Landing. She walked along the goat path that connects the *shtat* to the *shtetl* of her husband's origin.

Rifka Leeba was nearly at Dovid's childhood home when the *Hatikvah* lifted from the tarmac of the First Landing's airport. She stood outside that house and watched the lumbering vessel, with her husband and Hannah Leah aboard, as it crossed the sky. Rifka Leeba brought her right hand briefly to the *mezuzah* before knocking on her mother-in-law's door.

The door opened just a crack. Dovid's mother was none too pleased to see her daughter-in-law standing on the steps. The older woman's stare would have been enough to drive away anyone other than Rifka Leeba.

"Let me in, Mama," is what Rifka Leeba said.

Dovid's mother seemed to consider her options for just short of an eternity before letting go of the doorknob. Releasing the doorknob allowed Rifka Leeba to cross over the threshold without the older woman actually opening the door for her daughter-in-law.

Tea was reluctantly served, *shtetl* style, in glasses. Dovid's mother had steeped the tea in bitterness and spite, or so it seemed. She glowered in Rifka Leeba's general direction without looking directly at her daughter-in-law or speaking until they each drank their tea.

Dovid's mother spoke without a preamble. "*Nu*? Why are you here?" she snapped. With this, she scowled at Rifka Leeba or perhaps past her.

Rifka Leeba took a breath and then another one before she answered. "Dovid has gone and I have come to take care of you, Mama."

"What do you mean, 'Dovid has gone'? Did he finally throw you out of his house?" The older woman scowled and grimaced. "Did Dovid, at long last, figure out that you are a *kurvah*? Take care of me?!? Now, you have come to sponge off of Dovid's mother! I told him not to marry you. What are you doing here?"

"It's getting worse," thought Rifka Leeba. That's how she, Dovid, and Hannah Leah always referred to the old woman's state of mind. "It" was sometimes better and "it" was sometimes worse. "It" was a spectrum and that day "it" was pretty bad. "It" was why the rest of Mama's family had stopped visiting her. "It" is why Rifka Leeba told Dovid that she couldn't leave his mother on her own.

Rifka Leeba calmed her breathing. She kept her voice consistent and her tone evenly paced. "Mama, the *Hatikvah* has launched. You know that Dovid's been working on this, had planned this, for a very long time. You remember that. Right, Mama?"

"Don't talk to me like I am a child. Of course I remember that." Her words were crisp and this was said with a grimace.

"Well, Mama. That day has come. Dovid and Hannah Leah are traveling through the stars," Rifka Leeba said.

Dovid's mother shrugged and turned her hands upward. "OK," she said and then repeated that a few times, almost like a chant.

Rifka Leeba sighed. Her mother-in-law, without another word, left the room and went to bed. Rifka Leeba sat alone in the living room of Dovid's childhood home.

The following days were not much better. Dovid's mother did seem, eventually, to adapt to Rifka Leeba being in the house. Sometimes she remembered who Rifka Leeba was and why she was there. Sometimes she had no idea who it was living in her house.

Rifka Leeba kept the house clean and made sure that her mother-in-law was fed and bathed. Dovid's mother was not an easy person to live with, even on the best of days.

The first few weeks were additionally difficult for Rifka Leeba. Clouds of suspicion hung over the *Hatikvah* expedition. The shadows of those clouds were cast onto the families of the emigrants, those remaining on Planet Birobidzhan. The clouds of suspicion clung particularly heavily around Rifka Leeba and her mother-in-law.

The investors believed, without exception, and with good cause, that they had been bamboozled by Dovid and his associates. Of course, no one could specifically hold either Dovid's mother or his wife accountable for their financial losses. On the other hand, there was little remaining sympathy on Planet Birobidzhan for either of these women.

Rifka Leeba managed to scrape up some odd jobs to bring in a little household income. What work Rifka Leeba managed to get in those early years was offered begrudgingly. The pay was meager and often below the going rate. Those hiring acted as if it were an act of charity to offer Rifka Leeba even a bit of day work at substandard wages.

It was fortunate for Rifka Leeba and Dovid's mother that the house was in fairly good shape and that there was a kitchen garden. There was very little *gelt* coming in. They lived hand to mouth.

The *Hatikvah's* flight from Planet Birobidzhan to Planet Shney was a voyage of nearly ten years. It was nearly fifteen years after the launch of the *Hatikvah* that Dovid's drone arrived at the First Landing airport.

For nearly fifteen years there was no way for anyone on Planet Birobidzhan to know the conditions of the emigrants. Then, after the drone arrived, there was a ten year turnaround on any communication between the two planets. One can imagine the difficulty of establishing a trading partnership and retaining business relationships under such conditions.

For those first ten years of shuttle flights that followed the fifteen years of incommunicado, the expense of the transports was raised by the investors of Planet Birobidzhan. Most of these investors held a serious reluctance to spend good money after bad. The only income for the investors during those years was derived by selling passage to Planet Shney.

To recruit a steady stream of new emigrants required a committed nonstop stream of creative fiction on the part of the marketing teams that coalesced. They needed to project adventures and wealth. What they actually had to offer at this point, after all was said and done, was a long and mostly boring one way trip through the void in a newly designed and untested spacecraft. With luck, the trip would end with a safe landing on a cold and inhospitable world and a very uncertain future for the ticket holder. No guarantees of any sort were offered or should have been implied.

Such circumstances also complicated personal relationships. A dozen or so years after the launch of the *Hatikvah*, and before any word was heard from the emigrants, Rifka Leeba became pregnant. Tongues in the neighborhood wagged. Rifka Leeba ignored the whispering, the *loshon hora*, that went on mostly behind her back.

Her mother-in-law showed no particular surprise by Rifka Leeba's pregnancy. Quite often, she couldn't even remember who Rifka Leeba was or why she was in the house. When she did recognize Rifka Leeba, she would usually forget that Dovid had left Planet Birobidzhan on the *Hatikvah*. She would complain to her daughter-in-law that her son didn't visit enough or ask how his work at the toy store was going.

When Rifka Leeba gave birth to a son, she named the boy Nes, meaning miracle. She insisted, if asked, that Dovid fathered the child. Such a conception would indeed have been miraculous. Few people, however, actually asked her directly. They preferred gossip, slander, and innuendo.

Rifka Leeba's pregnancy was irrelevant to her mother-in-law. In fact, the older woman seemed to be oblivious of the pregnancy and even the child for more than a year after his birth. It was not until the boy began running about the house that she took notice of him.

Nes had not yet been weaned when Dovid's drone arrived on Planet Birobidzhan. The drone brought news from Planet Shney of a safe landing and an embryonic settlement. It also presented an actual measurable distance of around five years traveling that separated husband and wife rather than the abstraction that defined the previous years of separation.

With the renewed possibility of enterprise that the drone's presentation offered, there was a shift in attitudes concerning Rifka Leeba and her mother-in-law. The swindled investors began to consider the possibility of recouping some of their losses and maybe even turning a profit. They became less inclined to spite and the desire for revenge subsided. They stopped giving Rifka Leeba and her mother-in-law the evil eye or spitting in their direction.

Two distinct entrepreneurial associations arose in response to Dovid's drone. They represented distinct interests. At times, those interests were synergistic and at other times there was an element of conflict. One corporation represented the interests of the original investors and their descendants. The second corporation represented the interests of the settlers on Planet Shney and their families on Planet Birobidzhan.

When the first of the shuttle vehicles leaving Planet Birobidzhan for the new world of Planet Shney was fully booked, there was an actual measurable change in their household fortunes. From a share of the profits from that flight, Rifka Leeba received a small, but not insubstantial, payment. With each of the subsequent flights, another payout was received.

With the regular income, new horizons opened. This coincided with a bonding that took place between Nes and his grandmother. Dovid's mother seemed miraculously renewed and refreshed by a grandchild under her roof. She began to eat better, bathe herself, get some exercise and speak in complete coherent sentences.

Rifka Leeba began to feel more comfortable leaving Nes with the older woman on occasion, even for hours at a time. In the mother's presence, the older woman projected an air of confidence, capability, respect, and responsibility.

When alone with the young boy, Rifka Leeba's mother-in-law would call the child "Dovid" and assure Nes that she, not that "strange" woman, was his real mother. Dovid's mother would entice the child with cookies, toys, cuddling, various treats, and a wide array of privileges. She often took the *yingele* to the same park which she frequented with Dovid decades earlier. The boy played on the *shpilplats* where Dovid had played, listened to the *klezmorim*, ate *knishes*, chased the goats, and looked longingly into the window of the toy store on the circuitous walk home.

Indeed, Nes very much resembled Dovid at his age. There was a framed photograph of a young Dovid that hung on the wall. It could, however, very well have been a picture of Nes. Nes seemed to take the delusions of his grandmother in stride. By playing along with the older woman's winking deceptions, Nes benefitted from her open-handed generosity.

Rifka Leeba knew nothing of her mother-in-law's projections concerning Nes or of the boy's acquiesce to the aging woman's quirky perceptions. Her mother-in-law and her son kept their mutual secret.

Likewise, Rifka Leeba told no one about the good-natured elderly clothing store owner that smelled like aftershave, with the clean hands and a nice smile. The clothing merchant had made love to Rifka Leeba in the dressing room standing up, with her skirt hoisted above her waist. He impregnated her as he had her mother-in-law so many years before, with as little thought or concerns for potential consequences.

Nes basked in the love of these two women that each claimed to be his mother. He was well fed and happily spoiled. At a very tender age he became an expert at exploiting the differences between the parenting styles of the two "mothers" in his life to maximize personal benefits.

When Nes was quite young, Rifka Leeba would tell the boy that his father was unfortunately away from home and was very busy. She assured Nes that his father loved him. Dovid, she would say, was doing important work.

Later, after the drone brought word of the new settlement, Rifka Leeba told her son that Dovid lived far away on Planet Shney. The money that the family received as their share of the interplanetary enterprise, Rifka Leeba would tell Nes, came from the boy's father and the important work on the distant planet.

At bedtime, Rifka Leeba told young Nes far-fetched stories about Moishe Pipik, a boy that builds a spaceship from junk he finds and explores the stars and planets in his homemade rocket ship. Nes would dream of flying across the stars in a spaceship that he built himself so he could join his father. There, Nes would have a new life on a distant planet, emulating Moishe Pipik, alongside his heroic and almost mythical father, Dovid.

The older woman would tell Nes that his father was probably in the alley drinking with his no account *dreidl* gambling friends or passed out in the arms of some *kurvah*. Sometimes, when Rifka Leeba was not around, she would send the boy out to the alley to look for her *mann*. After a bit, Nes would return and tell his grandmother that his "*tate*" was not to be found in the alley. The older woman would then mutter something about *kurvahs und schnapps* before offering the boy a *kikhl* or a piece of fruit.

In this way, Nes grew up with two strong willed, overbearing mothers and two apparently absentee fathers.

40

THE EDUCATION OF YOUNG NES

Nes began *cheder* a little before his fifth birthday. He quickly learned the *Aleph Beis* and he became an avid reader, although not particularly studious. Nes' mind wandered the stars. His reading preference was for adventurous works of fiction. In class, his attention would drift. He tended to get fidgety, waiting to be released from the confinement of structured studies.

When Nes began his schooling, leaving his home early every morning, six days a week, the thin thread that connected Dovid's mother to what we understand as reality started to rapidly unravel. Nes would step over the threshold, close the door behind himself and walk the short distance to the *cheder*. Dovid's mother would sit at the kitchen table as her breakfast, nearly untouched, turned cold. If Rifka Leeba entered the kitchen, her mother-in-law stared daggers in her direction.

Dovid's mother would slip out of the house and search the alleyways and old haunts for her *mann*. She would harass bar tenders, innkeepers, madams, and pimps, demanding information on her husband's whereabouts. Sometimes she would forget her way home while out and about on her fruitless search for a husband that she had long since buried. She would be brought home by a neighbor, an apprentice from a local tavern, or by one of the younger *kurvahs.*

Rifka Leeba began to confine her mother-in-law to the house. The older woman's condition deteriorated rapidly. By the time *Pesach* approached, Dovid's mother was almost always on the couch. She would relieve herself in a bed pan when she managed to avoid soiling her clothing and bedding. The elderly woman barely spoke for days on end. When she did speak, the words were slurred and there was little coherence.

The night of the *Seder* was bleak. Nes and Rifka Leeba performed a perfunctory and joyless ceremony by themselves at their dinner table. The *borscht* was blood-red. The Angel of Death felt much too real in the symbolic-steeped rhythmic chorus of *Chad Gadya.* Dovid's mother took no notice of any of the goings-on. She slept on and off.

Nes was on an extended break from his schooling for the holiday. Over the next few days, his grandmother insisted that the boy stay close by. She would call him Dovid and cling to him. The only food that she ate was chicken broth that Nes patiently fed her one spoonful at a time.

Nes was sitting by his grandmother, holding her hand, when she passed away. Tears rolled down the boy's cheeks.

Rifka Leeba arranged for a funeral. The mother-in-law was buried in a grave next to her husband. The entire family came to the funeral out of respect for Rifka Leeba. No one besides Rifka Leeba and Nes actually mourned the passing of the bitter old woman. As the coffin was lowered into the grave, Nes cried without pause as he silently mouthed the word "Mama" over and over.

Over the next few nights, Nes would cry out "Mama!" from his bed. Rifka Leeba would come and sit by the boy, attempting to comfort him. "Mama is here," she would say, as she attempted to wrap her son in her arms. Nes would push Rifka Leeba away. "I want my real Mama!" he would shout. Rifka Leeba would leave the boy and both mother and son would then cry themselves to sleep in separate rooms.

When the mourning period ended, Nes returned to his daily routine of half-hearted attendance in the *cheder*. Rifka Leeba committed herself to bringing order to the house and a sense of stability for herself and her son.

A couple of weeks later, while Nes was in class, Rifka Leeba passed the clothing store where Nes had been conceived. The store was shuttered and draped with black cloth. Rifka Leeba approached the building and read the sign on the door. The elderly shopkeeper had suffered a heart attack and had passed on. His funeral was scheduled for the following afternoon, at the same cemetery where her mother-in-law and father-in-law were laid to rest.

As the *melamed* concluded the *cheder's* daily lesson, Nes found his mother was waiting for him. She was dressed in somber clothing. She took the boy's hand and they walked together to the cemetery.

The funeral for the shopkeeper was well attended. He had a large family, many friends, and business associates as well. The shopkeeper's wife and grown children huddled together closest to the grave. The man's sons all had an uncanny resemblance to Dovid. Rifka Leeba stood in the very back of the crowd. She spoke to no one. She held Nes' hand firmly.

When the graveside ceremony ended, as the crowd slowly dispersed, the widow approached Rifka Leeba. The widow limply shook Rifka Leeba's hand and with no enthusiasm thanked her for coming to the funeral. The widow looked askance at Nes and patted the boy's head with no affection. Then the shopkeeper's wife turned her back to Rifka Leeba and rejoined her family.

Rifka Leeba and Nes made a brief stop at the graves of her in-laws before they silently walked back to their home.

41

A DREIDL SPINS AS IT WILL

Nes' sense of loss when his grandmother passed away was astronomical. When the old woman was laid to rest, Nes was somewhat unsure about whether she had been his grandmother or his real mother. He certainly grieved at his grandmother's death as if it had been the loss of a mother.

Also, following his grandmother's death, Nes heard no more about the ne'er-do-well that was supposedly his *tate*. So, in a sense, he lost both a mother and a father at once.

The relationship between Rifka Leeba and Dovid's mother had never been warm. For years the two women had truly hated each other. Yet, Rifka Leeba felt responsible for the older woman. She had committed the latter part of her own life to caring for Dovid's mother. For Rifka Leeba, the death of her mother-in-law left a hole where there once was purpose.

That the shopkeeper passed away so soon after Dovid's mother was a shock that Rifka Leeba was unable to discuss with anyone. It was not that she was in love with the man. She most certainly was not. However, there was reassurance in the liason as well as a physical release. His death left Rifka Leeba feeling empty and reminded her of her own mortality.

Nes' relationship with Rifka Leeba became more frazzled and distant. Rifka Leeba was not quite there for the boy at this critical time. Assuredly, Rifka Leeba still tucked Nes into bed at night. She still fed him breakfast in the morning.

Six mornings a week Rifka Leeba kissed the boy on the top of his head and sent him on his way to the *cheder*, on his back a rucksack with books and a snack. Nes, however, had lost all interest in the lessons offered by the *melamed*. His limited focus evaporated. Sometimes he sat in the back of the room doodling and daydreaming. Sometimes Nes would simply ditch *cheder* altogether and entertain or educate himself.

The boy roamed far and wide on his own. His path soon included the *cheder* only sporadically. Admonishments from the *melamed* had little to no effect on the boy. At a very tender age, Nes felt orphaned on every conceivable level, cut adrift, and very much alone. He was essentially an untethered five year old.

Nes continued to look for the man that his grandmother had spoken of as his *tate* in all of the places that she had implied his father might be. As a result, Nes explored and frequented the most nefarious quarters of the *shtetl*. The gamblers and *kurvahs* took pity on the boy. They took him in and looked after him, in their way.

The gamblers allowed Nes to hang about. They would give him a few coins for running errands such as fetching food or a bottle of schnapps. They taught him how to palm cards, deal off the bottom of the deck, use a loaded *dreidl*, and other such unscrupulous tricks. They taught him how to hold his liquor and where to puke when he had too much.

Nes also learned from the gamblers how to use a *dreidl* as a tool for divination of sorts. Nes carried a *dreidl* with him at all times throughout his life and would discreetly spin it before making any important decisions.

The neighborhood *kurvahs* spoke tenderly to Nes. They would hold his hand and pinch his cheeks while calling him endearing names. When the *kurvahs* at the bordello closest to his house were not busy with paying customers, they sometimes let the boy into their rooms to cuddle him in their soft beds. Some would let the boy attempt to nurse.

Nes sometimes made it home for dinner, when he didn't get his fill of greasy food in a gambling hall or enough gourmet delicacies in a bordello. Sometimes he made it back by bath time. He almost always slept at home, occasionally coming in through the window. Early in the morning, Rifka Leeba would wake Nes, feed him breakfast and send him off once again.

Nes really didn't have much of a home life at that point and the educational opportunities offered by the *cheder* no longer appealed to the boy in the least.

On a fairly typical day, Nes might start out at the *cheder*. Mid morning, Nes would excuse himself to use the outhouse. Instead of returning to class, he would wander down the alley and then up the back steps of a bordello to join the *kurvahs* for breakfast. The *balabusta* of the bordello would put young Nes out the back door before paying customers began arriving shortly after noon. From there, Nes would either find himself an alley *minyan* spinning a *dreidl* or head to a pool hall.

It was fortunate for Nes that the Birobidzhan Pilots Association somewhat balanced out those other influences. Nes' wanderings led him down the goat path that connects the *shtetl* to the *shtat* and brought him to First Landing. There he found, at the airport on the outer edge of the *shtat*, camaraderie, and intellectual stimulation.

He was accepted into the Association because of his familial connections more than because of any particularly evident skills. He enjoyed playing with model airplanes and rocketry. He also valued the camaraderie of the Association. Mostly, however, he was drawn to their library.

The years passed. It was the library that provided a more consistent emotional support than that of the bordellos. The older flyers of the Birobidzhan Pilots Association also offered generally better guidance than the gamblers. But, Nes, nonetheless, kept his options open. He didn't give up on his old associates for the new.

So it was that Nes, still shy of the *Bar Mitzvah* age, was at the airport on the day that the first of the ships returned from Planet Shney, arriving unannounced at the airport.

The rich cargo consisting primarily of an array of highly useful and valuable minerals was unloaded and stored in a warehouse at the airport. The minerals from Planet Shney were nearly all immediately earmarked for the solar panel industry. The value was immediately evident and buyers were quickly found. The freight also included a fine selection of furs. These were stacked in neat piles on shelves in an airport warehouse. The pelts were soft and luxurious. Utilization of the furs, however, was not so immediately evident.

Nes was particularly impressed by the pelts of exotic fur from Planet Shney. The young fellow knew instantly that he wanted to learn to be a furrier. He determined that he would find himself an apprenticeship position in that trade.

On Planet Shney, cold weather is the norm. Even the summers are quite cool. Planet Shney is populated by seemingly unlimited colonies of semi-aquatic beaver-like creatures. These creatures are easily hunted and the pelts offer up a very comfortable fur, somewhat similar to sable fur if the historical records from Planet Earth are correct.

Wearing fur on Planet Shney is the norm. Everyone owns fur hats, fur lined boots, gloves with fur lining, as well and fur coats. It is also common to make rugs and wall hangings from fur and to line the cribs of babies with the soft pelts.

Furs, at the time, were quite rare on Planet Birobidzhan. The weather on most of that world rarely justifies such clothing. There were very few furriers on Planet Birobidzhan as there had never before been a substantial supply of pelts to work with. The fur bearing creatures of Planet Birobidzhan were simply not plentiful enough to be seen as a truly harvestable resource that could support an industry. Working with furs had been more of a hobby than a business.

On Planet Birobidzhan, the fine furs that originated on the distant Planet Shney were at first quite limited, but would soon become a steady commodity. This luxury item would spark an entirely new industry from scratch. As committed as Nes was to seeking out a furrier apprenticeship position, none was to be found anywhere in the vicinity of his house.

The boy was in a quandary. He spent untold hours mulling his situation. Many of those hours, he was in the library, absent-mindedly leafing through old books. It was there that he saw the ancient photos of Nineteenth Century *Yidden* on Planet Earth and Nes had a flash of insight and a flooding of inspiration.

Nearly all of the *Yidden* in the ancient photos were wearing *shtraymlekh*, elaborate fur hats. A *shtrayml* was worn with pride. Variations of this particular headgear had been worn on the Home Planet for hundreds of years, particularly by the followers of the Bal Shem Tov.

The various sects each adopted their own varieties of hats. Also, a man's social position could be determined by the elaborateness of the *shtrayml*. The hats were expensive. The wealthier the man, the more elaborate the headgear he wore.

The fur hats were donned particularly for holidays, *Shabbos*, and special occasions. Some young men would receive their first *shtrayml* for their *Bar Mitzvah* while others for their wedding.

The wearing of *shtraymlekh* on Planet Earth decreased significantly in the Twentieth Century and came to an end in the Twenty-first Century. The wild beasts that provided *mentshn* the beauty and warmth of their pelts had mostly come to extinction. The habitats of these beautiful creatures had mostly dissappeared due to environmental degradation at the hands of humanity.

Nes determined that the time was ripe to reintroduce the *Yidden* of Planet Birobidzhan to the ancient Home Planet tradition of the *shtrayml* now that quality fur was available. Nes deduced that since there were no professional furriers to apprentice with, that he would teach the trade to himself.

Nes further concluded that as Dovid's son he was entitled to an exclusive franchise on the fur trade. He was determined to negotiate a contract with executors of Planet

Shney trade on Planet Birobidzhan. Nes wanted to be the *gantze shtrayml macher* of Planet Birobidzhan.

All of this certainly could be considered a high degree of *chutzpah* on the part of a boy, one that had not even reached the age of emancipation. Particularly audacious about this proposition is that it hinged on the claim of an impossible parentage. Perhaps Nes' uncanny resemblance to Dovid helped sway that decision in his favor. Dovid, of course, was far away on a cold and distant planet.

For years, Nes had shown little interest in academic pursuit. In *cheder*, Biblical studies and *Halachic* discussions never had much appeal. Nes' math skills were always rudimentary, at best. Yet, with the arrival of that first ship from Planet Shney, the Holy Books and math became the boy's combined obsession.

The furs from Planet Shney stimulated Nes' creative abilities artistically as well as for the manipulation of logic. The hat business led the lad to immerse himself in the study of *Kabbalah* and numerology. Biblical texts and the numerical values hidden within them took on new significance. Nes honed his math skills and found creative ways to reach empowered numerical combinations from words and phrases.

There are the Thirteen Attributes of Mercy. *Chai*, the Hebrew word for life, is valued at eighteen. The numerical value of the Tetragrammaton, the name of the Holy One that is never even muttered, is twenty-six. Surely, the power of these numbers can be reflected in the hats that Nes manufactured. Certainly, the number of furs used in the manufacture of a *shtrayml* and the spiritual essence projected by the headgear is reflected in the asking price for each unique creation.

That year, the boy spent a lot of time with an untold number of rabbis. Probably, when all is said and done, the youthful Nes interacted with rabbis more in that one year than most people will in a lifetime.

Nes had a clear understanding of which side of his bread the *schmaltz* was on. Nes had a fine-tuned capability of determining which rabbis were most influential. He became an expert at calculations involving discounts and gifting that would help promote his budding enterprise. These were sophisticated skills for a boy that had not even reached the *Bar Mitzvah* age.

On Planet Birobidzhan, a *Bar Mitzvah* is generally a low key event. The *Bar Mitzvah* marks the coming of the age of emancipation. It is usually observed by attending *shul* on a *Mantik* or a *Danershtag* when the *Toyre* is read and the young man has a first opportunity for an *aliyah*.

Nes, in the year leading up to his *Bar Mitzvah*, had developed friendly relationships with a significant number of prominent local rabbis. For a youth with no particular religious inclination or rabbinic family connections, Nes had made a positive impression on the movers and shakers of the First Landing rabbinic establishment. Gifting many of those men expensive hats certainly helped. As a result, Nes' *Bar Mitzvah* was well attended by influential men all displaying the products of Nes' enterprise.

This is not to say that less prodigious friends were underrepresented. Men generally more at ease late at night in a pool hall or in an alley found themselves in a *shul* for an early morning *minyan*. In the women's section upstairs sat Nes' mother and a few relatives as well as representatives from several bordellos.

After turning thirteen, Nes' formal schooling, for what it is worth, came to an end. The young man had a business to run. Nes trained other boys and young men to manufacture *shtraymlekh* to his exacting specifications.

Nes traveled widely, visiting *shuls* and *yeshivas* worldwide. Nes, through sheer audacity, sold Planet Birobidzhan's religious authorities on the gregarious fashion of expensive hats made from imported fur. When traveling, Nes would spend his afternoons in the *shuls* and *yeshivas*. He would generally have his supper in the home of a prominent rabbi. After eating, Nes would find his way to a bordello or two where he would remain until nearly dawn.

Meanwhile, the ships from Planet Shney arrived at the Planet Birobidzhan Airport almost like clockwork, about once every other month. With each arrival, a folder addressed to the Birobidzhan Pilots Association was delivered. The contents of these folders ultimately proved to be quite valuable, enriching the Birobidzhan Pilots Association.

On the distant Planet Shney, Dovid had sworn that he was done with the business of space travel. He said that he wanted to spend his time with his grandchildren. However, he continued to sit up late at night researching, calculating, and designing. When each of the product-laden ships were loaded, Dovid included a satchel consisting of his notes and drawings which focused on improving the efficiency of interplanetary flight.

The innovations that Dovid suggested led to lighter, stronger, faster, less expensive, and more energy efficient ships. Although many of the changes were fairly incremental, incremental improvements do have a way of adding up.

As the changes in designs were implemented, the timing of the roundtrip was shaved down by a fraction here and a couple of percentage points there. The improvements primarily involved the use of minerals available on Planet

Shney but unavailable or extremely rare on Planet Birobidzhan. That is, until Dovid offered up plans based on an obscure theory from ancient Earth science that would change everything.

The use of pellet beams to speed travel between the stars had been envisioned by Twentieth Century Home Planet engineers but never put to a practical test. Pellet beam theory had been confined to laboratories and libraries. No one from Planet Earth had been willing to finance a test of a pellet beam system in the actual void. Dovid urged the Birobidzhan Pilots Association to take that task on, presented a blueprint for the system, and offered a scheme to finance the implementation.

Prospectors on Planet Shney had discovered gold. True enough, the gold was in an inhospitable region but the veins were wide, not very deep, and incredibly pure.

The gold flowed from the mines of Sibir to the growing *stadt* of Moskve. Of course, gold has industrial value and is also prized for jewelry, inlaid book covers, framed *ketubahs*, and other sorts of artistic uses. Before long, the supply of this soft metal was greater than those uses could absorb. The flow of gold continued unabated and the price plummeted. On Planet Shney bakers used gold to decorate cakes and gold dust was used by children as glitter for craft projects. The floor sweepings were thrown to the streets.

Gold was not so plentiful on other planets. The gold reserves on Planet Earth had long since been depleted, many generations before the first flight to Planet Birobidzhan. On Planet Birobidzhan, gold was virtually non-existent.

The cargo laden ships coming from Planet Shney arrived with loads of the soft, pliable yellowish metal. The wealth generated from the sale of gold, it was proposed, could finance a satellite and other specialized equipment needed for the pellet beam system.

A very limited amount of the gold imported to Planet Birobidzhan was used for electronics. Some gold was crafted into high quality jewelry. The bulk of the imported metal was minted into coins. Each coin was emblazoned with the image of the seven-branched Temple Menorah. The new gold coin shekels were quickly considered to be of higher value than the paper shekels that were in circulation on Planet Birobidzhan.

A technology that would significantly shorten the traveling time between distant points rekindled interest in sending a delegation to the Home Planet. The growing supply of Planet Shney gold suggested a leverage for that delegation if contact with Planet Earth was feasible.

Long ago, on the Home Planet, reaching back thousands of years of Earth history, gold gained a mythological value. Gold was made into religious statuary on every continent of the Home Planet. The gods of all the peoples of Planet Earth were represented in golden forms.

The *Yidden*, of course, refrained from the myriad of deities and the statuary that represented such gods. Gold was, nonetheless, used heavily in the Temple that King Solomon built in Yerushalaim. Around 34 tons of gold was used in that construction, transported by caravans from faraway Ophir. The inside of the Temple was overlaid with pure gold and gold chains were hung throughout.

Not long later, globally on Planet Earth, gold was formed into coins, bars and ingots. Empires rose and fell for gold and peoples were conquered and obliterated in pursuit of the wealth implied by possession of this soft and nearly useless metal. Gold had become the primary currency of Planet Earth.

Over two centuries had passed since Planet Birobidzhan's severance from direct contact with the Home Planet. It was reasonable to be concerned about the fate of humanity in general and that of the remaining *Yidden* in particular. Some suggested that the fate of our brethren might require action on the part of the delegation that would be sent to Planet Earth.

Considering the history of our people prior to the launching of the *Hatikvah* and the founding of a settlement on Planet Birobidzhan, a solid negotiating hand was called for. Gold, historically, facilitated the most complicated of negotiations. In the case of suppression or enslavement, gold was the ideal medium for *pidyon shvuyim*, the ransoming of captives. It seemed quite plausible that there would be millions of *Yidden* on the Home Planet that might need ransoming.

The Birobidzhan Pilots Association successfully launched a new satellite, placing it in orbit, the first step for using pellet beams to speed travel from Planet Birobidzhan. They then projected the pellet beams on a ship headed to Planet Shney. The expense involved was astronomical but the benefits were tremendous. The shuttle to Planet Shney passed ships launched earlier and arrived safely in just over half the time of the unassisted ships.

The experiment set in motion a diplomatic and economic expedition to Planet Earth. Earth remained, even after all the centuries of separation, the Home Planet. Earth continued to have a nostalgic pull on the *mentshn* of Planet Birobidzhan.

A selection process was put in place to choose the *mentshn* that would represent Planet Birobidzhan's economic and social interests. Eighteen men were chosen, each a representative of the various trends amongst the

Yidden of Planet Birobidzhan. Most were widowed. Some were unmarried. Nes was the youngest of those selected for this mission, and still unmarried.

In the period preceding the expedition to the Home Planet, Nes continued traveling extensively on Planet Birobidzhan. He marketed his *shtraymlekh* in the daytime. He dined with influential rabbis in the evening, where he would politely flirt with their daughters but judiciously deflect any suggested *shidduch*. Nes spent most nights in the reassuring and predictable comfort of a bordello.

It was certainly Nes' plan to stick to his preferred pattern when he arrived by airplane in Niu Niu Yark, on the last flight before Purim.

Nes had never been to this city for Purim, the busiest tourist event in Niu Niu Yark. Every room is rented at exorbitant rates. Some visitors resort to sleeping in the parks and alleys. Nes had the foresight to reserve a suite. He was surprised to find that his "suite" was a small room with a narrow bed in an old hotel, with a bathroom down the hall.

The young man left his luggage in the room. Carrying only his sample case of *shtraymlekh*, Nes began making the rounds of the largest *shuls* and yeshivas. He was dismayed to learn that the schools were all closed as well as all the rabbinic offices. Everyone was preparing for the massive celebration.

The lack of a rabbinic welcoming also meant that Nes was not invited home for a decently cooked home meal. He went searching for sustenance. The restaurants seemed to be overflowing with customers. There were long lines winding outside of most establishments. Nes settled for street vendor fare, which was selling briskly at two or three times the normal price.

Nes satisfied his hunger with *knishes* and sausages and then went looking for a welcoming bordello. He was again surprised to discover that the bordellos of Niu Niu Yark were all shuttered for an extended Purim break. The Niu Niu Yark *kurvahs* don't work on what they called amateur night. The professionals choose to stay home with their families rather than waste their time competing for attention on Purim.

Nes was regretting his ill-timed trip to Planet Birobidzhan's largest city. The parades and pageantry, however, were entertaining and the music from the *klezmorim* filled the air. He purchased *majoun* and schnapps from a street vendor. Nes' attachment to linear time faded as the *majoun* took effect.

Nes considered heading to his rented room, but the evening was still young. The air was balmy. The sky was clear with brightly shining stars. The music was pulsating. The party went on all around him and the *majoun* had taken control of his senses.

When Nes first encountered her, she was costumed as a fabled Bedouin. She was covered in cloth from the top of her head to her sandaled feet. Just below the sleeves, jangling bracelets were visible. Anklets with small bells were set just above her eloquently hennaed feet. Mascara accented her eyes, visible through the veil that covered most of her face.

Their eyes met as they stood side by side at an intersection, as the last decorated float of the official parade passed. The parade ended and the crowd filled the street. When the final float disappeared, Nes turned his head to look at the robed woman beside him. She was, however, no longer covered with cloth.

Besides the shimmering veil that covered most of her face, she was wearing little more than henna and gold paint. The henna and the paint also seemed to shimmer. The *majoun* that Nes had eaten added color and texture to what was already a vibrant evening.

Nes remembered being taken by the hand and led to a nearby park. He recalled the shadows, shades, and pulsating fluidity of light. Almost as if watching himself from the vantage point of an observer, Nes felt a disassociation from his actions as they found the relative privacy of bushes in the park. He watched himself as he entered her and brought her to climax.

When Nes awoke the next morning in his rented room, beside him in the narrow bed was the woman he had encountered so many hours earlier on the streets of Niu Niu Yark. Her hair was disheveled. Much of the gold paint was smeared. She slept contentedly, snoring ever so slightly.

Nes extricated himself from her arms and the tangled bedding. The light that came through the window of the small hotel room was diffused, contributing to the haziness of the morning. He quietly padded across the small room and out the door into the hallway. He headed down the hall to the shared *vashzimmer* to relieve himself and wash some of the sleep from his eyes.

Nes was pleased, on returning, to find a rolling cart by the room's door with a samovar of tea and a tray of *majoun* pastries. He wheeled the cart into the room and poured himself a glass of tea. He drank the first glass of tea *shtetl* style, with a sugar cube between his teeth. Subsequent glasses of tea he drank without sugar. Rather, Nes dipped a pastry into the tea and absorbed the full spectrum effects of the mildly stimulating tea and the somewhat hypnotic, bordering on hallucinogenic *majoun* working in conjunction.

Seated at a small table in the modest room, Nes watched his sleeping companion with some disorientation, a degree of quiet fulfillment, and satisfaction that felt like a new beginning to him in a yet undefined way. Nes was imbued with an unexpected sensation of hope and bliss.

Striving for clarity, Nes fiddled with his *dreidl*, attempting for divination. He spun repeatedly and drew conclusions from how the device spun and the way it fell. Without yet knowing the young woman's name, while she slept in the bed in that small room, Nes determined that his newfound hope and bliss derived from her and their shared *bashert* was sealed. The track of his life had been irrevocably altered.

42

THE RIVER FLOWS ON

Nes and Shprintza Freyda stood under the *chuppah* just after Purim. It was a minimal ceremony in one of Niu Niu Yark's smaller *shuls*. The rabbi muttered a few words. Nes smashed a wine glass under his boot. The couple kissed. Nes paid the rabbi and witnesses.

Immediately following that minimalist ceremony, the young people rode a public streetcar to the harbor of Seaside Mea Shearim. After walking to the docks, they boarded a ferry bound southward to the city of Eilat, for a spontaneous off-season honeymoon in the Tropics of Birobidzhan.

No friends or family attended the ceremony as neither the bride nor the groom were from Niu Niu Yark. Their meeting had been purely by chance and the marriage came about without plan or much thought. It certainly hadn't allowed time for inviting guests.

Nes had determined that they were destined to wed while Shprintza Freyda slept. Nes derived an uncanny sensation of hope and bliss from her essence before even learning her name. Discovering her name seemed to confirm his intuitiveness as well as provide proof to the effectiveness of his makeshift divination with a *dreidl*.

When Nes discovered that his newfound love was known as Shprintza Freyda, he felt assured that the qualities of hope and bliss he was experiencing were imprinted in her essential being and verified by the very definition of her given name.

When Shprintza Freyda learned Nes' name, she also felt that something truly miraculous had occurred. *Beshart* was evidently fulfilled by their chance encounter. Nes proposed while they ate breakfast and Shprintza Freyda accepted without reservations. The wedding was the following day.

The air was salty and balmy in Niu Niu Yark when they boarded the ferry. The ship sailed south into the true Tropics, on calm seas. It was the first time that either of these young people had been to that remote part of Planet Birobidzhan.

Everything about Eilat felt exotic and even foreign to them. This sensation is often true for new arrivals but it is more intensely felt off-season. The summers are hot in the Tropics. Much of normal enterprise simply winds down after Purim. With most of the tourists gone, the locals enjoy long *siestas* and partake in extended periods of inactivity.

The streets of Eilat are quieter in the summer. The town is void of bustling visitors. The wide array of tourist oriented services are no longer available after Purim. Fewer restaurants remain open and those serve meals that appeal to local palates rather than the tastes of outsiders; they offer combinations of food unfamiliar to most *mentshn* of Planet Birobidzhan.

Nes and Shprintza Freyda were enamored by everything. The spicy food of the Tropics. The music that sways with the palm trees. The poetic rhythm of the regional dialect.

The *shprakh* of the Tropics has the melodic variants of Spanish and Arabic words interspersed quite liberally. There is a sing-song quality to the local *zhargon*. Many familiar words are pronounced with the accent on a different syllable than what is standard on the rest of Planet Birobidzhan. Additionally, the "s" sounds are often exchanged for "t".

There is a relaxed attitude in the Tropics. The cultural standards are less restrictive. Perhaps it is the warmth of the Tropics that override the more restrained customs of the rest of Planet Birobidzhan. Women are more inclined to bare their arms and many wear shorter skirts than is the norm on the rest of Planet Birobidzhan. Couples in Eilat often walk holding hands or arm in arm when out for an evening stroll and no one seems shocked or offended.

Nes and Shprintza Freyda ate in the restaurants and the outdoor cafés. They relaxed together in the hammock that hung in the courtyard of the guesthouse. They took long walks on isolated trails. They made love on the colorful sand dunes and in the shade of the tropical trees. This was the first vacation for each of them.

Nes had traveled on Planet Birobidzhan extensively but never just for the pleasure of it. He was always traveling on business. In the Tropics, Nes hadn't even considered trying to make connections or attempt marketing his *shtraymlekh*. He couldn't even imagine anyone that lived in the humid soupiness of the Tropics ever wearing hats made of furs. Nes' sample case remained packed away in the closet of the guesthouse. Business was not on his mind.

Nes also had not visited a bordello since his chance encounter with Shprintza Freyda and their hasty marriage. Yet, while the young couple stayed in Eilat, they walked past the House of Veils Bordello several times a day.

At the House of Veils, the *kurvahs* relax on the veranda in varying stages of casual undress when not engaged with clients. In the off-season, there are far fewer paying customers. There is far more relaxing on the veranda, overlooking the street.

In the lobby of the House of Veils, there is a full bar with a piano generally in use, and often played quite well. The doors of the bordello stand open to the street. The interspersed aroma of baking and perfume waft invitingly to those walking by.

The House of Veils is the sort of establishment that, generally speaking, appealed to Nes' sense of aesthetics. It is a place that he might have found comforting not so very long ago. Nes hardly noticed the *kurvahs* when he passed those doors with his new bride at his side.

Shprintza Freyda had never left her *shtetl* on her own before going to Niu Niu Yark for Purim. She had never really traveled far even with her parents. She had only been to a few nearby *shtetls* that were not much different from her own.

Shprintza Freyda had gone to Niu Niu Yark by herself and without informing anyone of her intention. Just before boarding the ferry with Nes, Shprintza Freyda sent her parents a picture postcard. She informed them of the marriage and promised to visit sometime after the honeymoon.

So, the young couple drifted somewhat aimlessly in the *mañana* atmosphere of the Tropics of Birobidzhan. They extended their stay beyond their initial intentions. The tropical days became weeks that slipped into months. However, no vacation can last forever. They reluctantly boarded the northbound ferry back to the mainland.

As the ship sailed towards Niu Niu Yark, Nes began to consider how significantly marriage altered his life trajectory. For starters, he would, of necessity, be compelled to give up his potentially lucrative booking on the expedition to the Home Planet. After all, Nes was at this point a married man and soon to be a father. The summer clothing that Shprintza Freyda wore made it quite evident that she was already carrying their first child.

If Nes had been traveling on his own, he would have relied on his old connections and finagled a seat on the daily flight from Niu Niu Yark to First Landing. However, he was traveling with his pregnant wife. A bouncy flight in a small airplane didn't seem prudent.

The couple traveled by train. The train is considerably slower than flying but is far less jarring an experience and much more comfortable, particularly in a First Class sleeping compartment. They arrived well rested in First Landing early the following morning. The young people took a taxi to Nes' childhood home in the outlying *shtetl*.

Rifka Leeba had no foreknowledge of her son's arrival, much less an inkling of his marriage to the now very pregnant Shprintza Freyda. Rifka Leeba was drinking tea in the kitchen when she heard the front door open.

When Rifka Leeba saw Nes, a broad smile filled her face. He looked so much like Dovid when she first met him; the Dovid that she had loved with so much passion.

As her mouth opened to speak, Shprintza Freyda came within her field of vision. In that fractured moment that Rifka Leeba saw Nes' young wife, she saw the unmistakable resemblance to the *Purim Meydl* that arrived at her door so many years before with Dovid's daughter swathed in her arms.

The glass of tea that Rifka Leeba was holding slipped from her hand. The glass shattered on the hard tiles of the kitchen floor.

Rifka Leeba's eyes widened. Her mouth opened and closed without sound emitting. Then, she too fell, slipping off her chair and onto the floor. Nes rushed to his mother. He cradled his mother's head as Rifka Leeba passed on into the *Yenne Velt*.

The news of Rifka Leeba's passing spread quickly and the neighbors responded to the news in a most predictable way. Although precious few of them ever had anything good to say about Rifka Leeba while she lived, the house was nonetheless filled with a gaggle of neighborhood *balabustas*, set on the mission of assuring her a properly respectful memorial. The fragrances of the stews and *kugels* and casseroles that they brought became domineering.

Nes handed over the management of the house to these strangers. They tidied up. They hung black cloth over all the mirrors. They greeted and guided visitors. Nes sat on a hard bench in the parlor. He was shoeless and wore intentionally torn clothes to show proper respect.

Shprintza Freyda stayed by Nes' side during the proscribed mourning period. She occasionally rubbed her expansive abdomen. Perhaps this was to reassure herself and the unborn child. Perhaps this was to remind Nes of his responsibilities as she observed the complexities of his social interactions. These were the days when she learned who she had married.

Shprintza Freyda was a *meydl* from a very small and isolated *shtetl*. It was extremely daring for her to travel on her own to Niu Niu Yark. The intoxicating atmosphere of the Purim celebration in a city far from home offered her the anonymity for her uncharacteristically daring and seductive behavior that night.

It was purely coincidence that Shprintza Freyda and Nes met. Their whirlwind romantic encounter was fueled with alcohol and *majoun* and it was the whirlwind of this encounter that blew the two young people onwards to the Tropics of Birobidzhan. Dwelling in the Tropics is an exotic and somewhat hypnotic, dreamy experience for even the most jaded of travelers.

Truth be told, Shprintza Freyda had barely any clues as to who Nes really was. She knew that he was some sort of hat merchant. She was aware that he had the leeway to take an extended vacation and she barely considered that he paid for accommodations and meals without concerns for finances. It wasn't until that week of *Sitting Shiva* that Shprintza Freyda became aware that she had married a *gantze macher*.

The house soon filled, it seemed, to the bursting point with the widest possible array of visitors. They came in waves over the week as Nes mourned the passing of his mother. The house was overflowing with *kurvahs*, gamblers, rabbis, and members of the Birobidzhan Pilots Association in addition to the ever present neighborhood *balabustas*.

Shprintza Freyda watched as the visitors arrived and they each, in turn, approached her husband to offer condolences in their own way. Nes was equally comfortable, it seemed, with the most saintly as with the most carnal and everyone in between.

Each visitor, in turn, seemed to address issues of great personal importance, speaking coded terms in hushed tones that were comprehensible to themselves and to Nes. Shprintza Freyda was awed by the strangers and their interactions with her husband as the cascading incomprehensible conversations unfolded under her watching eyes.

The *kurvahs* would, mostly one at a time but sometimes in pairs, sit close enough to her husband to make Shprintza

Freyda most uncomfortable. With a hand on his knee or thigh, the *kurvahs* would lean into him and whisper in his ear. Nes apparently was familiar with each of them. He returned the intimacy, whispering confidentially with every one of them, sharing their secret memories and implied promises.

The rabbis spoke to Nes in a dizzying admixture of esoteric philosophy and *Kabbalistic* mathematics. Obscure concepts embedded in words and phrases semi-revealed in numerical terms and values were exchanged between these elderly sages and her young husband.

The conversations with the array of gamblers were no less obscure than the dialogue with the rabbinic representatives. They spoke about the way a *dreidl* spins and the ways that the device might fall. They hypothesized about the order and display of playing cards in various games. They articulated about the angles, force, and finesse involved in billiards. All of these discussions seemed to be as much or more about *Kabbalah* and numerology as the esoteric discussions of the rabbis.

Throughout that week, the gamblers placed wagers on everything imaginable, including which piece of babka a fly might land on. Outside, behind the family house, there was an ongoing, nearly nonstop, *minyan* of *dreidl* spinning every day except for *Shabbos.* Prominent rabbis often joined in between their more conventional *minyans* and heartfelt condolences.

Perhaps the Birobidzhan Pilots Association members' *zhargon* was the least comprehensible and most esoteric of all. In a casual manner they peppered their conversations with strange terms such as the Galilean Cannon and Dovid's Slingshot. They interspersed it with mind-bending numbers representing velocity. They spoke of the structural strength of various metallic alloys and the combustion rates concerning a variety of fuels. They spoke of the folding of space and time by traveling through wormholes as if it was as common as a walk in the park. If all of this wasn't mystical, there was no other way for Shprintza Freyda to wrap her head around it.

The neighborhood *balabustas* replenished the food on the serving table and assured that there were ample plates and silverware. They kept the very busy house orderly and clean. Otherwise, the *balabustas* looked on with a generalized scorn and a barely disguised air of moral superiority.

The *balabustas* were somewhat ingratiating without any affection. The *balabustas* dominated the background. Of all the strangers that were swirling about, these were the only ones that seemed familiar to Shprintza Freyda. The proficiency and aloofness of these women reminded Shprintza Freyda of the neighbors of her own *shtetl* so very far away.

During the week of official mourning, currency, both the paper shekels and the more prized gold coins, openly changed hands with great frequency. This was certainly true between the gamblers but with nearly the same frequency among the rabbis and also those of the Pilots Association. Only the *kurvahs* among all of Nes' friends and acquaintances were refrained from the fiscal exchanges.

With all of the hubbub, Shprintza Freyda watched as a steady flow of cash subtly flowed to Nes. In the process, Nes managed to exchange his booking on the highly speculative expedition to the Home Planet for accommodations on a flight to Planet Shney for the couple and their offspring shortly after the birthing, due sometime around Hanukkah. Their booking was for the flight on the scheduled launch midway into the month Shevat, as the flight in Tevet was already fully booked.

Nes arranged to have a message sent to Dovid via the next departing shuttle that week while *Sitting Shiva*. The message was to inform Dovid of Rifka Leeba's passing, the soon to be grandchild, and the intentions of Nes and Shprintza Freyda to settle on Planet Shney with the expected child. The message also informed Dovid which shuttle the young family anticipated to be traveling on. Of course, any messages sent from Planet Birobidzhan to Planet Shney take over two years to be delivered.

Throughout Nes' childhood, Rifka Leeba told him that Dovid was his father. Certainly by custom and tradition this was true. That was certainly how Nes perceived the relationship. Nes also profited considerably by the familial connection over the years.

Dovid likely had another perspective, at least to begin with. Rifka Leeba was his first, deepest, and truest love. It was heartbreaking for Dovid that his wife chose to stay behind on Planet Birobidzhan. Nes, of course, was conceived without Dovid's involvement.

When Dovid received the letter from the young man, much introspection resulted. Ultimately, Dovid determined that his love for Rifka Leeba transcended space, time, and any possible indiscretions. Dovid decided that he would welcome Nes into the fold, and help him and his nascent family to the best of his ability.

When the mourning period ended, the young couple were at loose ends. They remained in Rifka Leeba's house, which had been Nes' childhood home, but they had little to do but wait for time to pass. They waited for the birth and for the subsequent voyage to Planet Shney. Shprintza

Freyda was far from energetic. Her body swelled and the pregnancy weighed her down. She slept a lot.

Nes became bored and fidgety. He went for long walks. He visited his old haunts. The time away from the house stretched out as he went about fulfilling the promises that he had made to the *kurvahs* at the local bordellos. Each of the *kurvahs* insisted, however, that he return home at some point to fulfill his obligations to his wife.

Shprintza Freyda chose to ignore the smell of unfamiliar perfume and sweat that enveloped Nes each night when he eventually made his way home and back to her bed. She chose to forgive his propensity for dalliance. She knew that soon they would board the shuttle to Planet Shney. For more than two years they would share very cramped quarters and Nes' wandering would be curbed. On Planet Shney they would begin a whole new chapter in the story they were destined to create together.

Shprintza Freyda's pregnancy came to full fruition on the twenty-fifth of Kislev, the first day of Hanukkah. The midwives from the *Magen David Adom* assisted with the home birth. All went well without complications. A beautiful and healthy girl was welcomed and she was named Rifka Leeba in honor of Nes' recently departed mother of blessed memory.

Shprintza Freyda rolled Rifka Leeba every day in a perambulator to the nearby park. Fresh air and sunshine were precious commodities for mother and daughter. In a little over a month the young family would board the transit ship bound to Planet Shney. There would be no fresh air or natural sunlight while traveling through the void from one planet to another.

When the launch day came, Nes was excited. Shprintza Freyda was somewhat apprehensive. The beautiful Rifka

Leeba gurgled happily, comfortable in her mother's arms, nurtured and reassured at Shprintza Freyda's breast.

The sky was clear. The day was temperate and unseasonably warm. Perhaps Nes and Shprintza Freyda understood deep down the somewhat harsh reality. Rifka Leeba certainly had no way of comprehending the significance symbolized by something as simple as a warm and sunny day. The day of their embarkation would be the warmest day for the rest of their lives. Planet Shney is a very cold place.

As was usual, friends and families of those traveling crowded the tarmac to wave goodbye and to watch the ship lift off. Some were there specifically for Nes. Among the crowd were several of the local *kurvahs*. These young women each unconsciously patted their own abdomen. They each assured that Nes' legacy on Planet Birobidzhan included progeny.

Little Rifka Leeba had already celebrated her second birthday before arriving on the planet that would be her home. Even with all of the advances in technology, and even with the relative comfort of their accommodations, it was still a very long trip from Planet Birobidzhan to Planet Shney.

The family was very glad to disembark at the end of that voyage, particularly Rifka Leeba. She was very ready to stretch her tiny legs on land after so long entrapped on the ship. Nes, Shprintza Freyda, and Rifka Leeba were among the first passengers down the gangplank.

Dovid stood, slightly bent, in the observation shelter on the tarmac. Dovid was, by then, fairly advanced in age. He wore multiple layers of wool and fur to protect himself from the elements. The temperature in the shelter hovered around freezing, which was considerably warmer than out in the open. He was there to welcome his family to Moskve and Planet Shney.

The shuttle flight from one planet to the other had been fine tuned and normalized to such a degree that arrival times could be predicted within an hour or so. That was a true blessing. In the days of the earliest flights, predictions of arrival times were somewhat less accurate than predictions of how a *dreidl* might fall.

When the transport ship descended onto the tarmac and the gangplank was lowered, Dovid scanned the faces of the new arrivals. This was a practice that hasn't changed over the centuries. It was the same back on the Home Planet when sailing ships crossed the great oceans, passengers to be met by unknown relatives. Dovid would need to make an intuitive guess to determine which of the new arrivals on Planet Shney were the ones he was there to greet.

When Dovid saw Shprintza Freyda coming down the gangplank, time momentarily froze for him and then folded in on itself.

How familiar this lovely young woman looked. The memories were vivid and tinged with something akin to hallucinations. Dovid could not remember her name. Perhaps he had never known her name. The interchange was fleeting but passionate. It was a Purim many decades past on Planet Birobidzhan in the city of Niu Niu Yark. He was sure of the experience as could be and there on that gangplank was that lover that was a wisp of memories.

Then, as if awakened from a dream, Dovid remembered how much time had passed since that Purim so long ago and so very far away. He was fairly young then and now he was elderly. Surely that *meydl* of his memories would have aged considerably since then. Surely she would be nearly as old as he.

Dovid shook his head and took in a breath of the cold Moskve air. As he did so, he saw the woman that he was watching reach a hand to her companion on the gangplank. Dovid shifted his focus, seeing the man next to the young woman. Dovid blinked. The man next to her could very well have been Dovid himself, when he was a very young man, except for the elaborate *shtrayml* that he was sporting.

It took several minutes for Dovid's sense of incongruity to wear off. By then, Nes and Shprintza Freyda were approaching him. Little Rifka Leeba was in her father's arms, also appearing incredibly familiar to Dovid. There was no doubt in his mind that these were the people that he came to greet.

Everyone was a bit awkward and tongue-tied but warm hugs and kisses were exchanged amongst the adults of the family on the frozen tarmac of the Moskve Landing Field. Then Dovid turned his attention to the little one. "Who is this *tayere vonce*, this dear bedbug here?" Dovid asked, giving Rifka Leeba a *knip* as she squealed and laughed in Nes' arms.

"This is Rifka Leeba," Nes said to Dovid. Then, speaking to the child, he continued, "Say hello to your *Zaydeh*, *Ketschele*." Rifka Leeba giggled and squirmed a bit, feigning shyness. Then she jumped into Dovid's arms.

Dovid whispered into the child's ear and tickled her neck with his beard. Rifka Leeba smiled broadly, laughed unreservedly, and nodded happily.

What Dovid had whispered into the little girl's ear was that he always has sweet snacks such as candy or cookies in a secret jacket pocket. He told her that on that day he had dates that were sweeter than any candy and that she would be one of very few people on any planet to learn the location of that secret pocket. Dovid discreetly handed the child a date which she immediately crammed into her mouth.

Dovid also told Rifka Leeba that she was as sweet as a date and that he would henceforth call her Tamar. The truth was a bit more complicated than that. Dovid couldn't bear calling the little one by his wife's name. Just the thought of the name stirred up too many emotions.

Moreover, the child's resemblance to Dovid's daughter Tamar at that age was most uncanny. Tamar had always been Dovid's favorite child.

Tamar had been wandering *tsufus* in the wilderness of Sabir. She dwelled in a self-enforced exile and isolation. Dovid had no way of knowing definitively if his daughter was even still among the living, although he believed her to be. Dovid was almost unsurprised when he heard the notes on the wind as they neared his home.

Tamar stood alone on Tel Shomrim, overlooking the spaceport and the *stadt*. She played her violin for her own edification, wrapped in furs, sheltered by a small copse of trees.

The otherworldly sounds of violin were carried that cold winter afternoon, drifting intermittently by the wind currents, through much of Moskve's unique acoustic terrain. It had been years since those sounds had last been heard by anyone besides the wild beasts of Sabir or perhaps a stray trapper or prospector.

Baruch and Shmuli were walking from the Yerushalaim *Shul*, engaged in a *Halachic* dispute when the disembodied melodic strands intervened. The two fell silent, as each remembered the *meydl mit a fidele* that led them to Planet Shney.

Perez and Zerah each heard wisps of Tamar's violin in their respective homes. Each of the brothers considered briefly that perhaps they could do something to bring their mother a sense of peace, security, and belonging. They each, fairly quickly, determined that Tamar's life was beyond their comprehension.

The Mushrooms of Planet Birobidzhan shimmered in response to the strains of Tamar's violin under the snow covering of Planet Shney, in anticipation of the coming spring.

43

ADDENDUM: MOISHE PIPIK FLIES TO THE MOON AND SEEKS

Far di kinder fun der vayt
(For the children far away)

It was a very long time ago and very far away. In a *shtetl* called Brooklyn there lived a small boy named Moishe Pipik. Moishe Pipik was a good lad. He was smart and creative.

Although Moishe Pipik was an only child, he lived in a very crowded apartment. The apartment was situated in a crowded tenement building on a busy street in the very heart of Brooklyn.

The apartment was small but maybe it wouldn't have felt so crowded if he lived there with just his parents. However, besides Moishe Pipik and his parents, his *Bubbe*, his mother's mother, also lived in that small apartment.

Even with his grandmother sleeping in the "spare" bedroom, the apartment might have felt merely cramped but the apartment was always far more crowded than that. It seemed that there were always some extra relatives staying there.

There were always some family members going through a difficult stretch, between jobs and without a place of their own. Sometimes there were several relatives staying at once. They slept on the couch, in the bathtub, and on the kitchen floor. Sometimes there would be a "guest" sharing his bed. A small child might be sleeping in the bottom drawer of his dresser. In the summer, a person or two slept on the fire escape.

Both of Moishe Pipik's parents worked a lot. His father was at a job six days a week. His mother "took in" clothes to repair, besides all the cooking and cleaning involved in maintaining the home. She had learned to sew from her father, who had earned his living as a tailor among other endeavors. Moishe Pipik's mother often worked late into the night, sometimes falling asleep at the sewing machine that she had inherited from her father.

It really couldn't be said that Moishe Pipik's parents neglected him. They assured that he got all of the things that he really needed such as his daily meals and his weekly baths. Moishe Pipik's parents did truly love him.

What they couldn't provide the boy was all of the attention that he craved nor all of the things on his endless list of wishes and desires.

The other relatives filling the apartment to overflowing helped fill that void as far as his desires beyond absolute need was concerned. The neighborhood, as well, was crowded with people that were almost as nosy, loud and boisterous as his relatives. These neighbors watched out for Moishe Pipik, almost as if they were family.

Of all the relatives that frequently encamped at the family's apartment, often for weeks or months at a time, Uncle Morrie and Aunt Fannie were Moishe Pipik's favorites. Uncle Morrie was his mother's younger brother. Aunt Fannie, as near as he could tell, was actually a second or third cousin of his father's but she insisted on being called Aunt.

When Moishe Pipik was a little *pisher*, Morrie had been a merchant marine. Morrie traveled the world and would mail the family picture postcards from all the exotic ports where the ships docked. The postcards decorated the apartment, giving the place a low budget international flair.

As near as Moishe Pipik could tell, Uncle Morrie had some sort of job involving race horses. Unfortunately, the horses didn't always pay Uncle Morrie, which was a cause for friction with Moishe Pipik's father. Moishe Pipik figured that the problem stemmed from the fact that horses don't have pockets so the horses rarely carried money.

When the horses did pay off, Uncle Morrie would be quite generous. A couple of times he took Moishe Pipik to Coney Island, where they watched the skirts, ate ice cream on the Boardwalk and went to the Penny Arcade where Moishe Pipik saw the jumpy films of hoochie-coochie girls for the first time. Once, Uncle Morrie took the lad to the big museum in Manhattan to gawk at the dinosaur bones. Occasionally they would go to Ebbets Field to eat Cracker Jacks and Foot Long hot dogs while watching the Brooklyn Dodgers.

Nope. Morrie no longer shipped out. He did, however, tell elaborate tales of days when his travels took him to exotic places like Buenos Aires, Tangiers, Marrakesh, Havana and New Jersey. The stories of strange and wonderful adventures involved Eskimos, Bedouin, Gauchos, Pickpockets, White Slavers, Pygmies, Horse Thieves, Card Sharks, and Indians. In those tales, Uncle Morrie was always heroic.

Uncle Morrie played checkers with Moishe Pipik. He also taught him poker and gin rummy.

The most wondrous and unexplainable thing about Uncle Morrie is that he would sometimes pull a nickel out of Moishe Pipik's ear. For no particular reason, at random and unexpected times, Uncle Morrie would draw the boy close, reach around and extract a shiny coin...and then, give the nickel to the boy!

Nothing pleased Moishe Pipik more than the feeling of a nickel pressed into the palm of his hand. He would smile broadly and then squeeze the coin in a tightly gripped fist.

Of course, a nickel would not remain long in Moishe Pipik's hand. He would run down the street to Finklestein's Delicatessen where he would promptly exchange the shiny nickel for the opportunity to fish a fat kosher dill pickle from the wooden barrel. The pickle barrel was nearly as tall as Moishe Pipik. With the tongs held firmly in his right hand, leaning over the huge barrel, Moishe Pipik would try to find the biggest and juiciest of the pickles floating in brine. Nothing pleased him more than exchanging a nickel for such a Heavenly Delight as a fat dill pickle.

When his Aunt Fannie would arrive, it was usually just before dinner time. She would be carrying a small suitcase and the clothes she wore would be crumpled and mussed. There would be a knock at the door. Aunt Fannie, standing there, would sniffle. Aunt Fannie would be holding back tears. She would sigh heavily, and shuffle her feet a bit.

Moishe Pipik's mother would also sigh. Then, his mother would usher Aunt Fannie in. No questions were ever asked. An extra plate would be put at the table. Moishe Pipik's mother would add some more water to whatever was cooking on the stove and somehow there was always just enough food to go around.

The first couple of days after her arrival, Aunt Fannie was always moody and outwardly unhappy. Aunt Fannie would say things to Moishe Pipik such as "Always stay a little boy!" and "Don't grow up to be like all those other men!"

When the mourning period for her lost romantic entanglement was over, Aunt Fannie's mood would improve and she would be upbeat and joyful. Then, Aunt Fannie was a lot of fun to be around and Moishe Pipik loved all of the attention that she showered on him, although he could do without so many hugs and a few less pinches. Moishe Pipik really didn't much like the smeared lipstick on his cheeks either, truth be told.

On the particular day in question Moishe Pipik awoke with a particularly strong desire for a pickle from the big wooden barrel at Finklestein's Delicatessen. He asked his mother if she would give him a nickel to satisfy his craving. She told him that she didn't have any extra money for frivolity. He was most disappointed but not particularly surprised.

Aunt Fannie was stretched out on the sofa. She was feeling very sorry for herself. She had a hot water bottle on her head and she groaned horribly, on the verge of tears. Moishe Pipik determined that there was no point in asking Aunt Fannie for anything that morning.

Uncle Morrie was sitting at the kitchen table. He was drinking coffee, smoking a cigarette, and studying the Daily Racing Form. Moishe Pipik asked his uncle to look in his ears and see if there were any nickels hidden in there. Uncle Morrie grunted before taking a look. "I am afraid," he said, "that the nickel mine is played out for now." That was certainly not encouraging news.

Moishe Pipik always carried a rucksack to school, just like the other children of the neighborhood. In his rucksack, he always had a notebook, pencils, and a few crayons. Sometimes there was a snack. Always there was his small drawstring pouch where he kept his marbles as well as any treasures that he happened upon.

All the way to school that morning, Moishe Pipik walked in the gutter between the sidewalk and the streets. He kept his eyes peeled, hoping to spy coins that had fallen there. He didn't find a single one on that long walk to school. Moishe Pipik arrived at school, as he usually did, a little late and a bit rumpled.

Sorry to say, however, Moishe Pipik was not a particularly attentive student.

A typical day at Moishe Pipik's school went something like this. The teacher helped the children learn their *Aleph Beis*. All the children watch the teacher write the letters on the blackboard and they all copy the letters into their notebooks.

Everyone, that is, except Moishe Pipik.

When the teacher writes an *Aleph* א on the blackboard, all the children see an א but not Moishe Pipik. He sees a robot. The other children write א in their notebooks. Moishe Pipik draws a robot.

Next, the teacher writes a *Beis* ב on the blackboard, and Moishe Pipik sees a hippopotamus. The other children write ב in their notebooks. Moishe Pipik draws a hippopotamus.

The teacher writes a *Gimel* ג but Moishe Pipik sees a rocket ship preparing for liftoff. The other children carefully jot ג into their notebooks. Moishe Pipik carefully sketches a rocket on a launchpad.

School ended no time too soon for the boy. His craving for a fat kosher dill had not waned whatsoever during the proceeding hours. Yet, he was no closer to satisfying his desire, still lacking a nickel. Moishe Pipik dilly dallied on his way back home, as he considered his options.

Moishe Pipik detoured past the lot where the boys of the neighborhood would gather for games such as stickball, tag, mumbly-peg, and marbles. That day there was a circle of boys shooting marbles in the lot. Moishe Pipik joined in the game.

Marbles is a game involving both luck and skill. A circle is drawn on the ground, players place marbles within the circle and then take turns by aiming a slightly larger shooter at the marbles with the intention of dislodging the marbles from the circle. Any knocked free of the circle becomes the property of the player that has knocked them loose.

Moishe Pipik was fairly skilled at the game so evidently luck was not with him. In hardly any time, Moishe Pipik's drawstring bag was nearly empty. All that remained was his shooter, one cat's eye, a couple of very plain marbles, a button, and a pebble.

From there, Moishe Pipik wandered about the neighborhood, scheming and dreaming and hoping for a pickle. Surely there was a way for at least one nickel to come into his possession, or perhaps even acquiring a pickle by some other means.

Then, Moishe Pipik remembered that time once when he happened to be in the alley behind the delicatessen when the delivery truck was there. The driver, for no particular reason, as if a miracle, just gave him a pickle. Well, lightning can strike twice so Moishe Pipik ran to the alley but of course there was no delivery truck there on that day.

What Moishe Pipik did find in the alley was a wooden banana crate. Well, it wasn't a pickle but it was a fortuitous discovery. It was just what the boy needed to fulfill one of his lifetime goals. Moishe Pipik hoisted the wooden crate onto his back, resting it on his head. In this way, Moishe Pipik walked back to his building and up the steps to his apartment.

When Moishe Pipik got home, he found his mother busy scrubbing the kitchen floor. Hardly looking up, his Mama asked him, "What did you learn in school today?"

"I learned about rocket ships. Also, about robots...and... umm... hippopotamus...esses...ummm."

"Hippopotami, I think, is the plural, but I am not sure," said his mother. "Ask your teacher tomorrow."

"Okay, Mama," Moishe Pipik responded. He headed, with his crate, across the apartment and out the window to the fire escape.

On the fire escape, Moishe Pipik went straight to work. The banana crate served as the cabin for the rocket ship that he had always dreamed of building. With some bits of wire, string, wheels, bicycle pedals, tin cans, and such, Moishe Pipik built a rocket ship like none other. He wasted no time, blasting off in his rocket ship that very afternoon, directly from the fire escape.

This is how Moishe Pipik became the first person to fly to space and land on the Moon, not that he ever received much recognition for that feat.

The flight went without a hitch and was much quicker than Moishe Pipik had expected. When he arrived on the Moon, he was greeted with much fanfare. The Moon People pulled out all the stops. There was a marching band and a huge banner with the words "Welcome Moishe Pipik" in great big letters. They all yelled "Speech! Speech!" The cheers were thunderous when Moishe Pipik took the stage and expressed his heartfelt appreciation for their kindly reception.

Moishe Pipik's biggest regret concerning that trip, however, is that he didn't pack a camera. Photographic documentation of the voyage would have certainly bolstered his claims about visiting the Moon.

Lacking a camera, Moishe Pipik made a few sketches in his notebook. Unfortunately, in all of the excitement, he misspelled the word "Welcome" on the banner. Also, in his excitement, he added a giraffe, an elephant, and a hippopotamus to the picture even though none of those animals were actually there. Sorry to say, his drawings were not that convincing.

Additionally, Moishe Pipik had asked the Moon People if he could take some cheese home. He was informed that he had arrived on a day when the cheese mine was closed for repairs. So, most unfortunately, Moishe Pipik had no souvenirs from his trip to reinforce his assertions that he had traveled to the Moon.

Moishe Pipik's return flight was unremarkable and without a hitch. He was back on the fire escape in no time flat. It was still hours before his supper would be served. Moishe Pipik's mother was at work by the stove, stirring a large pot. He tried to tell his mother about his trip to the Moon but she was much too busy to listen and shooed him away.

Moishe Pipik's Aunt Fannie was once again moping in the living room. His Uncle Morrie had gone to the racetrack. The boy still had the unfulfilled desire for a delicious kosher dill and he still lacked a nickel. He headed back out into the streets of Brooklyn.

Moishe Pipik knew what had to be done and he went about doing it. He moved with the intensity and purposefulness of a shark, approaching neighbors in search of temporary employment. To anyone who would listen, he explained how he really wanted a pickle from the delicatessen and therefore really, really needed a nickel.

Over the next couple of hours, Moishe Pipik swept sidewalks, steps, and foyers. He emptied a litter box and took out some trash. He weeded several flower pots and walked a dog. Somehow, even with all the efforts, the goal remained elusive. Moishe Pipik found himself in front of Finklestein's Delicatessen without a nickel to his name. He sat down on the curb, held his head in his small hands, and began to cry.

The crying started out as just a whimper but it graduated into a full-fledged Niagara Falls sort of downpour. The tears fell into the gutter and threatened to flood the entire street.

When Mr Finklestein looked out the big plate glass window of his delicatessen, he saw what assuredly was the saddest little boy in the whole world. Mr Finklestein wiped his hands on his white smock and walked out the front door of the delicatessen. The bell on the door tinkled as he left the building and crossed the sidewalk.

Moishe Pipik was absorbed in his very personal sense of loss and private misery. He took no notice of Mr Finkelstein until the man's rotund shadow was directly over him. Then, Moishe Pipik looked up. He saw the kindly shopkeeper through his bleary reddened eyes, and began to stifle his tears.

"What's the matter, my Dear Moishe Pipik?" asked the good shopkeeper in the white smock.

Moishe Pipik, gasping and nearly choking on his river of tears, said most emphatically "Today is the worst day of my life!" He then dropped his head back into his hands and began crying once more.

"Listen, young fellow," Mr Finklestein said as he handed Moishe Pipik the handkerchief from his breast pocket. "How about you blow your nose, wipe away your tears, and come with me into the delicatessen. Maybe we can see what we can do to salvage your day. I have some experience with bad days. Maybe it won't turn out so awful after all."

Mr Finklestein took Moishe Pipik's small hand and the two of them walked inside. Mr Finklestein set Moishe Pipik up on a stool behind the counter, near the cash register. There, they would be able to talk while Mr Finklestein could keep an eye on his store and help any customers that may show up.

"So, Moishe Pipik! Tell me all about it. What happened today?" This is what the shopkeeper said to the boy.

So, Moishe Pipik proceeded to give an account of his day. "This morning, all that I really, really wanted - all that I could think about - was a pickle. You know how much I love the pickles from your big barrel." The boy gave the shopkeeper a knowing nod. Mr Finklestein returned the nod. Moishe Pipik continued his narrative.

"I asked my Mama for a nickel, but she said no. I asked my Uncle Morrie if he could pull a nickel out of my ear but he told me that my head was empty. That's how my morning began."

"Hmm," said Mr Finklestein.

"I looked for nickels in the gutter on the way to school but, no luck. After school, I lost my marbles...at least, most of them."

"Then, I built a rocket ship and flew to the Moon. They didn't have any cheese because the cheese mine was closed for repairs and I don't have any photographs so probably nobody will believe that. My Mom sure didn't."

Moishe Pipik showed Mr Finklestein the sketches from the trip.

"Well, now..." said Mr Finkelstein.

Moishe Pipik put his drawstring bag on the counter as he began to explain the next phase of his very long day.

"So, I went to work to see if I could earn a nickel. Mrs Apelblum asked me to take out her trash. She didn't have a nickel. She gave me seven pennies." Moishe Pipik put the seven pennies into a small pile on the counter.

"Mrs Bassowitz asked me to walk her dog. She didn't have a nickel. She gave me a dime which is much smaller than a nickel." Moishe Pipik sadly placed the dime next to the pennies.

"Mrs Czernec asked me to sweep her steps. She didn't have a nickel. She gave me a subway token." Moishe Pipik added the subway token to the collection of coins on the counter.

Mr Dannenberg also asked me to do some sweeping for him. He didn't have a nickel. He gave me three stamps." The stamps were placed on the counter.

"Mrs Ehrendorf had me clean out her smelly cat's stinky litter box. She gave me three empty soda bottles." These were in Moishe Pipik's rucksack and he placed them on the counter.

"Mrs Feldman asked me to pull all the weeds from her flower pots. She didn't have a nickel but she gave me two cookies and they were pretty good. Not as good as a pickle but better than a poke in the eye with a sharp stick, I suppose." Moishe Pipik smiled a bit as he wiped some cookie crumbs from the corners of his mouth.

Mr Finklestein patted Moishe Pipik on the head. "Let's do some math," he said to the boy. Moishe Pipik grimaced. He hated math but he tried to be brave.

Mr Finklestein counted five of the seven pennies as he picked them up off the counter. "Five pennies, young man is worth a nickel." He placed the five pennies into his cash register and replaced it with a nickel. Moishe Pipik's eyes brightened.

"This thin dime here doesn't look like much." With that, he dropped it into his cash register and placed two nickels on the counter in its place.

"What do you suppose that subway token is worth?" Mr Finklestein slipped the token into the cash register and replaced it with three nickels.

"These are three cent stamps. That's nine cents." Mr Finklestein placed a nickel and four pennies onto the counter.

"The soda bottles," Mr Finklestein continued, "each have two cents deposits." He put the bottles into a crate and put a nickel and a penny on the counter in their stead. Moishe Pipik's eyes widened.

Moishe Pipik began to count the coins, placing them into piles. Eight nickels made quite a stack. There were also seven pennies. Moishe Pipik happily traded five of those pennies for another nickel.

Moishe Pipik left Finklestein's Delicatessen with EIGHT fat kosher dill pickles wrapped in wax paper with brown paper wrapped around that and all placed lovingly into a paper sack by Mr Finklestein. Moishe Pipik held the largest pickle from the barrel in his right hand and ate it on his way back home.

By the time that Moishe Pipik had returned to his apartment, his family was already seated at the dining table. Moishe Pipik slid into his seat, next to Aunt Fannie. Aunt Fannie's mood had much improved. She squeezed the boy until he squealed and kissed him loudly on his cheek, leaving a significant amount of smeared lipstick on his face.

Uncle Morrie and Moishe Pipik's father had reconciled any ill feelings between them as Uncle Morrie had made a generous contribution towards the rent. He had also brought home a freshly killed chicken which Moishe Pipik's mother cooked and served even though it was a weekday and not *Shabbos* or a holiday.

Uncle Morrie and Moishe Pipik's father were sharing a bottle of schnapps. They each had a glass and the bottle sat between them. Moishe Pipik's father filled the cap - a thimble's worth, perhaps - with schnapps and passed it to the boy. Moishe Pipik tossed the pungent liquid down his throat and gave a little shudder.

Everyone was having a fine time. Uncle Morrie refilled the cap and slid it across the table back to Moishe Pipik. He also gave the boy the bag of chocolates that he had bought for him on his way home from the racetrack, handing him the bag under the table.

Moishe Pipik ate his fill and then some of the chicken and potatoes that his mother served that evening. He stealthily chomped down the chocolates as well.

Moishe Pipik wobbled away from the table, quite satiated. The boy went to his room, taking the eight remaining pickles from Finklestein's Delicatessen with him. He sat in his closet, eating one pickle after another, and thinking that it had turned out to be the absolutely best day of his life. That is, until the churning sensation in his stomach began.

44

THE GLOSSARY

abi guzunt - interj. As long as you're healthy [you can be happy]

Aish Zerah - (eish zerah) literally translate to: "a strange fire"

Aleph Beis - alphabet, the first two letters of the alphabet (א,ב)

ales iz gut - all is well

aliyah - an honorific tradition in a synagogue where a man approaches the Torah while it is read, literally going up in Hebrew

apikores - heretic

arayn - shtel arayn, "put in" when gambling with a dreidl

aun vas - and what

Baal Shem Tov - Israel ben Eliezer, known as the Baal Shem Tov or as the Besht, was a Jewish mystic and healer who is regarded as the founder of Hasidic Judaism.

babka - a sweet braided bread

balagan - a total mess (derived from Russian)

balabusta - a good homemaker, also can mean a landlady

Bar Mitzvah - literally, son of commandment, it is a coming-of-age ritual that takes place at the age of 13

Bar Mitzvah Bochur - a thirteen year old

bashert - generally used to refer to a soulmate, actually translates better as destiny.

bebl - a bean

Beit Din literally house of justice, it is a religious court

berakhah - a blessing

berala - a teddy bear

bissel - a little

bochur - boy or young man

borscht - a type of soup, generally cabbage or beet

bromayzer - Jews Harp

bubbie - grandmother

bulbe - potato, derives from Lithuanian bulve

bulbes is the plural of *bulbe*, potatoes

Chad Gadya - an allegorical song about a small goat, traditionally part of the Passover *Seder*

chai - life, the Hebrew letters (חי) refers also to the number eighteen

challah - a braided white bread eaten particularly on Shabbos and Holidays

chaverim - friends, companions, associates, members of an organization, partners

cheder - a one room school, literally a room in Hebrew

cholent - a slow cooked stew usually for the Sabbath

chuppah - literally, "canopy" or "covering" this refers to the Jewish marriage ceremony

chutzpah - extreme self-confidence or audacity

Danershtag - Thursday

das iz alts - that is all

daven - to pray

Derekh Eretz - respect, literally the way of the land

Der Profesor - The Professor

dire gelt - rent, literally apartment money

donning tefillin - putting on phylacteries, a set of small black leather boxes with leather straps containing scrolls. This is a daily religious practice (except for *Shabbos* and Holidays) which is performed by men in the morning while *davening shacharis.*

dreyen - to spin a dreidl

dreidl - a top associated with Hanukkah, dreidel

dybbuk - a malicious possessing spirit

Eretz Yisrael - the Land of Israel

er zitst bay der mizrekh-vant - literally he sits by the eastern wall, a highly respected person

esrogim - citrons, a citrus fruit associated with Sukkos (Sukkot)

es tut mir layd - I am sorry, literally it causes me pain

farsheteyt - understand

farvas - why

fentster - window

ferd - horse

ferd flig - horsefly

fidele - fiddle, violin

flig - fly

foigel - bird

Freyda - bliss

fremd feyer - foreign fire

galus - exile, Diaspora

Gan Eden - Garden of Eden, Paradise

gants - whole

gantze - whole

gantze mishpacha - the whole family

gefilte fish - literally stuffed fish, a dish made from a poached mixture of ground deboned fish

gelt - money

Gimel - third letter of the alphabet (ג). When gambling with a dreidl, if it lands on Gimel, one takes the *gantze* (whole) pot.

Glatt Kosher - stringently kosher

gornisht - nothing

gonif - thief

goyim - gentiles

groys - big

guzunt - health

halachic - Jewish Law

hamantaschen - a three cornered pastry associated with Purim

hamsa - a palm-shaped amulet popular throughout North Africa and in the Middle East

hartsikn dank - heartfelt thanks

Hasidic - a mystical Jewish movement founded in Poland in the 18th century (see Baal Shem Tov)

Hatikvah - hope in Hebrew

Havdalah - the ceremony that marks the end of the Sabbath

Hebraists - Hebrew scholar or advocate

hechsher - certification of food being kosher

henna - a dye used by Sephardic and Mizrahi women in a pre-wedding ceremony

Haredi - ultra-Orthodox

hoyz - house

hoyz flig - house fly

Ikh vis nisht - I don't know

Kabbalists - Kabbalah is an esoteric method, discipline and school of thought in Jewish mysticism. Kabbalists are the practitioners of Kabbalah.

Kadish - literally holy, a prayer of mourning

kashrus/kashrut - pertaining to dietary laws (kosher)

keinehora - from the Hebrew, Kein Ayin Hara, meaning no evil eye. It is said to ward off harm, often accompanied with spitting.

ketschele - kitten, little kitten, a term of endearment

khaveyrim - friends

khius - animals

kibbutz - a communal farm

kibbutzniks - people that live on a kibbutz

kibbutzim - plural of kibbutz

kikhl - cookie

kikhlekh - cookies

kind - child

kinder - plural of kind

klezmorim - musicians

kneidelach - matzah ball, a dumpling

knip - a pinch

knipple - a woman's secret stash of money, from the word knip, meaning a pinch.

knish - a deep fried or baked snack

kosher - food fit to eat according to law and customs

krom - store

kugel - a casserole made of noodles or potatoes

Kukuriku! - This is the sound that roosters make in Yiddish, Hebrew, Russian, Polish... Why do English-speaking roosters say "Cock-a-doodle-doo!"? *Ikh vis nisht.*

kurvah - a whore

kvelled - delighted, joyed

kvetching - complaining

lakht - laughs

latkes - potato pancakes

l'chaim - To Life! Used as a toast

leben - a living

Leviathan - a Biblical sea monster

luftmenschen - spacemen or literally air (luft) men (menshen). Singular is *luftmentsh.* A *luftmentsh* is commonly understood as one with his head in the clouds, an airhead, or one more concerned with intellectual pursuits than earning a living. It can also mean a beggar, a petty trader, a peddler, or a one with no visible means of support who lives on air. A middleman or hustler that derives an income without producing anything of value can also be called a luftmentsh.

macht a leben - make (earn) a living

Mamaloshen - literally mother tongue, Yiddish

Magen David Adom - Red Shield of David, or Red Star of David. It is the Israeli affiliate of the International Red Cross

majoun - a North African candy made with hashish and dates

mamzers - bastards

mañana - tomorrow (Spanish)

mann - husband

Mantik - Monday

Mantik aun Danershtag - Monday and Thursday. The Torah is read on those days. They are also traditional market days. It is sometimes used to mean frequently

mayn - my

mazel - luck

mechayeh - a pleasure

Meditsinish Gortns - medical gardens

Megillah Esther - the Scroll of Esther, the Book of Esther, read on Purim

melameds - teachers

Menorah - candelabra

mentsh - a man, a good person

mentshn - people, human beings

meshugganah - crazy

meydls - girls, young women

meydl mit a fidele - a girl with a violin

mezuzah - literally a door post, it is a parchment in a decorative case affixed to the doorframe

mikvah - ritual bathhouse

mincha aun maariv - afternoon and evening prayers, usually practiced with little or no break between the two sets

minyan - a quorum for prayer

mishegoss - nonsense

mishpacha - family

mit - with

Mitvakh - Wednesday

mitzvah - a religious commandment

Mizrahi - North African and Middle Eastern Jews

mohel - performs ritual circumcision

Moishe Pipik - a nonsense name, literally Moses' Belly Button

Mommala - a term of endearment for a small child, literally little momma

Moshe - Moses

Moshiach - Messiah

munn - poppy seeds

muzik - music

nachas - pride or gratification

nikal - a nickel

nisht - not

nisht gornisht - nothing

neshumeh - soul

oder - or

oy - Used to express surprise, pain, grief, worry, etc

offen - on

payos - side curls, based on an interpretation of the Tanakh's injunction against shaving the "sides" of one's head.

peniz - pennies

peniz oder a nikal - pennies or a nickel

Pesach - Passover

pisher - a very young person, literally one that urinates

planirt plan

potch - a smack

Profesor - Professor

punim - face

Purim Meydls - Purim Girls, in this story it refers to young women that become pregnant during the celebration of Purim. This is a totally fictionalized concept.

Rabbi - Jewish teacher or religious leader

Reb - an honorific similar to Mr.

Rebbetzin - a rabbi's wife

rishon - first in Hebrew

Sabbatai Zevi - a Messianic figure (false Messiah) in the 1600s

schlep - walk

Seder - a Passover meal steeped in ritual

Sephardic - Jewish diaspora population associated with the Iberian Peninsula

Shabbos - Sabbath, Saturday

shacharis - morning prayers

Shechinah - God's divine presence, often understood as the feminine aspect of God

shtrayml - (**shtreimel**) a fur hat worn by some Ashkenazi Jewish men ***shtraymlekh*** is the plural of *shtrayml*

schlepping - carrying, hauling

schmaltz - chicken fat

schmoozing - chatting

schnorrer - begger, sponger

shidduch - arranged marriage

Shin - A letter in the alphabet (ש). When gambling with a dreidl, if it lands on *shin,* one must *shtel arayn* (put money into the pot).

shney - snow

shneya - second in Hebrew

shochet - a ritual slaughter, a butcher

Shomer Shabbos - literally guarding the Sabbath, this refers to a strict observance

Shomrim - watchers or guards (Hebrew)

shofars - ram horns

shpilplats - playgrounds

shprakh - language

Shprintza - hope

shtel arayn - put in (when gambling with a dreidl)

shtisl - a pot. *A bisl aun a bisl vert a ful shtisl* - a little and a little make a full pot.

shraybmashin - typewriter

shtarkers - hard guys, gangsters

shtetl - a small town

shtick - gimmick, talent

shtikel - a piece

shtot - a city

shul - synagogue or house of prayer, school, from German Schule

shviger - mother-in-law

siesta - a short afternoon nap (Spanish)

Sit Shiva - the seven days of mourning

Sontag - Sunday

Sukkos/Sukkot - the harvest festival which is a major holiday

tallis - ritual prayer shawl worn by men

tallis katan - an undershirt with ritual fringes

Tamar - the name is also Hebrew for date

tayere - dear

Tanakh - the Jewish Bible, (Torah, the Nevi'im, and the Ketuvim). Christians call this the Old Testament

Tantele - term of endearment for a small child, literally little father

Tate - father

tefillin - (phylacteries) are a set of small black leather boxes with leather straps containing scrolls of parchment

Tel - hill or mound (Hebrew)

tish - table

toches - bottom, rear-end

toyre - Torah, the Five Books of Moses

traif - not kosher

Tsatske aun Muzik Krom - Trinkets and Music Store

Tsenter Shtot - City Center

tsibeles - onions

tuches - butt

tuches offen tish - a serious commitment, literally to put one's butt on the table

tsufus on foot

tzimmes - a sweet side dish usually made primarily carrots with fruit, the German zuomuose. Tzimmes colloquially means a big fuss or commotion.

tzitzis - knotted ritual fringes

vas - what

vashzimmer washroom, bathroom

vayb - wife

Vayikra - the Biblical book of Leviticus

vilde - wild

vilde khius - wild animals

vindow - window
vonce - bedbug, sometimes a term of endearment
yarmulke - a skullcap
Yenne Velt - literally another world, Heaven, death
yeshiva - a religious school
yeshiva bochers - students, *boocher* is literally a boy
Yid - a Jew
Yidden - Jews
Yiddishkeit - the Jewish way of life, Jewish culture
yingele - a boy, a youngster
zaydeh - grandfather
zhargon - jargon
zhurnal - journal
Zoologisher Gortn - zoological garden, a zoo
THE END

www.ingramcontent.com/pod-product-compliance
Lightning Source LLC
Chambersburg PA
CBHW060627310726
48982CB00003B/704

* 9 7 9 8 9 9 9 0 2 8 2 0 4 *